I0787160

# The Flintridge Conspiracy

EUGENE H. STRAYHORN JR.

Copyright ©2024 by Eugene H. Strayhorn Jr.

ISBN 978-1-964097-90-9 (hardcover)
ISBN 978-1-964097-85-5 (softcover)
ISBN 978-1-964097-86-2 (ebook)

All rights reserved. No part of this book may be reproduced or transmitted in any form or by any means, electronic or mechanical, including photocopying, recording, or by any information storage and retrieval system without express written permission from the author, except in the case of brief quotations embodied in critical reviews and certain other non-commercial uses permitted by copyright law.

This book is a work of fiction. Names, characters, places, and incidents are the product of the author's imagination or are used fictitiously. Any resemblance to actual locales, events, or persons, living or dead, is purely coincidental.

Printed in the United States of America.

# CONTENTS

# PROLOGUE

It doesn't take much to change the course of a life—a cryptic message, an unforeseen encounter, a tempting offer. These are the sorts of seemingly minor catalysts that shift us from one path to another and alter our destiny.

Marcus Eldridge sat waiting in a booth toward the back of the restaurant. Looking out the window, he monitored the parking lot. The murmurings of interwoven conversations rumbled through the crowded dining room. Most patrons seemed to be in a festive mood. It was the Fourth of July after all, a holiday when Marcus normally would have been relaxing at home. The chance to kick back and put his feet up came his way so infrequently that he cherished each opportunity.

As chief administrative officer for the Flintridge Medical Center, Marcus was an important man. He was charged with overseeing the day-to-day operations of a 120-bed hospital, and he took his responsibilities seriously. As a confirmed bachelor, his work was his life.

*So, why am I here*, Marcus wondered, though already he knew the reason—curiosity. The invitation to meet had been delivered to his office in yesterday's mail. Typewritten on plane stationery and unsigned, the message had brazenly proclaimed that he would benefit from choosing to show up.

Normally suspicious of unrequested solicitations that promised personal gain, Marcus had been about to toss the letter in the trash when something had stopped him. Perhaps the simplicity of the wording had intrigued him. There was no pleading, no cajoling, merely the promise of a reward for hearing what the writer had to say; or perhaps, something else had captured his imagination: the promise of a change of pace, an experience outside his daily routine—an adventure.

A late-model SUV pulled into the parking lot. Black, and with no distinguishing logos or insignias, under other circumstances, the vehicle would not have warranted a second glance. After turning into a parking space, rather than exit immediately, the driver sat for a time, surveying the lot and checking his rearview mirrors. In due time, he climbed out and began striding toward the restaurant.

Marcus watched the man cross the lot. He was a fit-looking fellow with a military bearing. He wore his hair, nearly white, cut short and neatly combed. His shoulders were square, and his back was straight. Marcus estimated his age to be somewhere between fifty and sixty-five. It was hard to tell, though the man gave the impression that he could handle himself in a fight.

Upon entering the restaurant, the man hesitated, looking from table to table, as if doing a threat assessment.

Marcus, also looking around, was forced to admire the man's choice of meeting places. Two guys eating breakfast together wouldn't raise any eyebrows, and the noise level would mask their conversation.

When the man saw Marcus, a flash of recognition came into his eyes. He nodded and began striding in his direction.

Marcus racked his memory but could not recall having ever seen the fellow before.

"Marcus Eldridge?" the man said quietly as he stood beside the booth, looking down.

"That's me, and you are…?"

"Summers, Captain Jack Summers."

"Captain?" Marcus gestured for the man to be seated.

Captain Summers slid into the bench seat facing Marcus. "United States Marine Corps, retired." He reached for a menu and began reading. "Have you ordered?"

"I ate before I came."

"You must be an early riser."

"Force of habit—from my graduate school days."

"Aw, yes—a master's degree in business administration from Tulane University and a second master's degree in public health also from Tulane."

Marcus startled but tried not to show it. Clearly Captain Summers had done his homework. "Your note didn't explain the purpose of this meeting."

"Good. Get right to the point—I like that. The fact is I would like to offer you a chance to earn a significant amount of money."

"Oh yeah? Doing what?" Marcus couldn't help but feel he was being conned, but when he looked closely, he saw that Captain Summers was serious.

"Before we get to that, I need your oath that you will keep this conversation private. No one must know what we are about to discuss. Do you swear?"

"Seriously? What's with all this cloak-and-dagger nonsense? First you send a cryptic message asking me to meet you in a public restaurant just off the Interstate, five miles outside of town, and then you want to swear me to secrecy? What's going on?"

"Do you swear?"

"And if I choose not to?"

"Then this meeting never happened." Captain Summers began to slide out of the booth.

"Wait. Hold on." Marcus held up a hand to stop him. "You caught me by surprise, that's all."

Captain Summers paused and leveled his gaze at Marcus. "Do you swear?"

"All right. Yes. I swear. I won't tell anyone—ever. Now will you tell me what's going on?"

Captain Summers eased back to the center of the bench seat. He started to answer, but the waitress stepped up to take their orders. She looked at Captain Summers.

He said with a friendly smile, "I'll have two eggs over medium, bacon, a short stack of French toast, and a glass of orange juice."

"And for you, sir?" The waitress looked at Marcus.

"Just coffee."

The waitress departed, and Captain Summers leaned closer. Speaking in hushed tones, he said, "Are you familiar with the New World Militia?"

Marcus shook his head. "No, I'm not."

"We are an organization made up of American patriots dedicated to preserving the liberties bequeathed to us by our founding fathers, the heroes of this great nation. I am the Northwest Regional Commander—Oregon, Washington, Idaho, and Montana. We have a new project we are about to undertake, and we need your participation. In exchange for your involvement, we will pay you one million dollars to be deposited in the financial institution of your choosing."

"A million dollars," Marcus scoffed. "Is this some kind of a joke? If it is, it's not funny."

"I assure you we are not joking."

"A million dollars? Seriously? Why me? Why do you think I can help you?"

"Because you are the hospital's chief administrative officer. That means you are ideally positioned to ensure that we can complete our mission."

"What exactly is your mission?"

Captain Summers leaned farther forward. "We are developing a virus to be used in time of war."

"A virus?" Marcus exclaimed with incredulity.

"Keep your voice down," Captain Summers commanded sternly.

Marcus whispered, "You're creating a weapon of mass destruction? That's bioterrorism."

"No, it is not," Captain Summers countered. "It's self-defense. Hear me out. This country has powerful enemies that would take away our liberties and turn us into a nation of sheep. Someday soon, they are going to move against us with force. When the time comes, we need to be prepared. We need a nonlethal weapon that will temporarily disable the enemy, allowing us to overrun their positions without bloodshed. Imagine the victories that could've been secured at Normandy during World War II, at Khe Sanh during Vietnam, and at Fallujah during the Iraq war. Tens of thousands of lives might have been saved if we'd been able to incapacitate our enemies without firing a shot.

"The virus is being bioengineered in a secure virology lab, the location of which you do not need to know. However, to finetune its effects, we will need to test it on human subjects. Our proposal is that one of our militia members will sequentially infect seven patients who have been admitted to your hospital. We will then collect all of their lab studies and clinical data while the virus runs its course. At the end of forty-eight hours, the virus has been designed to disappear completely from their bodies, leaving no trace and allowing the patients to recover completely."

Marcus shook his head. "What is to keep this virus from spreading throughout my hospital?"

"The virus' virulence, that is its physiological impact, will be adjusted during the trials. At the same time, it's infectivity, that is its ability to spread person to person, will be kept near zero. The virus has been engineered so that it cannot survive outside the body longer than five minutes. Let me reassure you no lasting harm will be done to any of the test subjects."

"Look, I'm not a scientist. I'm not a doctor. I don't have a degree in microbiology. I'm an administrator, a bureaucrat."

"Which is precisely what we need."

"What exactly would I have to do?"

"Supervise the members of your team. Deal with any logistical problems that might arise. Two members of the militia have already volunteered. One is a physician, the other a respiratory therapist. They will do most of the work. Your task is to make sure everything goes smoothly."

"And if I don't agree to participate?"

"Then this meeting never happened unless you start shooting your mouth off. In that case, I promise that you will be dealt with most severely."

Marcus swallowed hard. There was no doubt that Captain Summers meant what he said. "You can promise me that no lasting harm will be done to the patients?"

"Nothing more than a bad cold from which they will rapidly recover."

"Who are the people I will be working with?"

"You'll meet them after you agree to participate."

"How do I know your offer of one million dollars is legitimate?"

"The money will be transferred into your bank account before the operation begins."

"I need to think about this."

"We had assumed as much." Captain Summers reached into his shirt pocket and took out a folded slip of paper. He unfolded it and handed it to Marcus. "That's a phone number and a code phrase. If you agree to join us, call that number and give them that code phrase. If we don't hear from you, we will assume your answer is no."

Marcus read what was written on the paper. "What is this? Ophis…?"

"Ophis Pterotos. In ancient Greek mythology, Ophis Pterotos was the winged serpent that guarded the frankincense groves of Arabia. It's also the codename for our operation."

"What makes you think I'll agree to this?"

"Because you desperately need the money. You've made some truly awful investment decisions, haven't you?"

Marcus flushed.

Captain Summers's breakfast arrived. He ignored it.

With obvious concern, Marcus said, "What if something goes wrong?"

"It will be your job to see that it doesn't." Captain Summers sat up straighter. "Look, you have forty-eight hours. If you agree to proceed, the million dollars will be wired to your bank, so you'll need to provide the person you talk to with your routing number and your account number."

Marcus sat back. "I knew it. This is a scam. You're setting me up to steal my banking information."

"Why would we go to all this bother for $1,726.43?"

"What the…?" Marcus exclaimed in disbelief. "How do you know my bank balance?" *What else do they know about me?* he wondered, feeling vulnerable.

"I give you my word," Captain Summers replied evenly. "This is not a scam. The offer is real. You have forty-eight hours to decide."

Without further comment, Captain Summers rose to his feet and left the restaurant. As he passed a nearby table, he nodded to the two rough-looking men seated there. They stood and followed him outside. Then all three climbed into the SUV and drove off together.

Left alone, Marcus sat staring at the paper in his hand.

# ANOTHER BEGINNING

My name is Sterling, Doctor Blake Sterling. After completing my pulmonary medicine residency and passing my specialty boards, I had been recruited to join Pulmonary Associates, a two-man medical group in Flintridge, Washington—a sleepy suburb of Kennewick. I was about to become the practice's third physician.

From across the street, I stood gazing up at the four-story office building where I would soon be diagnosing and treating conditions related to the respiratory system. The building's plain brownstone façade fostered an impression of durability, permanence, and a no-nonsense attitude toward the healing arts, which was another way of saying it totally lacked style. During my years living in Los Angeles, I had seen warehouses endowed with more native charm. Still there's something exhilarating about staring up at the office complex where you are about to hang out your shingle for the first time.

It would be an understatement to say that I was nervous. *Terrified* would better describe how I felt. As a resident, I'd always had an attending physician to back me up. There was always someone looking over my shoulder, doublechecking my diagnoses, and reviewing my treatment plans. In private practice, I would be on my own. Of course, I could request consultations from other specialists, but for the most part, my patients would literally live or die based upon whatever choices I made. To practice medicine, a physician must shoulder almost unbearable responsibilities.

I had visited this office building once before—during the recruitment process. I had spent all of four hours one Saturday afternoon meeting with my prospective partners and getting a feel for the layout of the facility. During finals week, a one-day turnaround visit had been as much time as I could spend away from my studies. My memories of that trip were something of a jumble, lacking detail, like recalling a canvas painted in broad strokes with a wide brush.

What I do remember vividly was the warm reception I had received and the obvious camaraderie shared by the partners. In making my decision to join the group, I had assumed that the rest of the details related to launching a private practice would work themselves out. I was, after all, in God's hands.

I reached down and retrieved my backpack from the passenger seat of my eight-year-old Nissan Sentra. The pack contained a few personal items, a couple mementos to decorate my new office, and several textbooks, which I considered essential reference material. I had brought them along just in case, not knowing the strength of the practice's library. In training, I had learned that a well-written textbook was worth its weight in gold.

Looking up, I noted the wispy clouds that dotted the azure sky. It was a warm day in early August, and Flintridge temperatures were climbing toward ninety degrees. Still it was not as warm as LA where I had spent the last ten years.

After sending an arrow prayer heavenward, I locked my car and crossed the road to begin the next phase of my life.

Pulmonary Associates rented the entire third floor of the brownstone medical arts building. Hematology/Oncology occupied the floor above, Flintridge Internal Medicine the floor below. Nephrology and the dialysis unit were on the ground floor. Rather than take the elevator, I chose the stairs. At thirty-one years of age, I was just turning the corner into middle age, and it seemed advisable to exercise whenever the opportunity arose.

The receptionist behind the glass partition—her nametag read Sally Fairchild—looked up when I entered the waiting room from the stairwell. I vaguely remembered her from my previous visit.

"Good morning," Sally said. "Your name please?"

"Sterling. Blake Sterling."

Sally consulted her online scheduling program. "I'm sorry. I don't see your name listed. Do you have an appointment?"

"I don't, but it's Doctor Blake Sterling. I believe I'm expected."

Sally studied her computer screen again. "Sterling…? No… Doctor Sterling? Oh? Oh! You're the new guy!" She flushed. "I'm sorry. I should have known. Please…come on around. We are expecting you. I'll take you to see Lois Carlton. She's our office manager, but I'm sure you already knew that." Sally blushed again.

I followed Sally through double doors leading to the interior of the building.

As I recalled from my previous visit, the third floor was laid out to maximize efficiency in treating patients. The doctor's offices were placed in the southwest, northwest, and northeast corners. The office manager supervised the practice's daily operations from the southeast corner. In groups of three, exam rooms extended between the corner offices along the western, northern, and eastern walls. The waiting room, the reception area, and the restrooms were positioned along the southern wall. A wide corridor circled the interior of the building, separating the offices and exam rooms from a large central space where the nurses maintained patients' medical records, staffed a small laboratory, and attended to all the other functions that kept a medical practice going.

I later learned that Doctor Richards occupied the northwest office and Doctor Tucker claimed the northeast office. That meant the southwest office would be assigned to me, which was fine. At least I would have a view of the Flintridge Medical Center, which was only a three-minute walk from the medical arts building.

Lois Carlton glanced up when Sally knocked on her door.

"Doctor Sterling is here," Sally announced before returning to the reception counter.

Lois rose from behind her desk and stepped around to greet me. "Welcome," she said, extending her hand.

"Thank you. It's good to be here." I smiled and returned the handshake.

Lois looked to be in her late middle years. Her oval face was beginning to show creases in her brow and at the corners of her light-brown eyes. Her shoulder-length dark-brown hair was pulled back at the temples. Other than a wedding ring and simple gold earrings, she wore no jewelry that I could see. Her pale-green blouse, along with her tan vest and dark-brown slacks, were clean and neatly pressed. Her outfit fit the image of a modern professional woman.

"How was your trip north?" Lois asked.

"Enjoyable…all in all," I replied.

"When did you get in?"

"Yesterday afternoon."

"And the apartment you rented—was it ready for you to move in?"

"It was. It's a good thing it's furnished. I didn't bring a whole lot of stuff with me."

Lois nodded. "I remember those days. In college I could pack all my worldly possessions in the backseat of a VW beetle. So…are you settled in and ready to go to work?"

"I am. Where do I start?"

"You'll be seeing office patients this afternoon. This morning, the doctors would like to show you around—introduce you to some people and make sure you know how things work. Let me tell them you're here."

Left alone in Lois's office, I looked around. As a whole, the space was neat and orderly. There were pictures of her husband and two young-adult children on her desk—one boy one girl. A nursing school diploma hung on the wall along with several pictures of Lois standing with people I presumed were local dignitaries. A row of cactus plants sat on a shelf in front of the outside window. They appeared to be thriving, although with cactuses you can never tell.

"Doctor Richards can see you now," Lois announced from the doorway. "If you would like to come with me."

I followed her to the northwest corner of the building.

Before handing me over to Doctor Richards, Lois paused outside his office and said, "By the way, where did you park?"

"Across the street out front."

She reached into the side pocket of her vest and drew out a small notepad and a pencil. After jotting down a four-digit number, she passed the slip of paper to me. "The practice leases a gated parking area. It's around behind the building. That's the entrance code to raise the barrier." She turned away but then turned back again. "One more thing—when Doctor Richards is done showing you around, come see me again, and I'll introduce you to your nurse."

*Wow*, I thought. *I get my own office. I get my own nurse. Gated parking. How much better can life be?*

I knocked on Doctor Richards's door. When a deep baritone voice said, "Come in," I opened the door and stepped inside.

Doctor Adam Richards was a handsome sixty-three-year-old Black man who carried himself with great dignity. His skin was a rich walnut brown, and there were touches of gray at the temples of his short, neatly trimmed hair. There was a twinkle in his dark eyes. He was clean-shaven, and when he spoke, if you listened closely, you could detect a slight Southern accent. He was the Pulmonary Associates' senior partner.

Adam sat behind a desk cluttered with all kinds of memorabilia, papers, and patient records.

I sat facing him in one of two straight-backed armchairs. In the other chair sat Doctor Jerry Tucker, the practice's junior partner. No— that's not right. I was now the new junior partner. That would make Jerry the middle partner, I suppose.

In any event, Jerry was a sturdily built man with a square face and a strong jaw. His eyes sloped slightly toward the bridge of his nose, giving him a hawkish look. Heavy cheekbones and a perpetual five o'clock shadow added to the impression that he was a rugged individual, not to be trifled with.

"Well, Blake," Adam said mildly. "We are certainly glad you're here."

"Indeed we are," Jerry concurred. "It will be nice to have a new pair of hands to share the caseload." He glanced at Adam, and I had the impression that an unspoken conversation was taking place. It made me wonder if Adam, because of his age, was beginning to slow his practice down a bit. When I took a closer look, I saw traces of weariness in his demeanor.

We began by discussing the fundamentals of private practice. The partners proceeded to fill me in on salient topics such as the on-call schedule, the importance of keeping good patient records, and financial considerations like billing and paying office overhead.

"Do you have any questions?" Adam asked after they had said their piece.

"Two questions." I turned toward the middle partner. "Online, you are identified as Doctor Barry Tucker, but here everyone calls you Jerry. Which is it?"

"His given name is Barry," Adam said. "He took the nickname *Jerry* to honor Jerry Rice, the football player."

"The best damn wide receiver the San Francisco 49ers ever had," Jerry affirmed proudly. "Tell me, Blake, are you a football fan?"

"I enjoy watching a game now and then, but I'm not well versed on the subtleties of the sport."

"A pity," Jerry said. "A good football game is like watching a well-trained military squad maneuver."

"And your second question?" Adam asked.

"Right. It's about your medical records. You dictate every patient contact. How come you haven't switched to electronic records?"

"Ask him," Jerry interjected brusquely. He pointed at Adam. "It's his fault."

"What he's referring to"—Adam sighed—"is that I refuse to sell the practice to the hospital, and allow them to transition us to electronic records."

"Why is that?" I asked.

"Several reasons," Adam replied. "First and foremost, I didn't take up medicine to become somebody's employee—constantly worrying about whether or not I'll make my quota for the month or whether or not I'm ordering too many tests or too few, and I especially don't want some bureaucrat telling me how to practice medicine and what treatments I can prescribe, but enough of this. We need to leave now if we're going to make the CME conference. Jerry, are you coming?"

"Not today. I have some paperwork to do. I'll be here when you get back." Jerry stood and returned to his office.

I followed Adam down the back stairs, and then we walked briskly toward the medical center.

Continuing medical education conferences were held every Monday at noon in the hospital's auditorium. This week's topic was aplastic anemia, a subject with which I was only modestly well-versed. I had studied the disease as part of my medical school training and during my internal medicine residency. After specializing in pulmonology, I hadn't given the malady much thought. The presenter was Doctor Terry Prichard, a hematologist who also practiced out of the brownstone building, though a floor above where I would be working.

I did my best to pay attention as the lecture progressed, though I was beginning to suffer from sensory overload—there was so much to take in, starting a new practice and all. I did learn something of interest—a tidbit of information commonly called a clinical pearl. It had to do with the origins of the disease. Current thinking was that stem cells could lose their ability to differentiate and proliferate due to a defect in their DNA. This meant that new blood cells were no longer being produced, a condition Doctor Prichard termed *stem cell exhaustion*. In other words, in some people, the bone marrow might simply forget how to make blood.

At the conclusion of the lecture, as the audience was starting to break up, Adam took hold of my arm and guided me toward a tall fellow standing at the back of the auditorium. "There is someone you need to meet," he said.

The man was long and lanky. He wore wire-rimmed spectacles and was partially bald on the crown of his head. He had an easy, almost disjointed way of moving, and there was no disputing that a penetrating intelligence lurked behind his cobalt-blue eyes.

"Blake," Adam said. "This is Sam Duncan. He is your thoracic surgeon. You need to get to know him. He may not look it, but he's very good at what he does." Adam gave the man a teasing wink. "Sam, this is Blake Sterling. Be gentle with him. He's still wet behind the ears."

Sam stuck out his hand. His face lit up in a friendly smile as he looked me up and down as if to size me up. "So this is the new guy. Welcome to Flintridge. I think you're going to like it here. Just be sure you take everything this old goat tells you with a grain of salt. Make sure he's not pulling your leg."

I returned Sam's handshake, noting that his skin was soft and smooth—the hand of a surgeon. With feigned innocence, I said, "Pulling my leg? Are you telling me that when I request a surgical consult, I don't have to mark the patient with a line that says 'cut here'?"

Sam laughed. "Very good. You're going to do fine. Look, I've got to run. I'm doing a wedge resection in twenty minutes." He turned to Adam. "You may remember him. Mr. Proust? Bullous emphysema? We're going to see if we can improve his tidal volume."

"Aw, yes. Give him my regards, and let me know how it turns out."

"Will do," Sam promised and then hurried off.

"We should be getting back," Adam said. "Lois hates it when we're late."

As we started to leave the auditorium, a voice behind us said, "Hello, Adam. Is this your new associate? I heard that you were introducing him around."

"Nothing escapes your notice, does it, Marcus?" Adam turned slowly to face the man who had spoken.

"Not much," the man admitted smugly.

When I turned to look behind me, I saw a small man standing, perhaps five feet seven inches and weighing maybe 155 pounds. He had on a charcoal-gray three-piece suit with a white handkerchief in his breast pocket. His tie bore alternating stripes of dark and light blue. He had wavy dark-brown hair, nearly black. A thin mustache rested below his long nose and above his narrow lips. His smile did not make it all the way to his hazel eyes.

I felt Adam stiffen slightly. He inclined his head toward me but kept his gaze fixed on the man in front of us. "Blake, this is Marcus Eldridge. He is the chief administrative officer for Flintridge Medical Center. Marcus, this is Blake Sterling. No doubt you already knew that."

"It's nice to meet you." Marcus did not offer to shake hands. Instead, he looked at Adam. "Have you had a chance to think about our latest offer? I'm sure you'll agree it's more than generous."

"What he is referring to"—Adam again spoke to me but looked at Marcus—"is Flintridge Healthcare's attempt to take over the practice I've spent thirty years creating…just like they intend to do with every other medical facility in the region."

"You make our efforts sound predatory," Marcus said with feigned indignation.

"Aren't they?" Adam retorted.

"On the contrary, they are entirely defensive. We've been over this before." Marcus looked at me. "If another hospital were to move into the area, it would provoke an intense competition to see who could attract the most patients. The way to avoid such an unfortunate conflict is for us to manage all aspects of the practice of medicine from the specialist to the vendor selling durable medical equipment. That way, patients are locked into the system. A new acute care facility would find it exceedingly difficult, if not impossible, to even get started.

"Besides"—Marcus returned his attention to Adam—"think of the security joining us would bring. You would have a base of primary care physicians who would be obliged to refer to you, and you're not getting any younger. Wouldn't it be reassuring to have the equity from your practice safely tucked away in a bank account? You have to admit we've made you an extremely generous offer."

"At what cost?" Adam replied simply. "All we'd have to give up is our independence."

"You would become part of a larger organization."

"Like being assimilated by the Borg," I said under my breath before I could stop myself.

"Excuse me?" Marcus said with a look of confusion.

"Nothing." I gave a dismissive wave of my hand. "Sorry."

"Marcus," Adam sighed. "Like you said, we've been through this."

"But you're still considering our offer, right?" Marcus said hopefully.

"It's true I haven't made my final decision, if that's what you're asking. Now if you will excuse us, we need to get back to the office."

Adam turned and walked away before Marcus could reply. I followed.

As we left the hospital, Adam commented, "Officious little man. He thinks this is his hospital. Unfortunately, in some ways, he's right. A word of warning—be sure you don't cross him. He can make your life very difficult if he chooses to do so."

Within a few short hours, I had been given a great deal to think about. My mind was still swimming as we climbed the back stairs. Then I remembered I was supposed to meet with Lois to be introduced to my nurse.

Ellie McDonough was a vivacious, cheerful young woman who seemed hardly old enough to have graduated from nursing school. She had reddish-brown hair—the color of polished mahogany—that she wore pulled back into a ponytail. A smattering of freckles dotted her cheeks and nose. The corners of her brown eyes crinkled whenever she smiled.

Lois had escorted Ellie to my office, introduced us, and then darted off to mollify a patient who was loudly complaining about a scheduling mix-up.

As I sat looking across my desk at Ellie, who stood facing me, I felt like a provincial schoolteacher interrogating a reluctant student. It was not a comfortable feeling. Until very recently, I had been a resident in training and, therefore, subject to the witticisms and criticisms of the nurses.

"So," I said as I sat back, trying to seem as if this interview was an everyday occurrence. "How is it you wound up being my nurse?"

"We drew straws."

"And you won?" I rewarded her with a pleasant smile.

"I lost."

"Oh." I looked but could not detect even a hint of subterfuge. Crestfallen, I offered, "I'm sorry. I hope it won't be as bad as you expect."

Ellie's face melted into a bright smile. "Just kidding. Actually I volunteered."

"You did?" I blurted out. "Why?"

"Somebody has to make sure you start off on the right foot."

"Thank you. I suspect I'm going to need all the help I can get."

Ellie stood up taller. "Are you ready to begin?"

"I am."

"Good. I'll go put your first patient in a room." Ellie turned on her heel and departed.

*That young lady has spunk*, I thought to myself. *I'm going to have to keep an eye on her…although I suspect she will be the one keeping her eye on me.*

I lowered my head and quietly prayed, "Dear Lord, thank you for this opportunity. You have prepared this path for me to walk. Please be with me, and keep me from screwing up too badly. Amen."

# AN ODD CASE

Wednesday afternoon, during my second day in private practice, something unusual happened. Midway through the afternoon, Jerry Tucker invited me to work out with him after office hours. Although worn down from trying to adapt to the rhythms of private practice, I had no wish to offend my colleague, so I agreed to meet him at his exercise spa, the Columbia Fitness Center.

Immediately after finishing with my last patient of the day, I rushed to the department store at the local mall to buy a pair of exercise sweats. I would have purchased a pair of cross trainers as well except I was pressed for time.

Jerry was waiting for me when I entered the lobby. He waved, and I stepped forward to join him. To call the Columbia Fitness Center a gym would be like labeling the Notre Dame Cathedral a quaint country church. In its brochure, the facility was advertised as an exercise spa. The entire establishment was plush. Softly melodic music played in the background. Muted accent lighting illuminated the central area where clients gathered. A number of other rooms were dedicated to a variety of physical activities including weightlifting, aerobics, racquetball, handball, and age-related exercise classes. There was a swimming pool, two saunas—one for each gender—and two locker rooms, plus of course a juice bar. A tennis court and a basketball half-court were available outside.

Jerry had already paid for a locker for me to use that evening. As a regular member, he maintained his own personal locker. He tossed me a padlock and its key.

In the locker room, as I started to change into my sweats, I suddenly realized that I had forgotten to bring an athletic supporter. It was too late to do anything about it, so I put my sweats on over my boxer shorts and hoped nobody would notice.

"Where do you want to start?" Jerry said as we left the locker room together.

"Your call," I replied. "I'll just follow along." I had no idea if a specific sequence was recommended or if you simply migrated randomly from machine to machine.

"Let's start in the aerobics room and get limbered up," Jerry suggested.

Exercise equipment of all descriptions lined the walls and covered most of the available floor space. There were stationary bicycles, treadmills, elliptical trainers, and other devices that might've been modeled after constructions used during the Spanish Inquisition.

Jerry advised that I start with a treadmill and work my way up to more vigorous selections. After showing me how to get the thing started, he began walking on the treadmill next to mine. I had already made up my mind that this was not going to turn into a competition. Although he was ten years my senior, he looked to be in far better shape than I was.

"So…what do you think so far? Are you settling in okay?" he said loudly enough to be heard above the machines' hum.

"I'd say it's going well. I'm enjoying the patients. Overall, they seem like decent hardworking folks." I increased the speed of my treadmill from ambled to fast walk. Jerry was already at brisk jog.

I cast a quick glance in his direction. "What's your assessment? How do you think I'm doing?" I knew both partners had been periodically reviewing my charts, so I had been taking extra care with my dictations, making sure my notes were clear and that my treatment recommendations fell well within the standard of care.

"I think you're doing fine." He amped up his treadmill to a long-distance runner's pace. "I understand you bumped into Marcus Eldridge the other day. What did you think of him?"

"Honestly, he strikes me as someone who carries a lot of responsibility on his shoulders." What I didn't say was that because of his responsibilities, he takes himself far too seriously.

"I gather he mentioned Flintridge Healthcare's offer to buy our practice."

"Briefly, yes."

"Adam doesn't see it, but it's really the way we should go. No more hassles with employee relations. No more worrying about whether or not we'll get the referrals we need to keep the practice afloat—not to mention the buyout. There is so much I could do with that money." Jerry's voice trailed off so that I had difficulty hearing him. Then he spoke up again. "What's your opinion? What do you think we should do?"

"At this point, I don't have an opinion. I haven't studied the issue carefully enough to make a choice."

"Yes, of course. Well, as you think about it, if you do have questions, let me know. I'll be happy to share what I've learned."

"I appreciate that. When do we have to make a decision?"

"Soon."

It worried me that my partners were at odds on such an important issue. It worried me even more that I was in the middle.

We continued exercising for another two hours. By the time we quit, I was dead tired and starving. After showering and changing back into my street clothes, I thanked Jerry for the workout and headed back to my one-bedroom apartment. I had intended to fix myself a simple dinner, but instead I stretched out on the bed and was promptly asleep.

A little after 6:30 a.m. Saturday morning, I pulled into the gated parking area for the brownstone building. Only three other cars were in the lot, so I had my choice of spaces. Like Pulmonary Associates, the building's other practices were also closed on weekends. I suppose I might have parked at the hospital, since that was my destination, but I liked the idea of being behind a locked gate. Perhaps I was being overly cautious. I mean, who's going to steal an eight-year-old Nissan Sentra?

Still better safe than sorry. After making sure my car was locked, I headed for the hospital.

This Saturday was my first weekend on call, and it was the tail end of my first week in private practice. So far, I was pleased with the way things had been going and the relationships I was building with my partners. I was enjoying practicing medicine, and I was glad I had joined Pulmonary Associates rather than one of the other groups that had offered me a position.

Being on call during a weekday was different than being on call over a weekend. On weekdays, each partner was expected to cover his own practice, which included making hospital rounds on his own patients morning and evening. The guy on call was expected to pick up any new referrals that might come in and to be available for emergencies. On weekends, the on-call guy not only picked up all new referrals and covered all emergencies, he also rounded on his own hospitalized patients plus the patients his partners were caring for as well.

This day, there were five names on the list I had been given. As I entered the hospital, I decided to start with Mr. Emile Goldstein and work my way down. Actually, I did not start with Mr. Goldstein because his name was at the top of the list but because he was in the ICU, and I prefer to begin my on-call days by seeing the sickest patients first.

As I entered the hospital through its main entrance, I launched another arrow prayer heavenward.

The Flintridge Medical Center's intensive care unit took up the entire west wing of the second floor. Entry through its locked double doors was controlled by a keypad, and I could not remember the combination. Adam and I had stopped by the ICU during my first day's orientation. At that time, he had shared the four-digit code, but regrettably, I had failed to write it down.

I buzzed the intercom to request admittance, but there was no reply. I buzzed again—same result. I looked around for assistance, but with no one else in sight, it appeared that my only option was to hang out until someone happened by. Fortunately, I did not have long to wait.

A man near to my own age of thirty-one and wearing green scrubs approached the double doors. He was pushing what I recognized to be an ultrasonic nebulizer on a wheeled stand. I assumed he was a respiratory therapist.

"Excuse me," I said. "I wonder if you could help me? I'm Doctor Sterling. I've just joined the Pulmonary Associates, and I have a patient in the ICU I need to see. Do you think you could let me in or, better still, tell me the code so I can let myself in the next time."

"You're Doctor Sterling?" the man said with a look of sudden comprehension. "We heard you were coming—the department, that is. I work in—"

"Respiratory Therapy—I'd assumed as much." I inclined my head toward the nebulizer. "And you are…?"

"Tyler Wickham. I'm the assistant department head." Tyler had sandy-blonde hair and medium-brown eyes. He wore a full mustache, probably to conceal the scar produced by his cleft lip surgery as an infant.

Tyler commented, "You're joining a good group. I've worked with Doctor Richards for almost seven years now. He and Doctor Tucker are A-OK."

I detected a hint of uneasiness when Tyler spoke, though I didn't pay his state of mind much heed. "I'm glad to hear that. So…can you let me in?"

"Sure—if you wouldn't mind showing me your ID."

I reached into my hip pocket and withdrew the laminated badge the medical staff secretary had presented to me on Monday. I held it up so Tyler could read it.

He looked my ID over and then said, "Thank you. It's 4-7-1-3," enunciating each number clearly as he punched in the code. A buzzing noise signaled that the door was unlocked. He pushed it open before the buzzing stopped and held it open. "What's your patient's name?"

"Emile Goldstein." I fetched a ballpoint pen out of my shirt pocket and jotted down the number on the palm of my hand. "4-7-1-3. Got it."

Tyler brightened. "Mr. Goldstein, sure. This is for him." He motioned toward the nebulizer. "He's due for his morning breathing treatment."

"What are you giving him?"

"Albuterol."

Tyler pushed the door all the way open and entered the ICU.

"Thank you," I said as I followed behind. "Who knows how long I might have been standing there."

"It was good to meet you." Tyler headed toward a patient's room. I noted its number—5.

"I expect we'll see each other again." I called after him as he disappeared inside. I looked around.

The unit seemed deserted except for a youthful-looking nurse. She sat at the nurses' station. Her attention was focused on a bank of cardiac monitors. The previous time I had been to the ICU, the unit had been bustling with activity. *Where are the nurses?* I wondered. Then I remembered what time it was. *Of course—change of shift. In all probability, they are giving and receiving report.*

And I was right. I stepped up to a rack of tablet computers arrayed in slots on a shelf beside the nursing station. I picked up one of the devices that would interface with the hospital's mainframe. No sooner had I logged in with my username and password than a gaggle of nurses, all wearing scrubs, emerged from a room behind the nursing station.

When one of them, an older woman with salt-and-pepper hair, saw me, she immediately charged forward. "You there. What do you think you're doing?"

"Making rounds," I replied innocently.

"Who are you?"

I explained again that I was the new guy who had just joined the pulmonary medicine group.

"If that's the case," she demanded. "Show me your ID."

When I complied, she snapped, "You should be wearing that, not carrying it in your pocket. How are we supposed to know who you are if we can't see your badge?"

"Sorry," I said as I dutifully clipped the ID to my shirt pocket.

The nurse bustled off to see to her duties, and I sat down at a workbench to review my patient's medical record.

Five minutes later, I had learned a great deal about Mr. Goldstein. Thirty-six hours before, he had arrived in the Emergency Department with a diagnosis of gastrointestinal bleeding. In short order, he had been stabilized and the bleeding brought under control to the point that he had been deemed worthy of being discharged. However, before he could be signed out, he had come down with an acute respiratory ailment. Within a span of a couple of hours, he had gone from being unimpaired to showing signs of impending respiratory failure. Doctor Peter Ramsey, the hospitalist treating him for his GI bleed, had then consulted Doctor Tucker, who had admitted him to the intensive care unit.

A variety of diagnostic studies had been performed including a full panel of blood tests and a respiratory function profile. Although not specific, the results were most compatible with an acute viral infection. The nature of the virus had not been determined.

As I was finishing my perusal of Mr. Goldstein's medical records, I noticed Tyler step out of Mr. Goldstein's room. The respiratory tech nodded to me as he passed and said, "He's all yours."

"How did he do?" I asked.

"Amazingly well," Tyler replied. "You'll see."

I rose from the workbench and entered room 5 to speak with Mr. Goldstein. The middle-aged man lying in bed hardly looked sick at all. He certainly did not fit the description of someone who had been struggling to breathe. In fact, his status at that time had been so tenuous that Doctor Ramsey and Doctor Tucker had seriously considered intubating him and putting him on a respirator.

"Good morning, Mr. Goldstein," I said as I approached his bed. "I'm Doctor Sterling. I'm covering for Doctor Tucker. How are you feeling this morning?"

"Superb. Can I go home?" The patient's voice was clear and strong, and there was no wheezing or panting.

"We'll see. You were pretty sick when they brought you in."

"Perhaps, but I am better now."

"I can see that." I spoke with Mr. Goldstein for several minutes, taking additional history, and clarifying several points I had gleaned from his medical record. I finished up by saying, "How about I listen to your heart and lungs? Would that be all right?"

"Go ahead."

I retrieved my stethoscope from the inside pocket of my blazer. After fitting the ear pieces in place, I performed my examination. "Your lungs sound remarkably clear," I said when I finished.

"Told you. Can I go home?"

"Maybe this afternoon. I have to check some follow-up lab studies first, but if they tell me you are as well as you look, I don't see why you couldn't be discharged."

"Excellent. When will I know? I need to tell my wife."

"I'll be making rounds again this evening sometime between four and six. We should know by then how your lab studies turn out."

"More tests?"

"Only a few in follow-up."

I said goodbye to Jerry's patient and left the room. As I was sliding the glass door closed, a portly woman walked by. I interdicted her and asked, "Are you Mr. Goldstein's nurse?"

"No, that would be Madison. She had to run a urine specimen to the lab. She should be back soon. Is there something I could help you with?"

"No, thank you, eh—Dolly," I said, reading her name tag.

I sat down at the workbench again to enter my progress note and order a few salient lab studies. I thought about including a viral culture since the patient's condition had been so severe but decided against it because he had improved so substantially. Knowing the name of the virus that had infected him would not change his clinical management.

"You were asking for me," said a dulcet voice that came from behind me.

Startled, I swiveled around and looked up into a beautiful pair of blue, almost violet, eyes.

Madison Lane looked to be in her late twenties. She had auburn hair that descended in gentle flows to her shoulder blades. Her oval face complemented her cute nose and delicate lips as did her flawless complexion. Standing approximately five feet six inches, she could not have weighed more than 135 pounds. I tried not to stare.

Momentarily caught off guard, I stammered, "Hi. I, eh…you're Mr. Goldstein's nurse?"

Madison nodded. "And you're Doctor Sterling."

"Right. Blake Sterling. Call me Blake. I've just been going over Mr. Goldstein's records. It seems incredible, but apparently, he's not the same man he was yesterday afternoon. Is that true? Am I reading this right?"

"That is correct. Throughout the night, he kept improving. To look at him, you would never know how sick he was when he came in." Madison sat down in the swivel chair beside me.

"That's rather odd—not your usual pneumonia, and his breath sounds are clear. What do you think is going on?" I asked.

"I would guess some sort of respiratory virus, although it could be an exposure to some toxic aerosol, I suppose."

"True, but exposure to what? There is no history of his having come into contact with anything that could produce this clinical picture." I tapped the tablet computer for emphasis.

"In a way," Madison said. "He reminds me of a patient we had a week ago—Agnes Gilroy. She was admitted for workup of a syncopal episode. Within twenty-four hours of her arrival, she was in severe respiratory distress, but then she started to turn around. Forty-eight hours later, she was feeling fine without any lingering physical findings. Weird."

"I'll say. Two patients with the same peculiar presentation—that is strange. Makes you wonder if there might be a common source."

I checked the time on the wall clock. It was 8:35. I needed to get moving. I still had four other patients to see. I finished writing my progress note, signed my orders, and wished Madison a good day. I then hurried off to continue my rounds.

Two hours later, after attending to the last of my partners' patients, I returned to the ICU. Something about Mr. Goldstein's case troubled me, though I was having a hard time putting my finger on precisely what that might be. Perhaps the rate at which his respiratory status had changed was what bothered me most. To go from normal to seriously impaired and back to normal in such a short span of time was decidedly unusual.

The intensive care unit had been completely refurbished a year before my arrival, so the patients' rooms, the nursing station, all the equipment, and the furnishings were virtually brand-new. Even in subdued lighting, polished surfaces throughout the unit gleamed brightly, a tribute to the housekeepers' diligence.

During quiet times, when there was a lull in patient care, some units might play soothing music to relax both the patients and the medical staff; yet this morning, there was no music, only the muted electric hum of monitors, fluorescent lights, and intravenous infusion pumps. *At least no code blue alarms are blaring*, I thankfully reminded myself.

I sat at the workbench, going over Mr. Goldstein's record for a third time, having virtually memorized most of it. Several times when Madison passed by, she looked at me and smiled. I reminded myself not to read too much into her taking notice. *She's just being friendly*, I told myself, though when she finally finished her morning duties, she came over and sat down beside me. "Learn anything new?" she said, indicating the tablet computer.

"No, but I feel like I'm missing something."

"I know. It's an odd case, that's for sure."

She crossed her legs and took in a deep breath, which she exhaled slowly. "I love this job…except when I don't." She chuckled.

To be polite, I said, "Are you from around here originally?"

"Yep. Washington state, born and bred. I understand you're from LA?"

*The grapevine is up and running*, I thought. Every hospital had one. In training, there were times when the rumor mill knew what I was doing before I did. "That I am. UCLA all the way. Go Bruins. Where did you go to nursing school?"

"Gonzaga in Spokane."

"That's a Catholic school. Are you Catholic?"

"Protestant. You?"

"I like to think of myself as evangelical—or at least nondenominational."

We chatted for a while until she had to go back to work.

Looking at Mr. Goldstein's record, I decided that another review would be counterproductive. I also decided that if his lab studies were acceptable and he was still doing well, I would discharge him when I made my evening rounds. I asked Madison to let him know so he could make arrangements for transportation.

On my way out of the unit, I encountered Marcus Eldridge. We were about to pass in the hallway when he stopped and said, "Doctor Sterling, good morning. Would you be willing to give me fifteen minutes of your time? I'd like to speak with you about something."

"All right. Where would you like to meet?"

"I have to take care of a problem on the third floor. It shouldn't take but a minute. I could meet you in my office. Do you know where it is?"

"I think I can find it," Marcus said as if I had insulted his intelligence.

"Good. I'll see you there in two shakes of a lamb's tail." Marcus hurried off—a soldier on a search-and-destroy mission.

I changed course and headed toward the administration wing, which was located at ground level.

When Marcus arrived ten minutes later, I was idly killing time, studying the photographs that lined the corridor outside his office. "These are some fine images," I said as he drew near. "Good composition and a solid appreciation of how light can be used to establish mood."

"You sound like you have some familiarity with taking pictures," Marcus said.

"It's been a hobby since I was in high school. This artist...I don't recognize his name."

"He's a friend of mine. I just like the way his pictures look—very dramatic."

*Dramatic but impersonal*, I thought. *Vacant streets and empty park benches. Artistically appealing but lacking humanity.* I kept my impressions to myself as I followed Marcus into his office.

Like the photos outside, the room seemed sterile, devoid of passion. The desk, the bookshelves, the citations and awards hanging on the walls were all neat and tidy but formal—detached. As I sat down in one of several thinly padded chairs with wooden arms, I noticed the items on the desk. There was a laptop computer, a pen and pencil set on a marble base, a silver letter opener, a phone charging station, and a desktop calendar. Everything was in its place. The only object with any warmth to it was a picture of a Pomeranian in a gilded frame.

Marcus shed his suit coat and hung it on a rack in the corner. He then sat down behind his desk.

"What did you want to talk about?" I asked. "Have I done something wrong?"

"I don't know. Have you?" Marcus gave a half smile that suggested he was teasing. "Actually, I simply wanted to visit for a bit. I like to get to know the doctors who staff my hospital. So…tell me about yourself."

"There's really not much to tell. I'm not sure what you're asking."

"I'm just trying to get to know you. Your parents, are they still alive?"

"No. They died in an avalanche while skiing in Colorado. I was raised by my grandfather. He was a plumber. We lived in Santa Monica, California. That's where I grew up. Granddad moved to Las Vegas three years ago when he retired."

"Do you have any siblings?"

"No. I was an only child."

"What about hobbies? Besides photography, is there anything that interests you?"

"I like hiking in the wilderness. I also play the guitar, though I'm not very good at it."

Marcus tilted his head. "You're not married, are you?"

"No, I'm not. I was engaged once, but my fiancée died. She was bitten by a sea snake while snorkeling in the Virgin Islands." I tried not to cringe at the memory of losing her.

"Oh, how terrible. That must have been extremely traumatic. Were you with her?"

"I was. It happened so fast. There was nothing I could do. The snake came out of nowhere. It was over in minutes…but enough about me. What about you? Tell me about yourself."

Marcus tilted back in his chair with his fingers laced behind his head. "There's not much to tell. Like you, I'm a bachelor—I live alone except for Pebbles." He picked up the picture of the Pomeranian, stared at it for a moment, and then put it back down. I don't really have any hobbies. My work is what I enjoy most."

"Being responsible for the daily operations of a tier-three hospital must be stressful."

"It can be, but it's what I do—it's who I am. So tell me…I realize you've only been here a week, but how has your experience been so far?"

"Better than I expected," I answered truthfully.

"I assume that's a good thing."

"It is."

"What about patient care? How are we doing in that regard?"

"Fine. I mean the patients I've encountered seemed to be well cared for."

"Any cases in particular that stand out? Anything interesting that you've come across?"

"There is one case that has me puzzled. He's currently in the ICU, but he should be going home this evening." I drew a thumbnail sketch of Mr. Goldstein's clinical course and shared my concerns regarding the rapidity with which his symptoms had evolved. Marcus listened but made no comment.

When I finished, he said, "So…what's your diagnosis? What's going on do you think?"

I shrugged. "I'm not sure. He probably picked up some exotic respiratory virus, though where he might have contracted it, I have no idea. I suspect we will never know."

"A pity," Marcus said under his breath. "Well, thank you for taking the time to visit with me. If ever something comes up that you think should be brought to my attention, my door is always open. Likewise, if there's anything you need or if I can be of assistance in any way, don't hesitate to ask. Technically, my job is to make your job easier." Marcus rocked forward and then stood up.

"I appreciate that. So far, I'm impressed by how well the hospital functions." I stood up as well.

"Glad to hear it." Marcus patted me on the shoulder as I left his office.

Outside in the corridor, I was about to head for the front exit when I noticed a man standing where I had been standing while waiting for Marcus. I was about to wave hello to Tyler Wickham when another man stepped up to join him. I recognized the second man immediately. It was Jerry Tucker.

*What's he doing here?* I asked myself. *He should be home relaxing on his day off.*

Neither man saw me, so I ducked into an alcove and watched to see what would happen. Within less than a minute, Marcus emerged from his office. After briefly speaking with the two men, they followed him back inside.

"What was that all about, I wonder?" I said softly but then thought, *Probably has something to do with the Respiratory Therapy Department, which is none of my business.* I put the matter out of my mind and headed back to my car. I still had time to go grocery shopping and maybe do some laundry before returning to start evening rounds.

Marcus gazed across his desk at Tyler Wickham and Jerry Tucker, trying to decide which man he liked the least. It wasn't that they were particularly obnoxious or had annoying personal habits, nor was it that they were overtly hostile or argumentative. It was that they considered themselves to be his equals or possibly even his betters by virtue of their membership in the New World Militia. They had made their point of view clear—that their roles as foot soldiers entitled them to special considerations. Marcus, however, was of a different opinion. Captain Summers had explicitly charged him with supervising the members of his team. That meant he was in charge, and he wasn't about to relinquish his authority. It was time he put his foot down.

Glowering at Tyler with a level gaze, Marcus declared in his sternest tone of voice, "You will not go anywhere near Mr. Goldstein again, is that clear? I don't want you having anything to do with him. Do you understand?"

"A breathing treatment was ordered," Tyler protested. "What was I supposed to do? Tell Doctor Ramsey to take his order and shove it?" He looked at Jerry for support. Jerry merely shrugged.

"You are the assistant department head," Marcus countered. "Assign another therapist."

"They'll say I'm slacking—not doing my job."

"Tell them you're taking inventory or ordering supplies," Marcus said with a show of exasperation. "If this operation goes south, I don't want the subject to know you even exist. Are we clear?"

"All right," Tyler said, his frustration evident.

Marcus would have preferred a crisp "Yes, sir," but the therapist's reluctant capitulation was sufficient. "What do you have to say for yourself?" Marcus said, scowling at Jerry.

"I spoke with Captain Summers. He is pleased with the way Ophis Pterotos is progressing. That means The Angel is pleased—"

"This Angel?" Marcus interjected. "Who is this Angel I keep hearing about? What's his name?"

"We don't know," Tyler seemed apprehensive.

"That's right," Jerry said more matter-of-factly. All we know is that he is extremely wealthy, and he owns a virology lab in Mexico. That's where he prepares the aerosols we administer. Personally, I feel less threatened by not knowing. Knowledge can be a dangerous thing."

"So, Jerry, what happens next?" Marcus said.

"In the morning, I'll be sending copies of Mr. Goldstein's medical records and lab studies to Captain Summers.

"How do you intend to send them?" Marcus said.

"By US mail, same as the last two times," Jerry replied.

"Doesn't it bother you," Marcus said. "Trusting the post office? Government mail isn't very reliable."

"Relax. It's worked twice before. It will work again this time. We should get our next vial of serum by the end of the week."

"And how are you going to administer this one?" Marcus said, turning his attention to Tyler.

"Same as before," Tyler said as if the technique should be painfully obvious. "I pick a patient being admitted with a non-respiratory, non-life-threatening condition. I wait until they are asleep and then I sneak into their room. I hold my breath and spray several puffs of aerosol toward their face from a foot away, then I leave as fast as I can."

Marcus nodded crisply. "Very good. Sounds like a solid plan." He smiled at Tyler. A little encouragement would go a long way toward smoothing ruffled feathers.

"One more thing—both of you need to keep an eye on the new guy. When you are around him, be careful with what you do and say. Doctor Sterling is already suspicious that something funny is going on with Mr. Goldstein. We wouldn't want him to start nosing around more than he already has. Jerry, if he starts acting like he knows something is amiss, you need to distract him, and Tyler, when you're around him, you don't know nothing 'bout nothing. Understand?"

"That should be easy enough," Jerry commented under his breath.

"Hey," Tyler snapped. "A little respect. You're not the one risking your life like I do."

"The virus isn't lethal," Jerry declared. "All you'd get is a bad cold. Idiot."

"Gentlemen," Marcus barked. "Enough of that. We are a team. Let's act like one. We will meet again in ten days. Until then, behave yourselves."

After the two men had filed out of the room, Marcus pulled his bankbook out of the desk's top drawer. He opened it and stared at the deposit recorded on the first line—one million dollars. He absolutely loved looking at all those zeroes.

# UNEXPECTED DEVELOPMENTS

**M**onday morning, I was again making my hospital rounds—if attending to one patient can qualify as making rounds. I had survived my first weekend on call with no adverse incidents. In fact, I had even picked up my first referral, and since Adam and Jerry would be seeing their own patients, that meant I had only the one patient to visit, a fifty-seven-year-old chain smoker whose chronic bronchitis had flared into an acute lobar pneumonia.

Mr. Philip Drake had been admitted to the third-floor medical wing. When I checked on him, I was pleased to note that the intravenous antibiotics I had prescribed—along with bronchodilator treatments to open up his airways—were having a beneficial effect. His breathing was easier, and when I listened to his chest, his lungs sounded less congested.

After finishing with Mr. Drake, I still had an hour before I was to begin seeing patients in the office. I decided to visit the doctor's lounge. Perhaps I could introduce myself to some more of my colleagues and spend a few minutes getting to know them. I had found in training that killing time with my fellow physicians and listening to their gossip was a good way to stay abreast of what was going down in the world of medicine.

The doctor's lounge was on the first floor, not far from the cafeteria. After descending the stairs, I began walking in that direction.

That's when I noticed the chapel on my right as I was about to pass by. Mostly out of curiosity, I stepped inside.

Subdued lighting bathed the room in a soft yellow glow. Soothing music played in the background. Half-a-dozen wooden pews flanked each side of a central aisle that led toward an altar at the far end of the room. An overhead spotlight illuminated an empty golden crucifix. A white linen runner lay draped across the altar. Altogether, the room had a quiet, restful ambience befitting a place of meditation and worship.

I slipped into a pew toward the center of the room and sat down. After clearing my mind, I allowed a sense of calmness to fill me. I then closed my eyes and bowed my head.

"Heavenly Father," I said softly. "Holy and righteous is Your name. Thank You for bringing me to this place, and thank You for the blessings You have bestowed upon me. May I be mindful of each and every one and never take any for granted. Be with me as I go forward this day. Guide and direct my path. Endow me with wisdom and sound judgment. Allow me to minister to the sick in Your name, and bless the work of my hands that I may glorify You. In Jesus's name, amen.

I gradually opened my eyes and sat back. When I did, I became aware of a presence behind me. I startled and looked around to find Madison Lane seated on the opposite side of the central aisle, one row back, watching me.

"That was beautiful," she said. "Sorry. I don't mean to intrude, but I couldn't help but overhear. I wish more of our doctors would follow your example. Do you come here regularly?"

"Actually, this is my first time. What about you?"

"I try to stop in before every shift. A little quiet time helps prepare me for the chaos in the ICU."

"I can relate to that. Sometimes I get so caught up in the hustle and bustle that I forget to worship the way I should."

Madison chuckled. "Exactly. It seems like the grind of daily life can erode even the best of intentions."

"How true," I agreed. "By the way, do you go to church?"

"I try to attend every Sunday, why?"

"I'm looking for a church where I can feel at home. I'm wondering how you feel about your church."

"I like it—quite a lot, actually. The Resurrection Bible Church is a little more sedate than some of the modern churches in the area, but their theology is sound. The reverend Elijah Thomas is the pastor. He preaches a good sermon. Next Sunday, you should come and see. I think you'd like it."

"Thank you. I'll give it a try. What time do they start?"

"I attend the 8:00 a.m. service, but there are services at 9:30 and 11:00 as well."

"Sounds good. Eight o'clock—I'll see you there."

Madison looked toward the altar. "Do you think it helps?" she said with an edge of uncertainty.

"Do I think what helps?"

"Praying, beseeching God to heal the patients we care for. Do our prayers make a difference, or are we just making ourselves feel better by showing that we care? I mean, how would we know? Let's say I have a patient who is really sick. I pray for her, and she gets better. Would she have gotten better anyway if I hadn't prayed? Don't get me wrong. I don't intend to stop praying. I would just like to know if my prayers are doing anything worthwhile."

"You have to assume your prayers make a difference. Otherwise, why would God have ordained prayers as a holy rite in the first place?"

"But how do you know for sure that they help?"

"Maybe we're not meant to know. Maybe prayers are intended to grow our faith. When we pray, we first must trust that God will hear our prayers and then act to answer our prayers according to his will."

"Trust—that's the heart of the issue, isn't it? Trust—that's what we're really talking about."

"It would seem so." I stood up to leave and allow Madison to have her quiet time. "I hope your day goes well," I said as I stepped into the center aisle.

"And yours." Madison gave me a bright smile. "I'll see you in church if not before."

As I walked back to the office, I thought about our encounter and wondered how it was that I previously had failed to truly appreciate how attractive Madison was—not strikingly gorgeous in the sense of a fashion model but genuinely pretty in a wholesome sort of way. I also noticed that she wasn't wearing a wedding ring.

As I began seeing patients in the office that Monday morning, the workload seemed fairly routine, right in line with what I had come to expect after one week on the job. I had been scheduled to see one patient every fifteen minutes, and for the most part, I was keeping up rather well. Midway through the morning, it occurred to me that the majority of the patients I was seeing had been referred primarily from Adam. I had assumed they would come from Adam and Jerry equally. In that I was new, and having not yet established my own practice, my partners had both agreed to transfer some of their patients to my care.

This was a win-win-win scenario. Patients transferred to me would be seen sooner than if they had been forced to wait for an opening in their regular physician's schedule. Some of the workload was lifted from my partners' shoulders. In addition, each transfer helped build a practice of my own.

A little before noon, the three partners were together in the all-purpose room where the staff tended to gather when not involved in caring for patients. We were enjoying a brief interlude while our next patients were being roomed—being prepared for their office visit.

Adam, Jerry, and I were talking about something innocuous, maybe football or local politics; I don't remember specifically. I do remember that the tie I was wearing felt uncomfortably tight. A tie was part of what I had come to regard as our office uniform: slacks, dress shirt, tie, and leather shoes. A suit coat was optional, but not required.

All of a sudden, from out of nowhere, Adam announced, "There's something I've been meaning to tell you for a while now. I've been putting it off because…well, I might as well just say it. I'm going to retire at the end of the month."

"What?!" Jerry exclaimed.

"I thought you enjoyed practicing medicine?" I protested, feeling anxious.

"I do." Adam declared. "Well, at least I enjoy patient care. The political side of medicine, not so much. Be that as it may, I've been at this a long while. I'd like to spend time with my grandchildren and travel to places I've never been—maybe do a little gardening. Now that you're here, Blake, I can leave without dumping everything on Jerry."

Jerry seemed visibly shaken. "Who's going to run the practice? You've always looked after things. You're the one who handles the finances. Who's going to meet with the accountant and the lawyers?"

"That will be your job—yours and Blake's. I'll expect you two to work together. You're bright enough to figure things out." Adam gave an encouraging smile.

"You wouldn't consider working part-time, would you?" I asked hopefully.

"I've thought about it, but it seems to me that a quick departure would be best. I've already instructed Lois to begin notifying my patients. A clean break will be best for them as well."

"How did you come by that opinion?" Jerry said.

Adam braced a hip against the counter where items essential to running the practice were stored. "Oh, they may be upset initially, but they'll soon get over it. That'll be far better than dragging things out and going at it piecemeal. If I were simply to cut back, the patients I transferred to you guys would feel slighted, and the patients I kept to manage personally would feel inappropriately privileged. No, they all need to be in the same bucket, so to speak."

Jerry's facial expression began to harden with traces of anger. I could tell he had been caught completely off guard. He said, "Have you notified the medical staff office at the hospital?" It was apparent that he was beginning to appreciate the scope of Adam's disclosure. His reactions were following a predictable pattern. Denial, anger, bargaining, and acceptance—the stages everyone goes through upon receiving distressingly bad news."

"I have," Adam affirmed.

Through pursed lips, Jerry said, "I imagine you're expecting to be bought out?"

"I am, but we can hammer out the details down the road. I want to make it as easy on you two as possible."

"Bought out?" I said in confusion. "What are you—"

"He's talking about selling us his share of the practice," Jerry interjected. "Every partner owns a portion of the practice based upon the amount of overhead they've paid in over the years. How much a partner is to be paid when he leaves will depend upon his proportional share of the paid-in overhead times what the practice is worth. The bean counters will have to determine the practice's fair market value. One thing is certain—buying Adam out won't be cheap."

Adam nodded. "Like I said, I'll work with you on that."

Adam's nurse entered the room and handed him a chart and said, "She's in room 4. Her breathing is a little tighter than it has been, and she's running a low-grade fever."

"Thank you," Adam said. "I'll be right there." He turned to face us. "I apologize for laying this on you so abruptly, but it had to happen sooner or later."

"You're not ill, are you?" Jerry said with genuine concern. "Is there something going on we should know about?"

"No. I'm in good health—far as I know, which is another reason I want to retire now. I'd rather not wait until I'm too old to enjoy my leisure years. We can talk more about this later. Right now, I need to get to work." Adam left the room to see to his patient.

After he was gone, Jerry laid a hand on my shoulder. "We need to talk about this. What are your plans for lunch?"

"I thought I would attend the CME conference at the hospital."

"There isn't one today. They've been moved to Fridays."

"Really? That's good. Mondays are busy enough as it is. I guess I'm free for lunch.

"Do you like Chinese? There's a restaurant not far from here that serves a wicked chow mein. We could go there."

"Any place is fine by me—just so long as I get my questions answered. I need to understand what just happened."

"You and me both."

When Ellie brought me a chart, I went back to work; but rather than focus on my patients and their complaints, I found myself dwelling on what was happening to the practice. Changes are inevitable, though not all changes are for the best.

Noontime customers thronged the Lotus Dragon restaurant. We'd had to wait twenty minutes to get a table, and I was concerned that we might be late getting back to the office. However, we were served promptly, making up for lost time. The chow mein was very good as Jerry had foretold.

"Let me understand," I said after taking a sip of my green tea. "When a partner leaves the practice, those who remain are obligated to buy his share?"

"That's the agreement," Jerry affirmed. "Perhaps if I give you an example, it will make all this clearer. As you know, the amount of overhead we pay is based upon what we bill. Currently the ratio is forty-five percent, meaning that if we bill a thousand dollars, we will pay 450 dollars in overhead. Imagine that over time, one partner bills a total of 10 thousand dollars, and the other partner bills 8 thousand dollars. The first partner will have paid 4,500 dollars in overhead charges, or 56 percent of the total overhead. The other partner will have paid 3,600 dollars in overhead, or 44 percent of the total.

"When the first partner retires, the second partner is obligated to pay him 56 percent of what the practice is worth—an amount that depends upon a number of factors including whatever capital assets the practice owns, whatever funds are in the bank, and a nebulous factor called goodwill, which is basically a dollar value assigned to the practice's ability to attract new patients. In a nutshell, goodwill is the quantification of a practice's favorable reputation in the community. You take all these factors and combine them together and then subtract whatever liabilities may be outstanding, and there you have the practice's net valuation.

"So if a practice's net valuation is, let's say, a hundred thousand dollars, the second partner will owe the first partner 56,000 dollars."

I nearly choked on my chow mein. "You mean that's what we're going to owe Adam?"

Jerry shook his head. "Those figures were just by way of an example. The actual amounts could be considerably different. I suspect they will be much higher."

I could hardly believe what I was hearing. "Really? What happens if we don't pay him?"

"He would have the right to sell the practice to a third party and proportionately distribute amongst us whatever someone would be willing to pay. In other words, all three of us would be bought out. The bottom line is we'd be homeless, so to speak."

A feeling of impending doom came upon me. "Now I understand why you were so negatively impacted. What are we going to do?"

"As I see it, there's only one thing to do. We're going to have to sell the practice and become employees of Flintridge Healthcare."

"What would that entail?"

"Pretty much what you would expect. We would be working for the hospital. They would own the practice. Our employees would no longer be employees of Pulmonology Associates. They would be employees of Flintridge Healthcare—meaning we would have very little say over who was assigned to work in our office. Our incomes would be determined by our billings as before, but our overhead would be higher than it is now because Flintridge Healthcare would expect to make a profit on their investment.

"Not only that, we would have administrative bureaucrats like Marcus Eldridge telling us what tests we can order, what drugs we can prescribe, and what we can bill for our services. The quality of our healthcare would no longer be measured by how well our patients do but, rather, by how much money we can bring in. Peer reviews would no longer be geared toward making us better doctors. Instead, they would be intended to make us more efficient employees."

My sense of foreboding increased exponentially, molding my face into a worried frown. "Selling out can't be our only option."

Jerry blotted his lips with his napkin. "If Adam expects a lump-sum buyout, I don't see that we have a choice. On the other hand, if he would be willing to be bought out over time, perhaps we could manage it, but that would mean we would be taking home substantially less money every month. I don't know about you, but my expense-to-income ratio is already uncomfortably high. I'm not sure that I could sustain a drop in revenue."

I put down my chopsticks and sat back. "I did not expect this when I agreed to join you guys."

Jerry looked offended. "Hey, I am as disturbed by this as you are. I had no idea Adam's retirement was on the horizon."

"I wasn't accusing you of deceiving me. It just came as a surprise, that's all."

"There is another possibility," Jerry said reluctantly. "We could borrow the money to pay Adam off."

"You mean the associates would borrow the funds collectively?"

"No, I mean each of us individually. Look at it this way. If you started out in practice on your own and weren't joining an established group, you would have to borrow to get your practice started. The net effect would be pretty much the same either way. You'd have to go into debt to have the opportunity to practice medicine."

We both sat quietly for a time, thinking about the problem at hand. At length, I asked, "Which option do you favor?"

"All things considered, I'd have to say selling the practice to Flintridge. What about you? What do you think is the best way to go?"

"I'm not sure. I need time to study this some more." After a moment of introspection, I asked, "What happens if one partner wants to go one way and the other partner wants to go a different way? What do we do then?"

"In all probability, such a disagreement, if it couldn't be resolved, would force a sale of the practice—either to Flintridge or to another entity. Adam is retiring. A debt is owed. There's no getting around that basic fact."

"When do we have to decide?"

"Before the end of the month—that's when he says he's leaving, and we will want to have an agreement nailed down before that happens."

The waitress came with our bill, and Jerry picked up the tab. I paid the tip. As he stuck the receipt in his shirt pocket, he said, "So… what did you think? Pretty good chow, right?"

"It was good," I agreed. "I assume it would have tasted even better under different circumstances."

"No doubt. Are you ready?"

I nodded in the affirmative, and we returned to the office to begin an afternoon of patient care.

Late Wednesday afternoon, I was back in the ICU. Once again, it was my turn on call. This time it was because I had swapped days with Jerry, who had requested time off to take care of a personal matter. Near the end of office hours, a request had been phoned in that I come to the unit to consult on Violet Shoemaker, a middle-aged woman with a condition known as Goodpasture syndrome—a disease wherein the body's immune system attacks both the lungs and the kidneys, resulting in significant bleeding. The goal of therapy is to remove the offending antibody that is damaging the patient's internal organs. This is done by a process called total volume plasmapheresis. Blood is withdrawn from the body, separated into plasma and cells, and the cells are then transfused back into the patient. When performed in combination with drugs that suppress the immune system, this therapy can be lifesaving.

It was a busy time of the day. The unit bustled with activity. A number of physicians were making afternoon rounds, which meant the nurses were busy scheduling tests, dispensing medications, and otherwise attending to the physicians' orders.

I had just finished examining my patient and preparing her for her first plasmapheresis. I had also met with her family members to explain the nature of her illness and describe the therapy I was recommending. Their apprehension was plain to see. I tried to reassure them as best I could, but I had to be honest. In medicine, there are no guarantees of a satisfactory outcome. I could not promise them that their loved one would respond favorably and be restored to good health.

In treating patients, you do what you can and pray it will be sufficient while recognizing that the ultimate outcome is beyond your control.

I sat down at the workbench to compose my consultation. I had almost finished documenting my visit when I felt a hand on my shoulder. I looked up to see Madison Lane standing behind me with a worried frown on her face. She said, "Violet isn't looking good. Her oxygen saturation is falling. It's down to 91 percent."

"It's the blood in her lungs," I replied. "It's interfering with her ability to take in oxygen. I'm afraid were going to have to intubate her. Call Respiratory Therapy and have them bring up a ventilator while I get set up to pass the tube."

Introducing a breathing tube into the airway of an awake patient is quite difficult. The body's normal reflexes aggressively resist allowing anything to enter the trachea. For that reason, patients need to be sedated before intubation. The problem is that once they are sedated, they stop breathing on their own. When a patient has been sedated, they need to be intubated immediately. Any extended delay can result in profound oxygen deficiency, which can damage the heart, the brain, or other vital organs.

After preparing for the intubation by assembling all the drugs and equipment we would need, I stood at the head of the bed, ready to insert the breathing tube. Tyler Wickham, the respiratory therapist, stood next to me, ready to assist. He held a self-inflating breathing bag called an Ambu bag. He would use it to breathe for Mrs. Shoemaker in case the intubation failed.

After reconfirming that we were set and ready to go, I nodded to Madison, who injected the sedating drugs into Mrs. Shoemaker's intravenous tubing.

The wall clock ticked off seconds while I paused to allow the drugs to have an effect. I then introduced the laryngoscope into the back of Mrs. Shoemaker's throat, gently but firmly elevating the tongue and opening the upper airway to bring the vocal cords into view.

That was when I realized we had a serious problem. Blood from my patient's lungs had accumulated in the back of her throat, obscuring my view of the vocal cords.

Visualizing the vocal cords is key to a successful intubation. With the cords in view, you can watch the endotracheal tube pass between them directly into the upper trachea. Doing a blind intubation—advancing an endotracheal tube without seeing where it's going—is often unsuccessful, and each failed attempt wastes precious time. If the tube winds up in the esophagus rather than the trachea, the patient cannot be ventilated; and the longer the situation is allowed to continue, the greater the risk of oxygen deprivation.

I immediately called for suction and began removing as much of the blood as I could. A great deal was thick and clotted and resisted my efforts to clear the upper airway. Precious seconds ticked by while I labored to bring the cords into view.

"Doctor Sterling?" Madison said calmly, though I could detect an urgency in her voice.

"I'm working on it," I declared without shifting my gaze away from the back of my patient's throat.

"Would you like me to bag her for a while?" Tyler suggested.

"Not yet," I responded. "There is one large clot in the way. If I can just break it loose…"

After another twenty seconds of working the suction catheter without improving my field of view, I barked more brusquely than I intended, "Twenty cc's of normal saline. I need it now."

Madison moved to comply with alacrity, but her efforts to draw up the liquid seemed to take forever. When she handed me the saline, I removed the needle and pointed the tip of the syringe toward my patient's upper airway where I thought the vocal cords might be. Firmly, I pressed the plunger, sending out a strong spray of liquid. I then set about to suction away as much blood as I could, but the clot still wouldn't budge.

"Let's do it again," I called out. I handed the syringe and the needle back to Madison.

"I could bag her while you're waiting," Tyler said with unmistakable alarm.

"I've almost got it," I declared as Madison handed me the syringe again. I sprayed another stream of liquid at the clot and then went back to working with the suction catheter.

Finally, the clot came loose, and the vocal cords came into view. As quickly and as carefully as I could, I passed the tube, watching it slide between the cords. When it was finally in place and its occlusive cuff properly inflated, I used the ventilation bag to deliver several quick breaths. With each compression of the Ambu bag, I saw my patient's chest rise and fall.

"We're in," I announced with a huge sigh of relief. I could feel the tension in the room beginning to dissipate. I looked at the wall clock. Three minutes and forty-five seconds had elapsed since the drugs had been administered. *That's a long time to ask a patient to hold their breath*, I thought.

When I turned to Tyler, I could tell he was upset; but rather than address the source of his disquiet, I said, "Go ahead and hook her up."

When he was ready, I called out the initial ventilator settings I wanted to use. They would be fine-tuned incrementally as determined by the patient's response.

When the ventilator was properly configured, Madison, Tyler, and I all watched the monitor that displayed the patient's oxygen saturation level. As her numbers began to improve, we relaxed even more.

"Thank you both," I said. "Let's hope this buys her the time we need to bring her immune system under control."

Tyler didn't offer a comment but simply left the unit, still troubled.

I returned to the workbench to finish my consultation and record a progress note detailing the intubation. When I finished, I sat back and knuckled my eyes. It had been a long day, and I was tired.

Madison came over and sat down beside me. "That was exciting." She sat her coffee mug down on the workbench between us and began idly fingering a roll of paper tape that had been left there. "I was thinking we might have to do a cricothyrotomy."

"I know. I could tell. That was about as close as I want to come to being forced to provide a surgical airway. By the way…" I turned sideways to face her. In so doing, my elbow knocked her coffee mug to the floor, breaking off the handle. "Oh, I'm so sorry," I said. "That was your own personal mug, wasn't it?"

"It doesn't matter," Madison replied graciously. "It was empty anyway." She bent down, gathered up the broken pieces, and threw them in the trash. "What were you about to say?"

"Only that I've thought about the question you asked the other day in the chapel—about whether or not praying makes a difference. I've decided to try an experiment." I reached into my shirt pocket and brought out a small spiral-bound notebook. "I'm going to record every prayer I pray on behalf of a patient. I'll write down what I pray for, being as explicit as possible, and then I will later go back and record the outcome, however the case turns out. If prayer has no effect, then there should be no correlation between my prayers and the ultimate result. If, on the other hand, prayer is effective, the outcome should reflect what I prayed for more often than not. It's not rigidly scientific, but at least it will give us a clue."

"I like it. Maybe I'll do the same thing, and we can compare our findings."

"Good idea. That will give us a better chance of seeing a clear result."

"It will be exciting to see how our results compare—not that it's a competition. I didn't mean that." Madison flushed slightly.

"I didn't think you did. Besides, we're not the ones who determine how our prayers will be answered. Therefore, we can't take credit for the outcome if our prayers are successful."

"True. Say, can I get you anything?" Madison said. "You look like you could do with a glass of orange juice or something."

Feeling guilty, I glanced at the wastebasket where Madison's broken mug now resided. I had been about to ask for a cup of coffee. Instead, I said, "Thank you, but I'm fine. Here in a little bit, I'll be heading out to get some dinner. Oh, that reminds me. This coming Saturday, I'm having a small dinner party for my partners and their wives. It will be an informal get-to-know-you event, and I was wondering if you might like to join us?"

"Me? You want me to have dinner with your partners and their wives?"

"Well…yes. Otherwise, there will be three males and two females, which will seem awkward. Besides, I enjoy your company. I like talking with you. It's not going to be anything elaborate or fancy, just some down-home cooking, maybe a meatloaf or a chicken casserole—I haven't decided. What do you say?"

"I'm flattered, but—"

"Oh, please don't say no. I'll do my best to see that you have a good time."

Madison thought for a moment and then said, "Very well. I accept."

"Excellent."

"Where, and what time?"

I filled her in on the specifics. After checking on my patient one more time and confirming she was still moving in the right direction, I took my leave and headed out to grab a bite to eat. As far as I was concerned, Saturday couldn't come soon enough. However, a lot can happen between Wednesday and Saturday—as I was about to find out.

As I started to leave the hospital, I thought about Tyler and his reaction to the way I had handled the intubation. I felt that I understood what was bothering him. *Best to address his concerns while they are still fresh*, I told myself. I turned and headed for the Respiratory Therapy Department.

Respiratory Therapy was homebased in a large rectangular space on the ground floor, not far from the Emergency Department. A sizable work area at the front was where the department's machines were serviced, calibrated, and sanitized. The department's ventilators, nebulizers, humidifiers, monitors, and other items of respiratory equipment were kept in a storage room toward the back. Beside it was the office reserved for the head of the department. Tyler sat on a stool in the far corner of the open space.

"Are you angry with me?" I said as I drew near to where Tyler was testing a humidifier to confirm that it was functioning properly.

"I'm not angry," he responded brusquely.

"What are you then?"

"What I am doesn't matter."

"You think I was wrong, don't you?"

"What I think is unimportant. The patient is improving. That's all that counts."

"No, it isn't. We are going to have to work together, and I want to know how you feel."

"You want to know how I feel? All right. I'll tell you. I think you took an unnecessary risk. You let your ego get in the way of doing what was best for the patient. You weren't going to allow that clot to defeat you regardless of how long it took to move it out of the way."

I countered, "Like you said, the patient is improving. It all worked out in the end."

"That's not the point. You took a risk you didn't need to take. What if hypoxia had triggered an arrhythmia? Or what if she had had a stroke? You could've stepped aside and let me ventilate her for a minute. I could have brought her oxygen saturation up near normal. Then you could have had another go at dislodging the clot. It would have taken longer, but it would've been far safer."

Suddenly I felt deeply embarrassed. There was truth in what Tyler was saying. I had been determined to demonstrate my prowess in passing an endotracheal tube, and I wasn't going to let a stubborn blood clot defeat me. "You're right. I should've stepped aside and let you bag her. It would've been the more prudent thing to do. Fortunately, God was with us. He kept her from suffering the consequences of my pride."

"I don't believe in God," Tyler declared flatly.

"You don't believe He exists or you don't believe He was looking out for Mrs. Shoemaker?"

"I don't believe He exists."

"Really? Then how do you explain the reality that surrounds us? Something had to create all that is."

"I can't explain it."

"And yet here we are."

"If God does exist, how do you explain what's happening to Mrs. Shoemaker?"

"What do you mean?"

"How can an all-knowing, all-powerful deity who supposedly loves us allow that poor woman to suffer like she is, drowning in her own blood?"

"There is suffering in this world because evil exists, and evil exists because—" Interrupted, I looked up when Marcus Eldridge entered the department.

"Oh, sorry," he said when he saw me talking with Tyler. "I didn't know you were here."

"It's all right," I said. "We were just reviewing a difficult patient I'm treating. Tyler had a suggestion as to how I might improve my patient care." I turned to Tyler. "I would like to continue this discussion some time…if you're willing."

"Sure…if you want." I could tell he was less than enthusiastic.

"Good. Until later then." I turned and left the department.

As I was walking back to my car, it occurred to me to wonder about the relationship between Marcus and Tyler. Perhaps it was just coincidence, but they seem to encounter each other more frequently than might be expected by random chance.

"What was that all about?" Marcus demanded after Blake had left the department.

Tyler responded, "Like the good doctor said, we were talking about patient care."

Marcus looked around nervously. "It didn't have anything to do with Ophis Pterotos, I hope?"

"Don't be saying that name out loud around here," Tyler snapped.

"Don't you be telling me what I can and cannot say. Who do you think you are?"

"What's going on?" Jerry Tucker asked from the doorway. "Is there a problem?" He checked his watch as he stepped inside. "Can we get on with this? My wife is expecting me to take her out to dinner tonight."

"Fine by me," Marcus said, still miffed at Tyler.

Ignoring Marcus's disquiet, Tyler said, "I've heard from Captain Summers. The next batch of virus is still being fine-tuned. It will be ready in about two weeks."

"Why so long?" Jerry said.

"I imagine it's because reengineering a virus is delicate work. It takes time to get it right. Anyway, Captain Summers wanted to be sure that we are prepared to test it as soon as it arrives."

Jerry looked around. "I assume we are alone?"

"Relax," Tyler said. "There's nobody here but us."

"Just making sure," Jerry said. "As far as I am concerned, we can deploy the virus anytime we choose. The only constraint is that it needs to happen on a day when I'm on call. That way, I'll get the referral. That will allow me to control what tests are ordered and what treatments are given."

"Shouldn't be a problem," Tyler said to Jerry. "But this time, I'll expect you to help me pick out which patient to infect. I don't like choosing them on my own. What if I mess up and give the virus to someone who is sicker than I realize?"

"Yeah, that could be bad," Jerry agreed.

"Jerry, what about Blake?" Marcus said. "Does he still have a burr under his saddle regarding patient number three?"

"I don't think so. At least he hasn't said anything. Far as I know, he hasn't been asking any questions either."

"Be sure you keep an eye on him. We wouldn't want his curiosity to cause a problem."

"Is there anything else?" Tyler said as if he was in charge of the meeting.

Jerry shook his head. So did Marcus.

"Well then," Tyler said. "I have something." He looked straight at Marcus. "Captain Summers wants you to be the one to pick up the virus when it's ready. He will text you with the time and place to meet."

"Why me?" Marcus protested. "Taking delivery of the samples—that's your job."

Tyler shrugged. "I'm sure he has his reasons. Also, you are to bring copies of patient number three's medical records with you when you go. Apparently, the ones we sent by mail never arrived."

Marcus looked at Jerry. His facial expression said, "Told you."

Jerry ignored him.

Tyler finished up by saying, "Between now and when we deployed the next sample, let's remember to keep our mouths shut." He again glowered at Marcus.

Marcus started to respond, but Jerry cut him off. "I don't know about you guys, but I'm tired. I'm going home."

"Good idea." Marcus abruptly turned and left the department.

"Officious prick," Tyler snarled under his breath after Marcus had gone.

"Play nice," Jerry said before he too departed.

# EXPANDED RESPONSIBILITIES

Early Friday morning, during the third week in August, I was rounding on Mrs. Shoemaker in the ICU. Forty-eight hours had elapsed since she had completed her first plasmapheresis, and her condition had improved substantially to the point that I could remove her breathing tube. In fact, her response to therapy had been better than anticipated. The medications we were using to suppress her immune system were causing some nausea. Otherwise, she was feeling more comfortable. Her family was quite pleased with her progress. I wrote an order to move her out of the ICU and open up a bed for someone who needed it more than she did. With a sense of satisfaction, I jotted her name down in my spiral-bound prayer notebook.

I had anticipated visiting with Madison, but she was busy caring for a cardiac patient who had been admitted in the wee hours of the morning. Rather than chat, I was forced to settle for a quick word in passing—an expression of goodwill and a hope that she would have a fine day.

When I checked the time, I found I had nearly an hour before I was scheduled to begin seeing patients in the office. I decided to visit the cafeteria and treat myself to a decent breakfast.

As I made my way through the serving line, I ordered scrambled eggs, bacon, a blueberry muffin, and orange juice. Carrying my tray, I headed for the doctors' dining room.

It's fascinating how people segregate themselves into cliques. When I entered the dining room, I noticed that the orthopedists were seated at one table, the surgeons at another, and a group of primary care physicians and medical specialists at yet another. I was about to join this last group when I saw Adam sitting by himself in a corner, reading a journal article while consuming a bowl of oatmeal. I turned in his direction.

"Mind if I join you?" I said, stepping up to his table.

"By all means." He gestured for me to sit down, which I did. "How goes the war?" he said before taking another bite of oatmeal.

"It may be too soon to tell, but I think we're winning." I reached for the salt and shook a little onto my eggs. "I know," I confessed when Adam gave me a sour look that expressed his disapproval. "But they're so bland otherwise. A man has to have a few vices. What are you reading?" I pointed my fork toward his medical journal lying open on the table.

"It's a review of the alpha-1 antitrypsin deficiency syndromes and how they lead to cirrhosis of the liver."

"I would have thought you'd be digging through a travel magazine, looking for tips on vacationing in Jamaica, or sightseeing in Europe. You're going to retire in a week and leave all this behind."

"Force of habit, I suppose, like an old fire horse put out to pasture—can't help preparing to run when he hears the fire bell. Besides, I hope I never grow too indolent to learn new things."

I frowned. "Aren't you worried you'll miss this more than you think?"

"Miss what?" Sam Duncan stepped up to our table. Being a thoracic surgeon, he was wearing a long white lab coat over a pair of green scrubs. "May I?" He nodded toward an empty chair.

"Of course," Adam replied. "Blake is concerned that I might find retirement boring."

"How do you feel about that?" Sam drizzled maple syrup onto his French toast.

"I imagine that regretting my decision to retire is a possibility but unlikely—if I keep myself busy enough. I guess we'll find out." Adam closed his magazine and pushed it aside.

"And how are you doing?" Sam said to me. "Getting used to private practice?"

"Gradually. There is more to it than I had realized."

"Such as?" Sam sipped his coffee.

"Practical stuff—dealing with finances, ordering supplies, employee relations."

"They can be tricky," Sam admitted. "Adam, how would you say he's doing?"

Adam chuckled. "He's farther along than I was when I was in his shoes."

"Probably because he has you to teach him. By the way"—Sam turned his head to look at me—"congratulations on your appointment."

I responded with confusion. "What appointment?" He couldn't be referring to my having joined the Pulmonary Associates. That was old news.

"Oh, that's right," Adam said sheepishly. "I've been meaning to tell you. You were selected to take my place on the Infection Control Committee. You're to be its chairman."

"No way," I protested with a smirk.

"It's true," Sam agreed, completely deadpan. "As chief of staff, I signed off on the appointment yesterday afternoon."

"This is a joke, right? You two are pulling my leg." I looked from Adam to Sam and back again. Neither man cracked a smile.

I shook my head. "I'm a pulmonologist, not an infectious disease specialist."

"Unfortunately," Sam said. "Somebody has to chair the committee, and since there is no infectious disease consultant on the medical staff, you're that somebody."

"What do I know about weird bacteria and crazy viruses?"

Sam countered, "You went to medical school, right?"

"Yes."

"And you completed a three-year residency in pulmonary medicine, right?"

"Yes," I agreed reluctantly, suspecting that I could see where he was headed.

"Then you know as much as anybody else on the medical staff."

"Actually," Adam interjected. "The job isn't that hard. You'd be surprised by how much you already know about controlling infections. If I can chair the committee, there's no doubt you can as well. Besides, your infection control nurse will do most of the heavy lifting. Mainly your job will be to supervise her work, and you'll have four committee members to help. Besides, if you do run into a problem that's beyond your capabilities, you can bring it to Sam's attention. He'll figure out a way to get you the help you need."

"I will?" Sam said, looking momentarily unsettled. Then with greater assurance, he said, "I mean, I will. At least I'll do what I can."

Adam glanced at the wall clock. He then gathered up his breakfast tray and his medical journal. "We have just enough time. Blake, come with me, and I'll introduce you to your infection control nurse. She can answer more questions than I can." He turned and started toward the exit.

I wolfed down my scrambled eggs and hurried to catch up. *Dear Lord*, I prayed as I bussed my tray. *Please don't let her be a crotchety old hag.*

The Flintridge Medical Center employed Heather Jean Oliver as its infection control nurse. Her small office was on the third floor, ideally positioned midway between the surgical wing to the east and the medical wing to the west. Seated at her desk, studying a medical record online, she looked up when Adam knocked on her open door.

"Good morning," Adam said as he stepped inside. "I've brought someone who would like to meet you"

"Let me guess." Heather stood up. "This is the new associate you've been telling us about." She smiled.

"He's also the new chairman of the Infection Control Committee," Adam added sagely.

"Really?" Heather's smile faded into a feigned look of complete surprise. "Why am I always the last one to know these things?" A moment later, the smile returned. She held out her hand to me. "Welcome aboard."

"In case you hadn't noticed," Adam commented. "Heather likes to tease." He tried to move aside, but the office was so small I still had to reach around him to shake Heather's hand.

"Trust me," I said. "You weren't the last to know. I was." I tried to keep the sullenness out of my voice, but a small amount managed to seep in anyway.

Apparently Heather picked up on my resentment. "It won't be so bad. We'll have fun working together. You'll see."

Her smile widened into a grin. She was a slightly overweight middle-aged woman with a round face, rosy cheeks, and dimples. She wore her graying hair done up in a bun at the back of her head. Her blue eyes twinkled mischievously. Wearing the right attire, she might have passed as Mrs. Santa Claus.

As a rule, I'm not keen on first impressions. It's hard to judge people fairly until you get to know them. However, if pressed for an opinion, I would have said that Heather was someone I might learn to like.

"You had an interesting case the other day, didn't you?" Heather offered offhandedly. "I believe it was the weekend before last—Mr. Goldstein?"

"How do you know about him?" I responded with mild surprise. "I don't remember Doctor Ramsey sending you a referral, and I know I didn't."

"I monitor every patient admitted with a possible infection especially if they are admitted to the ICU. It's my job to spot problems before they develop into major incidents. Mr. Goldstein was being well managed. The appropriate protocols were in place. There was no need for me to get involved. It was curious though how quickly his symptoms changed from none to bad, and back to none again."

"That was odd," I agreed. "By the time I saw him, he was on his road to recovery. There wasn't much left for me to do."

"Do you know what's really strange?" Heather said as if divulging a secret. "There were two patients before Mr. Goldstein who ran the same clinical course—rapid onset, rapid improvement."

"Two patients? I know about one. What was her name?"

"Agnes Gilroy?" Heather suggested.

"That's it," I confirmed. "But you say there was a third?"

"Billy Mitchell. She was admitted with a clot in her femoral vein. Within twelve hours she came down with the same acute respiratory syndrome. Within thirty-six hours, her lungs were clear. I didn't make much of it at the time—"

"Three cases are more than a coincidence," I interjected.

"I should have been informed about these cases," Adam declared, sounding mildly offended.

Apologetically, Heather said, "I'm sorry. I thought you knew. Doctor Tucker consulted on all three. I assumed he had been keeping you up to speed. Besides, there really wasn't much to tell. They all went home fully recovered. Anyway, I plan on digging a little deeper into these three cases when I get the time—mostly out of curiosity."

Adam glanced at his watch and then announced with a tone of urgency, "Partner, we need to get to the office. Lois will skin us alive. She hates it when we make patients wait"

Before leaving, I turned to Heather and requested, "Let me know what you find out, would you please?"

"Be glad to. Like I said, it's going to be fun." She waved goodbye as we headed for the stairwell.

"So," Adam said when we were out of earshot. "What do you think?"

"I think I like her. It's impressive that she can remember names, dates, and attending physicians involved in the care of patients admitted weeks if not months ago. Is there anything I should know about her?"

"Sometimes she tends to get ahead of herself. That's when you need to put on the brakes—remind her to take it slow and steady."

*And just how am I supposed to do that*? I thought. Out loud, I said mostly to myself, "I have a feeling that, like she said, it's going to be fun."

"Yep. You got that right." Adam chuckled. "Speaking of fun, you do remember that the CME conferences have been moved to Fridays?"

"That's today. Do you know the topic?"

"Acute kidney failure."

"I should make a point of attending."

"Also, you are aware, I'm sure, that you will be expected to present your own CME conference before the end of the year."

"Seriously?"

"Every medical staff member is expected to contribute."

"Wow. The hits just keep coming."

The low hum of conversations reverberated throughout the lecture hall. Physicians, nurse practitioners, and a lesser number of ancillary personnel casually took their seats. The auditorium was nearly two-thirds full. Doctor José Rodriguez stood behind the lectern, nervously thumbing through his notes. José was a dour man, not given to flippant humor or lighthearted mirth.

I had been introduced to Doctor Rodriguez one morning in the ICU. My first impression had been that he was a bright, well-educated physician who would make an excellent resource as a nephrology consultant, but he was not the sort of fellow you would want to grab a beer with.

Doctors licensed to practice medicine in Washington state were required to complete two hundred hours of continuing medical education every four years. The hospital's CME program was intended to help the medical staff meet this goal as efficiently as possible. One hour of credit was awarded for simply attending a lecture. An additional hour could be earned by completing a brief self-test at the conclusion of the presentation.

All in all, the CME program offered an effective way for medical practitioners to satisfy their licensure requirements while staying abreast of current trends in medicine. The only drawback was that the quality of the lectures depended entirely upon the presenters' ability to communicate. That truth was clearly in evidence when José began speaking.

I fought to keep my attention focused on what José was saying, but his monotonic presentation seemed perfectly tailored to put me to sleep. I was just about to drift off when José gestured in a way that summoned forth a memory from when I was nine years old. He stood with his right elbow resting on the back of his left fist. He held his right arm upright with his index finger extended as if emphasizing a point. It was the same posture my grandfather, William Oliver Sterling, had adopted from time to time during our various conversations. When I closed my eyes, I could still visualize him standing on the front porch of our two-bedroom bungalow, located three blocks inland from the Pacific Ocean in Santa Monica, California.

A radiant sun descended toward the western horizon, painting the hovering clouds in golden shades of yellow, orange, and bronze. The spectacular sunset was the sort for which the Pacific Ocean was renowned. The entire sky blazed with color, but the heavenly display had done nothing to staunch the flow of tears that ran down my cheeks or to ease my anguish. I had been living with my grandfather for almost a month. I had come to stay with him after my parents had been killed while skiing in Colorado. I had been told that they had ventured away from the groomed trails and onto a bowl-shaped hillside, triggering the avalanche that had ended their lives.

As I watched the sun slowly sink toward the ocean, the agony of my loss was exquisitely intense. When my grandfather emerged from the house, laboring to breathe, as was his nature on account of his emphysema, he found me sitting on the porch swing, sobbing bitterly. Rather than intrude, he stood by patiently, waiting for the candle of my grief to burn itself out.

When I noticed him watching me, elbow on his fist, right index finger pointed heavenward, I could tell he wanted to offer a comment.

"What?" I said between sobs.

Very gently, he replied, "You miss them terribly, I know. So do I. They are not here right now, and it hurts. It hurts so much you think your heart will shatter, but we will see them again. This I know."

"How can that be?" I said, my nine-year-old brain struggling to understand.

"We will see them after the resurrection, when all of God's children will be raised. We will be reunited in heaven."

"How do you know this?" I said angrily.

"Because your mom and your dad put their faith in Jesus. They accepted Him as their Savior, and He promised that whoever believes in Him will not perish but will have eternal life."

"People promise lots of things," I countered with hostility. "They don't always keep their promises."

"That's true," Grandfather admitted between breaths. "But Jesus will keep His."

"What makes you so sure?"

"I believe He will do what He said He will do because of the resurrection. You know what resurrection means?"

"It's when dead people come back to life."

"That's right. Jesus told his disciples several times what would happen—that He would be betrayed, convicted, mocked, spit upon, flogged, and crucified. He also told them that on the third day, He would rise again—and it happened just as He said. Jesus was dead, but then He was raised up to new life. Even now, He is alive and sitting on His throne at the right hand of God. The resurrection is proof that if we trust in Jesus, we will have eternal life. Do you trust Him?"

"I do," I answered without hesitation, unsure where I had gained the force of my convictions.

"Then you will see your parents again—maybe not for a while, but it will happen."

I felt an upwelling of peace, and the sobs stopped. When I regarded my grandfather again, I could tell he was even more short of breath. Talking had worn him out. I patted the bench beside me, and he ambled over to sit down. He laid his arm across my shoulders and said, "I'm proud of you, lad. Don't ever surrender your faith, not ever. It will see you through the good times and the bad. Stay strong in the Lord, and He will guide your path."

"I will, Grandfather. I promise."

Little did I know that in years to come, the veracity of the promise I had made would be sorely tested.

When José finished, a smattering of applause rose from the audience. I suspected that some folks were clapping out of appreciation that the lecture was finally over.

I trailed behind a group of internists as they left the lecture hall. In passing, I noticed Marcus Eldridge standing alone a dozen yards away. He waved when he saw me and began walking in my direction, causing me to wonder if I would be late getting back to the office again.

As if reading my mind, Marcus said, "I won't keep you. I only wanted to wish you congratulations on your appointment. The Infection Control Committee plays an important role in keeping our patients safe during their hospital stay. Being named chairman, that's quite an honor for someone new to the medical staff."

"Thank you. I just hope I can do the position justice."

"I'm sure you will. By the way, I understand you and your partners have been discussing the hospital's offer to buy out your practice. I would be interested in knowing if you've formed an opinion."

"Not yet. We're still sorting through the pros and cons."

"I would think it should be an easy decision. It's a strong offer. Not only is the buyout substantial, Flintridge Healthcare would take over those practice management functions that tend to drive physicians crazy. With our support, you would spend less time overseeing your practice and more time treating patients."

"Like I said, we're still evaluating your proposal. I'm sure Doctor Tucker will keep you informed."

"Doctor Tucker?" Marcus said with a degree of apprehension.

"I saw you talking with him the other day. I had assumed you were discussing the buyout."

"Oh. Yes, of course. That conversation slipped my mind—I talk with so many people."

"I see. On a different subject, I was wondering, I've heard some of the nurses complaining that the hospital is cutting back on overtime hours. Is that true? Are you going to be limiting the number of overtime hours a nurse can accumulate?"

Marcus nodded. "Unfortunately, it is true. It may not seem like it at times, but we're running a business. Overtime expenses are a substantial fraction of our payroll. We have to be cost-conscious whenever and wherever we can. Why do you ask?"

"Will you be hiring more nurses to cover the shortfall in patient care?" I asked with concern.

"Hiring more bodies would sort of defeat the purpose of cutting back, don't you think."

"Then how are you going to handle the shortage of nurses?"

"We plan on increasing staffing ratios. Each nurse will have to care for one or two more patients."

"Won't that increase burnout or push the nurses toward unionization?"

"Perhaps, but we really don't have a choice. If you're concerned about the nurses' income, talk with Medicare and the insurance companies. Tell them to pay us more for the patients we treat. As it is, we are between a rock and a hard place. I share your concerns for these staffing matters, but unless our revenues increase, my hands are tied."

"So it seems. I gather there is more to being a hospital administrator than I had imagined. In any event, thank you for taking the time to explain the issues, but I've got to run."

"Not a problem. We can talk again later if you'd like. Let me know when you make a decision regarding the buyout."

"Will do."

I hurried back to the office only to discover that my afternoon wouldn't be as busy as I had thought. In fact, I managed to finish early and return to the hospital before the gift shop closed.

"For me?" Madison said somewhat self-consciously. "Thank you...I think."

Standing in the middle of the ICU, in plain view of the rest of the staff, she began unwrapping the small gift box I had handed her.

"You shouldn't have," she said, making it sound more like a reprimand than an expression of humility upon being offered a gift. Her hands trembled ever so slightly as she tore through the packaging.

"All they had for wrapping paper was get-well themes. I suppose I could have wrapped it in a brown paper bag."

Madison lifted the box's lid. "A coffee mug?"

"To replace the one I broke."

She removed the mug from its container and held it up, "'World's Greatest Nurse'—that's a bit presumptuous, don't you think?"

"It was either that or 'World's Greatest Doctor,'" I chuckled.

"Thank you," Madison said mildly. "I appreciate the sentiment."

"You're welcome. I'm just sorry I was so clumsy. We're still on for tomorrow night, right?"

"Your dinner party—yes. What time again?"

"Anytime between 4:30 and 5:00. Look in the mug," I suggested.

She reached in and drew out a slip of paper, which she unfolded.

"That's a map to where I live. It shouldn't be too hard to follow."

"I'll be there."

"I hope I didn't embarrass you too much." I smiled innocently as I indicated the nurses, housekeepers, and patients who were watching us.

"I'll survive, but just remember, payback is a—"

"I know." I turned to leave, and Madison headed for the coffee pot in the utility room behind the nurses' station to try out her new gift.

"I'm not sure I agree with that," Flo Richards, Adam's wife, said. She was a stout Black woman with an oval face, high cheekbones, and almond-shaped eyes. When she smiled, she exposed a row of even white teeth. Her given name was Florence, but she preferred the abbreviated form. She sat opposite me at the picnic table I had stationed on the grass beneath a canopy in my backyard.

"All life is sacred," Flo continued. "How can it be morally justifiable to end a life prematurely?"

Somehow, euthanasia had become our topic for discussion, and it had soon become apparent that my guests held staunchly different points of view.

Seated next to his wife, Adam nodded his agreement.

Beside him, Linda Tucker, Jerry's wife, said, "I believe every mentally competent human should have an absolute right to determine the course of his or her own life. That includes ending it…if that is what they choose to do." She was a thin, angular woman with long fingers and a long neck.

The solar-powered torches I had stationed around the yard flickered, sending shadows dancing across the six-foot fence that encircled the yard. Rather than prepare a formal meal, I had chosen to host a serve-yourself backyard barbecue replete with hamburgers, hot dogs, and chicken breasts grilled over a charcoal fire. In addition, I had set out deviled egg potato salad, pork and beans, chips, and a tossed green salad with either ranch or thousand island dressing.

Seated to my left, Madison shook her head. "Dying is irreversible. It extinguishes any hope of fixing a choice made in error. It's also final. It eliminates the possibility that a change of circumstance might lead to a change of heart."

Jerry, seated next to Madison and across from his wife, said, "I'm inclined to agree with Linda…with certain caveats. Before a person seeking euthanasia can be granted permission, they must have a legitimate reason for wanting to end their life. Such reasons might include incurable cancer or intractable pain. They would not include depression or an attitude of despair."

Linda countered, "Why exclude psychological pain? Mental anguish can be as devastating as physical pain—even more so. In some cultures, ending one's life is seen as an acceptable means of atoning for intolerable shame. Some psychological burdens are simply too oppressive to bear."

"That is true," Adam said. "Psychological pain can be overwhelming, but it's often treatable either with medications or counseling or both, and as Madison pointed out, death obviates the possibility of recovery. Blake, you haven't joined in yet. What's your opinion?"

"It's a difficult subject," I replied. "I do support the right of individuals to choose their own destiny. However, there is something uniquely special about life. My faith compels me to believe that God has a plan for each and every person and that He expects us to see His plan through to the end. To intentionally end a life prematurely is, in fact, a violation of God's will and, therefore, is a sin. Euthanasia leaves no room for God's grace to affect an unanticipated outcome—a miracle, if you will. Besides, as I see it, dying isn't the issue. We will all die. How we live is what matters—with faith, hope, perseverance, and love hopefully. Killing yourself is just wrong."

Madison laid a hand on my forearm. "Well said."

"Even so," Linda said. "The decision should be left up to the individual, not to the government. People should be free to decide for themselves if they will live or die."

"But there needs to be government oversight," I said. "Especially when it applies to euthanasia—to ensure that it is done humanely and in compliance with whatever standards society deems applicable."

"That is exactly the point my wife was making," Jerry said. "Why should society, i.e., the government, determine what standards are fitting for the individual?"

"In large measure," I replied. "Government involvement is necessary to protect the individual from fraud, incompetence, and abuse—in much the same way that the practice of medicine is regulated. As physicians, we first must demonstrate our competence by passing examinations, and then if we fail to adhere to the proper standards of medical care, our licenses will be revoked. This is how the public is protected."

"In a free society," Jerry said. "The citizenry would be responsible for protecting themselves rather than having some bureaucrat control what they can and cannot do."

"I might agree with you," I said. "If every citizen had the ability to accurately assess a provider's qualifications. Most people can't distinguish a good doctor from a snake oil salesman. They have neither the time nor the expertise to make a valid judgment."

Jerry was about to respond when his cell phone rang. He answered it as he rose from the table. He then stepped away to carry on his conversation. When he returned, he announced, "That was the Emergency Department. They have a patient coughing up blood, and I've been asked to consult."

"It's not Violet Shoemaker, is it?" I said apprehensively. "I do hope her Goodpasture's isn't acting up."

"That's not the name I was given."

Adam looked to his wife. "You know, we probably should be going too." When Flo nodded her agreement, he stood up and said to Jerry, "If you'd like, we can take Linda home so you can go straight in."

"That would be appreciated." Jerry glanced at Linda. "You okay with that?"

"Of course." Linda also stood up.

Flo stood up as well and stepped around to take my hand. "We had a lovely time. Thank you for inviting us." She seemed on the verge of adding something to the effect that we should do this again but then caught herself, as if unsure how her husband's pending retirement would impact their future social calendar. Instead, she leaned past me and said, "Madison, it was a pleasure meeting you. I'll look forward to seeing you again."

Madison rose to her feet and replied, "Me too. Before I arrived, I wasn't sure what to expect, but you've made me feel quite at ease. Thank you."

When my partners and their wives finished their goodbyes, they departed. Madison turned to me and announced, "I'll help you clean up."

"No need. I've got this."

"I want to—if you don't object?"

"Are you kidding? I enjoy your company." Together we cleared the table and carried the dirty dishes and the remnants of our meal indoors.

"So…what did you think?" I said as I returned the mayonnaise and the mustard to the drawer in the refrigerator door.

"I like Doctor Richards. It's a shame he's retiring."

"Yes it is. I thought for a time that he might change his mind. You can tell he's going to miss practicing medicine. What about Doctor Tucker? How do you feel about him?"

"He seems restrained—closed off, as if he's holding something back. What it is, I'm not sure."

"Yeah. As we were talking out there, I had the same thought."

We finished washing the dishes and putting the leftovers away.

"Thank you for coming," I said as I walked Madison to her car. "Did you have a good time?"

"I did. I wasn't sure that I would, but yes, I did. Oh, while I'm thinking of it, will you be at the 8:00 a.m. service tomorrow?"

"I intend to be there. I enjoyed last Sunday. Reverend Thomas has a talent for preaching. I like the way he stays close to the written word. It bothers me when pastors put their own spin on the Scriptures."

"Good. I'll see you in church then."

As I stood on the sidewalk, I watched Madison drive off. In thinking about the evening, I realized that I had learned several things about her. She loved being a nurse and was determined to excel at her profession. She had a droll sense of humor, which you might miss if you weren't paying attention. She could at times be impatient with those whose opinions differed from her own, and she had a strong affinity for Chocolate Mousse Royale ice cream from Baskin-Robbins.

I pulled in and parked my Sentra in the lot adjacent to the Resurrection Bible Church. This was my second visit. As I approached the sanctuary, I again had the impression that the building seemed out of place. Its gleaming white exterior, tall windows, and soaring steeple looked to be better suited to a New England countryside than to the outskirts of Flintridge, Washington.

The sanctuary was filling rapidly. Founded at the turn of the millennium, the church was again teetering on the verge of outgrowing its physical infrastructure. Twice the sanctuary had been enlarged to accommodate an expanding congregation.

The reverend Elijah Thomas's charismatic personality partly accounted for the church's steady growth. As senior pastor, he delivered the lion's share of the Sunday sermons and was generally regarded as a gifted orator. It was, however, the content of his messages rather than his preaching style that attracted new members. Modeled after the Calvary Chapel movement of the sixties and seventies, the church's evangelical theology focused on teaching straight from the Bible rather than allowing humanistic themes to warp the message.

When I entered through the carved double doors, I noticed that Madison had arrived early. She was seated toward the middle of the sanctuary and was saving me a place. She looked quite prim in her Sunday attire: a pale-blue cotton blouse, beige slacks, and chocolate brown pumps. I had chosen to wear a teal-colored dress shirt with a yellow-and-tan tie, black pants, and black leather shoes. She looked up and smiled when she saw me sliding into the row to sit beside her.

The service began with the choir leading us in singing "Rock of Ages." We then sang "Holy, Holy, Holy," one of my favorite hymns. For some inexplicable reason, I recalled that the anthem was first published in 1826 by Reginald Heber, vicar of Hodnet, Shropshire, England. *Strange*, I thought. *The odd bits of trivia we accumulate, never fully comprehending why they stick in our minds.*

Reverend Thomas's Sunday message was taken from the book of Matthew, chapter 8. He recounted that when Jesus and his disciples were crossing the sea of Galilee, a storm came up and threatened to sink their small fishing boat. The disciples were sorely afraid for their lives, but Jesus was asleep. They woke him, and He rebuked the storm, but then He chastised them for their lack of faith.

"This seems a simple enough story," Reverend Thomas declared, spreading his hands wide. "Except for several salient points. First off, the disciples were professional fishermen. They earned their living sailing the sea of Galilee. They were accustomed to bad weather. For them to be mortally afraid, it must have been an extraordinarily dreadful storm. Also, we note that Jesus rebuked the storm. Combined, these two elements suggest that the storm was demonically empowered. This is supported by Matthew chapter 17 in which Jesus rebukes the demon which had possessed a young boy, and the demon fled from the child."

Reverend Thomas's analysis captured my attention. I have never really known what to make of demons. I believe they exist because the Bible treats them as real beings. However, my training in the scientific disciplines leads me to consider other explanations to account for the afflictions that beset humanity. For instance, what is mental illness—a derangement of the brain's physiology or possession by a malevolent supernatural entity? It was an intriguing question.

The reverend continued, "Another point to be made is that the disciples were afraid, and yet Jesus scolded them for their lack of faith. This supports the assertion that fear is the antithesis of faith. True faith drives out fear. If we trust in God, no matter how severe the tribulation, He will see us through. To be afraid is to suggest that we don't fully trust Him."

Now this was something I could wholeheartedly endorse. To my mind, faith equates to accepting God's plan for our lives, knowing that He will see us through to the end, and that the end will be good.

Reverend Thomas paused and looked down upon the congregation. "The final point I would like to share is that Jesus allowed the storm to rage until it threatened to sink the boat. Had he chosen to do so, he could have prevented the storm entirely. Too often, we pray to be protected *from* the storm when, in fact, we should be praying that Jesus will see us *through* the storm. Many of the ordeals we endure are intended to grow our faith. Rather than strive to avoid them, we should allow the afflictions we suffer to build our character and increase our trust in the Lord."

As I listened to Reverend Thomas's words, I tried to imagine a time when I had feared for my life. To my amazement, I found that I could not recall even a single instance. That being the case, I tried to envision what it would be like being convinced that at any moment I was going to die. Would my faith be strong enough to see me through, or would I, like the disciples, cower in fear? *How can anyone possibly know what they will do under such circumstances?* People claim they're not afraid to die, but how can they be sure? It would be like tightrope walking across a deep canyon. Unless you are actually doing it, you cannot know for certain how the experience will affect you.

Brave soldiers freeze up in the heat of battle. During difficult landings, pilots have been known to plow their planes into the ground because they lost their nerve. I thought about Peter, who claimed he would never abandon Jesus but then denied Him three times when challenged after Jesus was arrested.

As I saw it, the heart of the matter was that when the time comes to face your demons, you need to trust God and pray that He will grant you the faith to carry you through.

When the service ended, I looked at Madison and found that she had been watching me.

"Where were you?" she said with a bemused smile.

"Thinking about unlikely situations and improbable events," I said lightheartedly. I had no desire to burden her with my morbid musings. "Are you hungry? Would you like to grab a bite of brunch?"

"I would love to, but I promised a friend I would take her shopping. She's pregnant, and she needs to buy some maternity clothes."

"Perhaps another day then—maybe next Sunday."

"I will look forward to it."

We said goodbye, and I headed home to spend the rest of the day mucking around inside my own head.

Alfred's was nearly deserted when Marcus entered and looked around. The dingy restaurant was located directly opposite Flintridge on the far side of Kennewick, well away from the more popular venues like the Columbia Center Mall or the Uptown Shopping Center. Although it was approaching the dinner hour and Marcus was hungry, he soon lost his appetite as he inspected his surroundings. There were smudges on the windows, grime on the floor, crusted food on the table tops, and flies buzzing around what looked to be week-old slices of pie in a countertop display.

Just as he had done before leaving the hospital, Marcus consulted the appointment app on his cell phone, confirming that it was Thursday afternoon and he was in the right place. Hopefully, the man he was meeting would show up soon. Sneaking around, putting up with the cloak-and-dagger melodrama was giving him an uneasy feeling.

Marcus made his way to a booth on the far side of the restaurant. He tried not to touch anything as he sat down. "Just coffee," he told the waitress when she stepped up to take his order. He placed the package he carried on the bench seat beside him, close enough that he could feel it against his leg. Wrapped in plain brown paper and tied with twine, there was no way to tell what was inside.

Just as Marcus was about to again check the time on his watch, Captain Jack Summers appeared in the entryway. He too carried a package except his was smaller—approximately the size of a cigar box. It too was plainly wrapped. When he saw Marcus, he crossed the room and sat down facing him.

"And here I thought I would be the one waiting," Captain Summers said in lieu of offering an apology for being late. He continued holding his package in his hand rather than set it down on the table or on the seat beside him. "Nothing for me," he told the waitress when she appeared at his elbow.

The woman scowled resentfully as if envisioning the meager tip she would earn, having served the table nothing but a single cup of coffee. She left in a huff.

"Who is The Angel?" Marcus asked without preamble.

"How do you know about him?" Captain Summers said, suspicion narrowing his eyes.

"I was talking with Tyler—"

Interrupting, Captain Summers tsked with his tongue. "I'll have to have a word with that boy."

"I was told that he's some sort of rich benefactor and that he has a lab in Mexico where he bioengineers the virus like some mad scientist. Is that true? Is he the one paying the bills?"

"If anyone asks you about him," Captain Summers responded mildly. "Tell them you don't know anything—because you don't—and let's keep it that way, shall we? Now, tell me, how are things at the hospital? Any problems so far?"

"You mean regarding Ophis Pterotos?"

Captain Summers shot a cautionary look across the table.

"Nobody heard me," Marcus declared defensively. "Relax. You are way too uptight."

"Relax?" Captain Summers snarled. "Perhaps you don't appreciate what's at stake here, or maybe you are unaware of the penalties for domestic terrorism."

Marcus paled. "What do you mean domestic terrorism?" Until that moment, he hadn't considered what they were doing from that point of view.

"I would say developing a bioweapon for military use qualifies."

"Hold on, I—"

"You what? What did you think we were doing? Or were your eyes too full of dollars signs to care?"

"I didn't sign up to be a terrorist." Marcus protested.

"Yes, you did, and you've been paid."

"No way, man. I'm out. You can have your money back."

"You'd walk away from one million dollars?"

"I just did."

"That's not the way it works. You are going to see this project through to its conclusion."

"And if I don't, what will happen?"

"What do you think will happen?" The look in Captain Summers's eyes was so severe that Marcus felt as if his guts had been tied in a knot.

"Now," Captain Summers continued. "Do you have something for me?"

Marcus retrieved his package from the bench seat beside him. His hand trembled when he handed it over.

"This is patient number three's medical record, I presume," Captain Summers said.

Finding that his mouth had gone dry and he was unable to speak, Marcus nodded.

"Good," Captain Summers said. "Then I have something for you." He passed the package he still held in his hand across the table. "You'd be wise not to open that. Tell Tyler and Jerry to be careful with this batch—it's more virulent than the last version."

"Why are you doing this?" Marcus said. He seemed defeated.

"For God and country," Captain Summers declared proudly.

"What could you possibly hope to gain?"

"Victory when our enemies move against us—not that such things would matter to you. We both know why you got involved. The only thing you care about is the money."

"That's not true," Marcus countered forcefully. "I care about the hospital and the work I do."

"Of course you do. That's why you're willing to infect patients with an unknown pathogen. Just do the job you were hired to do, and all this will soon be over."

Captain Summers slid out of the booth and departed, leaving Marcus feeling abashed and resentful.

Carrying the cigar-box-shaped package ever so gingerly, Marcus also left the restaurant without bothering to leave a tip.

# UNPOPULAR DECISIONS

At 1:00 a.m. on Friday, the first day of September, Tyler Wickham was alone in the Respiratory Therapy Department. At that hour of the morning, the department was quiet, as was the rest of the Flintridge Medical Center, except for the Emergency Department, which was busy as usual. Tyler had volunteered to work the night shift in place of a colleague who had requested time off to be with his girlfriend. It wasn't that Tyler harbored any particular desire to help out a fellow therapist when the need arose. Rather, he had a mission to perform and only a limited amount of time to see it completed.

The previous day, during his meeting with Captain Summers, Marcus Eldridge had taken possession of the reengineered virus. Upon returning to the hospital, he had hastily transferred the sample to Tyler's care, clearly anxious to be rid of it. During the handoff, Marcus had repeatedly stressed how dangerous the virus was and how careful Tyler should be, as if a trained therapist might be ignorant of the risks.

Tyler bristled at the memory of their conversation. Marcus might outrank him in matters that pertained to the hospital, but when it came to the militia's business, Tyler was the one with seniority.

The cigar-box-shaped package sat open on the counter in front of Tyler. He had put on a full biohazard suit to open it, carefully removing the brown paper wrapping, taking his time and working deliberately.

Upon lifting the lid on the box, he had discovered a test tube half full of amber liquid. Cushioned in foam rubber padding, the sample looked exactly like the first three specimens. Only by deciphering the test tubes' encrypted labels could they be distinguished one from another.

Also in the squat box was an ordinary-looking orange-colored medicine bottle that contained a dozen antiviral tablets. These had been specifically engineered to kill the virus and were to be used as emergency therapy in the event something went wrong while handling the sample. They were believed to be highly effective, though they had never been tested on humans.

Tyler transferred the test tube to a weighted stand specifically designed to not tip over. With the greatest care, he extracted the stopper that sealed the test tube. Using a pipette attached to wall suction, he drew up two cc's of liquid, which he transferred to the glass reservoir of a bulb atomizer. After screwing the reservoir back into the atomizer, he placed the disposable pipette in a zip-up plastic bag that would later be incinerated. He firmly reinserted the stopper into the test tube and then transferred the test tube into a long, slender bullet-shaped metal cylinder with a screw-on cap. As with the previous three samples, the metal cylinder, along with the bottle of antiviral tablets, he would give to Jerry for safekeeping. Jerry had been charged with holding onto the tubes until the last virus sample had been tested. When the clinical trials were concluded, all the specimens would be destroyed together.

His preparations complete, Tyler removed the headpiece of his biohazard suit. He had begun to sweat, and he used a towel to dry his face and neck. The atomizer was safe for the moment. The virus would not be released unless someone squeezed the bulb or broke the reservoir.

After he had finished cleaning up and after wriggling free of his biohazard suit, Tyler began to prepare himself mentally for the next stage of his mission.

Pushing a wheeled handcart loaded with various respiratory therapy supplies, Tyler entered the intensive care unit without arousing suspicion. He wore a long white lab coat, green scrubs, and paper shoe covers over his tennies. He looked the part of a technician going about his nocturnal duties, one of which was to service the wall-mounted oxygen outlets used in patients' rooms throughout the hospital. He carried the atomizer containing the virus—protectively swaddled in a square of soft fabric—in his lab coat pocket.

This was Tyler's third visit to the intensive care unit in the last two hours. On the previous two occasions, he had studied the unit's patients and learned their diagnoses. He was searching for an individual who satisfied a set of specific criteria. He needed a middle-aged male with a non-respiratory, non-life-threatening malady who was expected to remain hospitalized for at least three days.

At the end of his first visit, Tyler had despaired of finding a suitable candidate. At the end of his second visit, however, he noted that a patient had just been transferred in from the Emergency Department.

Thankfully, Mr. Leland Wright fit the profile. He was a fifty-three-year-old gentleman with septic cholecystitis, a serious infection of the gallbladder. He was moderately ill, but with proper care, he was expected to make a full recovery. He was a nonsmoker, and there were no other medical issues to complicate his serving as test subject number four.

Tyler had phoned Jerry at home to solicit his opinion. After listening to Tyler's report, Jerry—still half asleep—had agreed that Mr. Wright seemed like a suitable candidate, and he had advised Tyler to proceed. What both men had failed to take into account was that in six hours Blake would be coming on-call and would remain on-call for the next twenty-four hours—until 8:00 a.m. Saturday morning.

The time had come for Tyler to complete his mission. This was also the part he dreaded most. In theory, his task was straightforward. He would slip into the patient's room under the guise of servicing the wall oxygen equipment. Mr. Wright, having been sedated by his pain medications, would either be groggy or sound asleep. Tyler would unwrap the atomizer, and while holding his breath, he would deliver two quick puffs a foot in front of Mr. Wright's face. Tyler would then exit the room immediately, and for the next five minutes, he would stand watch in case one of the nurses elected to enter the room. If that were to happen, Tyler would do his best to distract the nurse for as long as possible, allowing the aerosolized virus to die off.

The problem was there were any number of places where the plan could go terribly awry. A member of the ICU staff could challenge his presence in the ICU, noting that the wall oxygen units had recently been serviced. Mr. Wright's gallbladder pain might be severe enough to keep him awake. The atomizer might dysfunction. Tyler could fail to exit the room quickly enough, thereby becoming infected himself. A nurse desiring to enter the room might be undeterred by Tyler's interdiction.

In preparation, Tyler donned a surgical cap, a pair of neoprene gloves, and an N95 facemask. He then fully buttoned up his lab coat and, steeling himself, forged ahead.

As noiselessly as possible, he slid the glass door open and stepped inside Mr. Wright's room, gratefully noting that the patient appeared to be asleep. Tyler then quietly closed the curtains that surrounded the bed, blocking the view of the interior from outside the room. With great care, he retrieved the atomizer from his lab coat pocket and cautiously unwrapped it.

Tyler then paused to listen, making certain that the commotion inside the ICU had not changed. Satisfied that his presence had not yet been noticed, he inhaled deeply and held his breath. With one hand supporting the atomizer's reservoir and the other hand grasping its bulb, Tyler aimed the tip toward Mr. Wright's face. He squeezed the bulb twice and then once again for good measure. A silvery, slightly iridescent mist floated toward his victim's nostrils.

Still holding his breath, Tyler quickly rewrapped the atomizer in its protective cloth before exiting the room. The next five minutes seemed an eternity. Eventually, when no one came to inquire after his reason for loitering, he breathed a sigh of relief and left the unit.

In the empty corridor outside, he shed the facemask, surgical cap, and shoe covers, which he stowed in a trash bag from his cart. Next he took off the lab coat and the gloves. Both of these he trash-bagged as well, along with the wrapped atomizer. On his way back to the Respiratory Therapy Department, Tyler looped by a housekeeping station. There he added his trash bag to others waiting to be collected and incinerated.

*Now*, Tyler told himself. *Nature will take its course.* He had done his duty. Captain Summers and the other leaders of the New World Militia would be pleased. Perhaps they would offer him a promotion.

It was twenty minutes past noon by the time the last patient of the morning finally signed out and departed. The Pulmonary Associates' office staff promptly locked the doors and began decorating in celebration of Adam's retirement. As office manager, Lois supervised transforming the central work area into a party room. Crêpe streamers of blue and gold were hung from the ceiling and on the fronts of desks and counters. Multicolored balloons were inflated and strategically taped to desks, chairs, computers, and other pieces of office equipment. The Internet radio was switched from the usual spa station to a lively pop music channel.

Party hats and noisemakers were handed out, and soon it seemed everyone was in a festive mood, including Adam who, being the center of attention, looked somewhat embarrassed. Flo Richards, Adams wife, had been invited to the party. She stood behind where her husband sat in his place of honor, a look of pride in her eyes.

A work counter was cleared, and several nurses began setting out serving trays that offered a variety of Mexican dishes. These included Spanish rice, refried beans, tacos, and enchiladas, along with tortillas and a mixed-green salad. To drink there was coffee, iced tea, and a large cooler of lemonade. A line formed, and people began filling paper plates with their selections. They then moved off to find a place to eat. Several wound up sitting in wheelchairs with their paper plates balanced on their laps.

Jerry and I had held back on joining the serving line until our employees had been fed. As we watched the festivities unfold, Jerry leaned closer and whispered in my ear, "How do you think he's going to do in retirement? I've worked with the man for nearly ten years now, and I don't believe I've ever seen him so uncertain."

At first, I failed to appreciate what Jerry was seeing. To my mind, Adam seemed happy, though a little uneasy perhaps; but then when I looked closer, I noticed apprehension in his eyes. Apparently, He wasn't as keen on retirement as he had led us to believe. I felt inclined to wonder if he was having second thoughts and was moving forward with retirement simply because he had announced that it was going to happen.

I began to worry that the celebration would interfere with our ability to see afternoon patients. When I shared my concern, I was informed that our schedules had been left open to prevent just such a conflict.

After most of the employees had finished their meals, Lois stood up and stepped forward. Holding a small gift-wrapped box in her hand, she looked at Adam. "I can't believe you are actually retiring." She cleared her throat and in a more formal tone of voice said, "Doctor Richards, words cannot adequately express the love and affection we have for you. For all these years, you have been our employer, our teacher, our mentor, our inspiration, and our friend. We're going to miss you severely, but we wish you well. May you prosper in whatever you choose to do from this point forward. As a token of our regard, we got you this." She handed the box to Adam. "Whenever you look at it, remember how much we care for you."

When Lois stepped back a pace, I noticed that her eyes were moist.

Adam opened the box. Inside was a top-of-the-line smartwatch.

"It's already paired with your cell phone," Lois announced. "It's fully configured and ready to go."

"How did you get access to my phone?" Dumbfounded, Adam examined his gift. He then cocked his head to look up at his wife, who shrugged and looked away. He glanced back at Lois. "Thank you. It's a lovely watch, and I will wear it proudly, but I don't need a reminder. I will remember each and every one of you and how much you have meant to me."

The phone rang. It was an outside line. Ellie, my nurse, answered it. She listened for a moment and then said, "He's right here. I'll tell him." She hung up and turned to me. "That was the ICU. They have a patient they would like you to consult on, and they need you as soon as possible."

After receiving the consultation request, I walked-jogged to the hospital, which was faster than driving. During my second week in practice, I had actually timed myself to see which would get me there the quickest. Fortunately, I enjoy walking, and it's good exercise.

When I entered the ICU, Doctor Peter Ramsey, the hospitalist, was waiting to speak with me. A small energetic man with a pleasant demeanor, he was Leland Wright's admitting physician, having been asked by Doctor Morton Stone, the patient's general practitioner, to take over Mr. Wright's care while he was still in the Emergency Department. It was Peter who had requested my consultation.

It's no wonder that patients have trouble figuring out who's actually taking care of them. In complicated cases, as many as seven to ten physicians from a variety of specialties may be involved, not to mention members of the ancillary medical teams. Keeping track of who's who can be a daunting task especially when you're not feeling well.

Peter wore a worried look when I approached him at the work counter. "Thanks for coming so quickly," he said. "This guy is getting worse by the minute. When I first saw him in the ED, his lungs were clear, and he was breathing easily. That was around 8:00 p.m. yesterday evening. He was still breathing well when I checked him just before midnight. A little after six this morning, he began showing signs of pulmonary involvement. Since then, he's gone steadily downhill. His O2 sats are dropping, and he's beginning to manifest some cyanosis. I'm worried that he could code at any minute."

Peter's description reminded me of Emile Goldstein, the patient I had covered on-call shortly after entering private practice. However, rather than assume they had the same pathology, I decided to reserve judgment until I had completed my own evaluation.

Out of the corner of my eye, I noticed Madison standing a dozen feet away. She was helping another patient. When she looked up and saw me, she smiled. I smiled back. *Damn she's pretty*, I thought, but for the moment, I put her out of my mind.

"Where is he?" I said to Peter.

"He's this way. I'll introduce you." He led the way to room 237.

Often a physician, when he first encounters a patient, will gain a sense of how that patient is doing. Are they fundamentally well or are they acutely ill? Are they comfortable or are they in pain? Are they coping or is their condition, whatever it might be, getting the better of them? One look at Mr. Wright told me he was a train wreck that was about to slam into the ICU. His bedside monitor confirmed that his oxygen saturations were dangerously low.

I turned to Peter, but before I could speak, he said, "All set up and ready to go. I would have intubated him myself, but you got here too quickly. The respiratory therapist is on her way with a ventilator."

*On her way*, I thought. *Good. That means it won't be Tyler.* I had nothing against the fellow, but I didn't feature being reminded of what had happened the last time.

Peter approached the bed and started to introduce me, but it was clear that Mr. Wright wasn't paying attention. He was too keenly focused on trying to breathe.

Rather than wait for the respiratory therapist, we decided not to delay the intubation. With Peter assisting, passing the tube went very smoothly, and we were able to resuscitate our patient with a self-inflating breathing bag until his ventilator arrived.

There is one thing about intubating patients that I truly do not like. Inserting a tube into a patient's windpipe makes it extremely difficult to take their history. I have always elected to do my own histories and physical exams rather than rely on someone else's observations. In this case, what with Mr. Wright intubated, that was not an option. After placing Mr. Wright on a ventilator and with his oxygen saturations beginning to stabilize, Peter and I sat down to discuss his case. I already knew the highlights. It was the fine points—the minutia—that was lacking.

Peter explained that our patient had come to the hospital with abdominal pain. An ultrasound had confirmed the presence of gallstones, and his blood work had suggested a smoldering infection. Peter had started him on broad-spectrum antibiotics given intravenously.

It turned out that Peter had taken a surprisingly good history, yet there were still details I did not know. Had the patient recently had the flu? Had he been around anybody who was sick? Had he coughed up any blood? Was there a family history of lung disease? Were there any sick animals in the house? Had he ever used tobacco for an extended period of time? Things like that.

Whereas intubation makes history taking difficult, it makes doing a physical examination relatively easy. Since intubated patients are generally sedated, you can poke and prod, look and feel as you need to. However, when I finished doing a physical, I had not learned much more than before I had begun. I could find no telltale signs of an underlying medical condition. Other than gunky lungs and a few wheezes audible when I listened to his chest, there were no clues to indicate what had caused his deterioration.

If the history and physical examination fail to lead to a diagnosis, lab studies can sometimes come to the rescue. However, in Mr. Wright's case, they were of little help. All they told me was that he had a diffuse pneumonia of uncertain type, probably caused by a yet-to-be-identified virus.

After I finished recording my consult in Mr. Wright's medical record, I wrote two pages of orders, the first of which was to place Mr. Wright in strict respiratory isolation. Hopefully, the tests I was requesting would lead to a proper diagnosis, and the treatments I was prescribing would speed his recovery. I said a prayer for him and wrote his name in my prayer notebook.

I hated having to wait, but I figured that within twelve to twenty-four hours, I would know considerably more than I did at that moment. In the meantime, there was someone I needed to talk to. When I was satisfied that my patient was finally stable, I headed off to track down my infection control nurse.

I finally located Heather in the medical wing on the third floor. She was assessing the condition of a thirty-four-year-old bus driver with a drug-resistant cellulitis, an infection of the skin. She looked up as I drew near where she sat reviewing the patient's chart. "I was wondering if I would bump into you this afternoon," Heather said with a wry smile

"So I gather you know about Mr. Wright?" Having been seated for the last half hour while completing my consult, I chose to remain standing.

Heather nodded. "I had planned on stopping by the unit to check on him, but I thought I should finish up this patient first. This guy probably has MRSA." From medical school microbiology, I recalled that MRSA—pronounced mersa—stands for Methicillin-Resistant Staphylococcus Aureus. Staphylococci are a particularly aggressive species of bacterium.

Heather continued, "Imagine the harm a highly drug-resistant flesh-eating bug could cause if it were to get loose in the hospital. That's why this fellow needs to be on wound-and-skin isolation. His family may not appreciate having to don a gown and gloves just to visit their loved one, but inconveniencing them is better than letting a serious pathogen escape into our patient population.

Heather finished entering her recommendations into the tablet computer she was using then closed the file and handed the device back to the patient's nurse.

"I'm curious," I said when she turned to face me. "What happens if a doctor doesn't comply with your directives?"

Heather grinned, accentuating her dimples. "That's where you come in. You get to counsel the errant practitioner and explain why it would be in everyone's best interest if he or she were to get with the program."

"Let's say I do my best to convince the blackguard but he or she still refuses to comply. What then?

"You meet again, but this time you take the chief of staff with you. Together the two of you persuade the stubborn clod to be a team player."

"And if that doesn't work…?"

"I ask the hospital administrator to suspend the offending physician's hospital privileges. His patient is then reassigned to another physician who will implement my recommendations."

"Is there a procedure whereby a physician can appeal your recommendations?"

"There is. That's where the Infection Control Committee comes into play. The doctor presents his case, I present mine, then the committee decides who's right, though disputes rarely escalate to the point of involving the committee. Most doctors see the light if it's properly presented to them. After all, we're on the same team, and we share a common goal—keep as many people as possible as healthy as possible for as long as possible. Now tell me about your patient. What do you think is going on with Mr. Wright? Is it the same syndrome?"

"I don't know," I admitted truthfully. "I suspect it may be, but I can't be sure until I see how his disease progresses. You had intended to look into the first two patients. Did you have a chance to do that?

"I did."

"What did you learn?"

"Not a whole lot that was new. I called both Billy Mitchell and Agnes Gilroy. They both claim they are fully recovered, though they were quite ill for a time. Neither would admit to having a history of lung disease. I also called the lab to see if they'd held back any blood samples from when they were admitted. They hadn't, unfortunately. Otherwise, I would've requested viral cultures on both patients. As it is, that isn't going to happen. It will happen for Mr. Goldstein, however. The lab still had a sample of his blood. I assume you ordered viral cultures on Mr. Wright."

"You assume correctly. I asked them to culture both his blood and whatever sputum he can raise."

"That's good. From a public health point of view, is there more we should be doing?" The look on Heather's face implied that it was a rhetorical question and she had several recommendations in mind.

"What do you suggest?" I asked casually.

Heather nodded. "One of the first things would be to speak with the families, see if these patients shared any activities in common—business meetings, travel, shopping, community gatherings, club attendance—that sort of thing. Next, I would evaluate their home and work environments. Sometimes a careful analysis will turn up a common source of exposure. Also, I would get in touch with the County Health Department and with other hospitals in the region to see if they have logged any similar cases."

"Those are all good ideas. One thing we need to keep in mind is that just because patients follow a similar clinical course, that doesn't mean they have the same malady. It could all be coincidence. We'll be in a better position to judge after we see how Mr. Wright progresses. Look, I'm going to loop by the unit to check on Mr. Wright again. If anything turns up this afternoon I'll be at my office. Please give me a call. Otherwise, I'll talk to you tomorrow."

"Sounds like a plan," Heather agreed.

I took the stairs down one floor to the ICU.

Mr. Wright's breathing was about the same when I looked in on him. The thing that worried me, however, was that although his mental status was unchanged, his blood pressure was below normal, and he was beginning to spike a fever. That implied that the antibiotics he was receiving weren't adequately covering his infection. I thought about requesting an infectious disease consultation to help sort out his medications, then I realized that at the Flintridge Medical Center, the closest thing to an infectious disease consultant was me. The irony almost made me laugh—almost.

"I gather it was touch and go for a time," Madison commented as she stepped up to join me.

I was standing just outside Mr. Wright's room gazing in. Except for an emergency, I would have to put on a cap, gown, and gloves to enter. "He's not out of the woods yet."

As usual, Madison looked quite fetching. She wore her auburn hair drawn back into a ponytail, mother-of-pearl burettes at her temples. "Are you on call this weekend?" she said.

"No, I'm off. I was on call last weekend. That's why I wasn't in church. This time, it's Jerry's turn in the meat grinder."

"Isn't this the week you start your new schedule now that Doctor Richards has retired?"

"Don't remind me. Not only will we have to take call every other weekend, to make the schedule come out correctly, we'll have to cover the Monday following our weekend on-call as well. That's three days in a row. I didn't expect this when I joined Pulmonary Associates."

"Are you sorry you did—join them, that is?"

"Not yet, but… actually, no. I'm not sorry. Things can get a little dicey every now and then, but I'm enjoying private practice, and I couldn't ask for a better office staff. With time, I will get used to the new schedule, I suppose."

"Maybe you should pray about it," Madison suggested.

"Now that is a very good idea. Would you pray with me?"

"Of course." Madison edged slightly closer.

I closed my eyes and in a lowered voice said, "Heavenly Father, we thank You for the opportunities you place before us. We pray that you will sustain us as we strive to serve the patients You bring us. Give us wisdom and sound judgment, and refresh our minds that we may be clearheaded and mindful of all the information we need to retain to practice medicine well. We pray especially for Mr. Wright. Allow the power of Your Holy Spirit to defeat his infection and heal his body. Restore him to good health if that is Your will. We ask all these things in the name of our Lord and Savior, Jesus Christ. Amen."

"Amen." Madison echoed. "Well said. Do you think you will be in church this weekend?"

"I should be…unless something unexpected turns up. You?"

"Yes. I plan on being there."

"Great. Save me a seat, if you wouldn't mind. Maybe we could do lunch afterward. What do you think?"

Madison smiled. "I would like that."

"Excellent. I'll look forward to it. Well, gotta run. I still have a few office patients to see."

"And I have a dressing to change." Madison turned away to gather the supplies she would need.

Monday morning, in the first week of September, I arrived at the hospital early. I'd had the weekend off and was feeling refreshed despite having spent considerable time completing tasks I had been putting off such as washing my car, balancing my checkbook, and getting my laundry done. Such is the life of a bachelor. Without a helpmate, everything is do-it-yourself.

When I entered the ICU to begin my morning rounds, I noticed Jerry sitting at the work counter, reviewing a medical record. He looked beaten down in the way his shoulders slumped and his head sagged forward. I assumed he'd had a rough weekend on-call, and I wondered if he had been up all night. It seemed a reasonable possibility, judging by the haggard expression on his face.

One glance toward room 237 told me that Mr. Wright was still on a ventilator. I had hoped he might have recovered enough to be extubated, but that apparently was not the case.

"Good morning, Jerry," I said as I sat down beside my partner. "Rough weekend, I gather."

"And then some. Your patient there"—he inclined his head toward Mr. Wright's room—"kept me up most of the night."

"His pneumonia isn't clearing? That's a surprise. I had expected that by now he would be much improved."

"Quite the contrary. He's been spiking fevers to 103. His chest x-ray shows increased consolidation in both lungs, and he is hypotensive. I'm fairly sure he's septic. I drew some blood cultures. The preliminary results should be available later today. To make matters worse, I suspect he's had a mini-stroke: He's harder to arouse, and he's not moving his right side much. I would have ordered a CT scan, but he's hemodynamically unstable. I've started him on dobutamine to keep his blood pressure up. He is now at ten micrograms per kilogram per minute, and I've added vancomycin to maximize his antibacterial coverage. I put him on one gram IV every twelve hours by slow infusion."

Jerry regarded me with red-rimmed eyes. He seemed unusually morose. I detected a sorrow in his demeanor that exceeded the physical and emotional depletion that would have resulted from fatigue alone. I hadn't known the man long, but he seemed genuinely distressed by Mr. Wright's deterioration.

"I'm sure you've done everything you can," I said in an effort to provide a measure of consolation. "We do our best, but the outcome isn't up to us."

"It will be a miracle if he survives. I wish I had done things differently."

"It's not your fault. Like I said, we do our best, and then we pray." As I spoke the words, I was reminded of the prayer I had shared with Madison. I made a mental note to again speak with her about unanswered prayers and learn if she'd had any additional thoughts on how to deal with them.

Changing the subject, I said, "Is Ramsey up to speed on what's been going on?"

Jerry nodded. "He just left. He agreed that we're doing everything feasible."

I laid a hand on Jerry's shoulder. "I suppose all we can do now is wait and see if he'll pull through. By the way, I assume you've been in touch with the family. We need to prepare them in case Mr. Wright doesn't make it."

"They were in last night. I'm pretty sure they understand what's going on. It's the wife I worry about. She seems rather fragile. If he dies, I don't think she's going to do well."

"I will call them later this morning and see if there's anything we can do to comfort them." Dealing with grieving families is one of the hardest duties that befall a physician. "Well," I said more optimistically. "He's not dead yet. Let's see if we can think of something else that might make a difference."

Jerry wished me well and left the unit. I felt a surge of sympathy for the man. Sometimes it's difficult—keeping your patient's troubles from touching you emotionally.

I turned toward Mr. Wright's room. Before entering, I suited up in shoe covers, a paper gown, gloves, splash-resistant safety glasses, and a facemask. After completing a targeted physical exam, I shed the protective garments and returned to the work counter where I sat down with the patient's chart to review the lab results. Jerry had been right. There were strong indications that Mr. Wright had suffered a small stroke. If he survived his pneumonia, I would have to get neurology involved. Early rehabilitation could minimize the severity of the damage, but currently, he was much too ill for such interventions.

As expected, my patient's metabolic profile was a mess. His liver function studies, his serum electrolytes, his blood gasses, and even his blood sugar were abnormal. When I called the lab, I was told that the blood cultures were negative—thus far, nothing was growing, which didn't count for a lot since more time would be needed to be sure the cultures were indeed negative.

When I finished with the chart, I was forced to agree that everything that could be done was being done. With a sigh of resignation, I headed off to see my other patients before reporting to the office.

The woeful phone call I had been expecting rang through at 4:15 a.m. on Tuesday morning, the day following my encounter with Jerry in the ICU. Technically, my on-call shift wasn't supposed to start until 8:00 a.m., but I had left instructions with the nurses to notify me in the event that there was a significant change in Mr. Wright's condition.

The nurse on the other end of the line—I didn't catch her name—frantically informed me that Mr. Wright had suffered a cardiac arrest and that cardiopulmonary resuscitation, or CPR, as it is commonly called, was underway. Doctor Ramsey, who happened to be admitting a patient at the time, was running the code. I asked if I could speak with him, but when the nurse relayed my request, she was told that he would get back to me when things calmed down.

Rather than wait for Peter to call, I informed the nurse I would be in as soon as possible. I hung up the phone and immediately began getting dressed. I figured I would shave on the way to the hospital. I keep an electric razor in my Sentra for just such occasions.

Regrettably, I found that I hadn't charged it in a while; and when I tested it, the battery was dead.

As soon as I entered the ICU, I could tell I was too late. The nurses and the support personnel were moving far too slowly for a resuscitation to be ongoing. When Doctor Ramsey emerged from Mr. Wright's room, he was stripping off his neoprene gloves. The paper gown he was wearing was hanging open in the back. He shook his head when he saw me and crossed the room to where I was standing.

From a dispenser on the counter, he slathered on hand sanitizer and rubbed it in thoroughly. "Would you want to write the death certificate, or should I?"

I replied, "You can since you are…since you were his primary physician. I'll notify the family if you'd like.

"Oh, yes please." Peter made a sour face, indicating how he felt about doing family notifications. "So…what would you suggest we put on the death certificate? What would you say is his final diagnosis?"

"Respiratory failure due to multifocal pneumonia complicated by cholecystitis."

"Multifocal pneumonia? That's rather ambiguous."

"You're right." I reached for the phone. "Let me call the lab. Maybe we can be more specific." When I ended the phone call, I announced, "They are growing a virus, but they haven't identified it yet. Maybe you should put down viral pneumonia, type NOS—not otherwise specified."

"That's not much better than multifocal pneumonia. Maybe we should wait twenty-four hours and see what grows."

"I could live with that," I replied. "Sorry, bad choice of words."

Just then, Heather Oliver entered the ICU. Apparently, she too had asked to be notified in the event of a significant change in the patient's status. After I finished speaking with the family members and conveying our sympathy, Heather and I sat down to discuss what to do next.

"So? What do you think?" Heather said. "Were Mr. Wright and Mr. Goldstein suffering from the same disease? Or were their illnesses only superficially similar?"

I scraped my thumb along the edge of my jaw, feeling my unshaven beard. "At this point, I'd have to say they were different pathologies. Mr. Wright's clinical course differed substantially from Mr. Goldstein's. Even so, it might be prudent to err on the side of being excessively cautious. Let's put out a directive requiring all patients admitted with pneumonia to be placed in strict respiratory isolation at least until we know more about this…whatever this is."

"Everyone?" Heather blurted out with alarm. That's going to annoy a lot of people."

"Wouldn't that be preferable to allowing an unknown pathogen to gain a foothold in the hospital?"

"You're right. I'll pass the word."

There was nothing more for me to do in the ICU, and it was too early to begin rounds on my other patients. I decided to visit the cafeteria. Maybe a light breakfast would help me clear the cobwebs from my mind.

In the cafeteria, I ordered oatmeal, to which I added small scoops of raisins and mixed nuts, a fruit cup, whole wheat toast, and a carton of apple juice. Rather than head for the doctors' dining room, I made my way to an empty table across from the serving line. From where I sat, I could gaze out through the large picture windows at the city of Flintridge.

The weather outside was mild, and it promised to be a beautiful fall day. A few of the deciduous trees on the hospital campus were beginning their autumnal turn. Soon the forests surrounding the town would become a riot of color. Then winter would not be far behind—or so I had been told. One thing about growing up in Southern California—you don't get to experience the change of seasons like people in other parts of the country.

Fragments of conversation ricocheted through the large dining hall. I tried not to listen. Most of the snippets were obviously gossip and, therefore, more speculation than fact. I have always been amazed at how insular hospitals can be—in the world but not part of it. I smiled. A world within a world—it seemed an apt description.

"What's so funny?" said a female voice behind me. I turned my head to look and found Madison smiling down at me.

"I was just thinking about life in a microcosm."

"Sounds interesting. Mind if I join you?"

"By all means." I started to stand, but Madison waved me back into my chair. "There is no need to be so formal." She put her tray down and then sat down facing me. "By microcosm, I assume you were referring to our hospital environment?"

"I was. Hospitals are a world unto themselves. I remember when I was in training. Stretches of days would drift by, and then I'd realize that for a week—or more—I hadn't set foot outside the hospital. It's like your whole life gets compressed down to a few rudiments—eat, sleep, and work."

"It's often more complex than that." I noticed that Madison's breakfast consisted of a hard-boiled egg, half a grapefruit, and a slice of dry wheat toast with black coffee. I wondered if she worried about gaining weight.

"How so?"

"Too often there is an emotional component we can't avoid. I heard about your patient, Mr. Wright. Sometimes even our best efforts aren't enough."

"It sort of feels like God turned His back on the poor man."

"Does that make you angry?"

I tilted my head to peer at Madison. "Why do you ask?"

"I heard it in your voice."

"Yeah. It kind of does. Scripture says that we are supposed to bring our petitions before the Lord with prayer and thanksgiving, but sometimes when I pray, it feels like I'm talking to the wall. I pray fervently, like we did with Mr. Wright, and yet nothing happens. It sort of feels like God has shut down our access to His throne of grace, leaving us to fend for ourselves." I held up a hand, palm out. "Before you say anything, I know that's not true, but that's how it feels. Unanswered prayers test my faith more than almost anything else."

"I understand. It's like you're shouting for help, and nobody's listening, but that's why it's called faith—because you have to trust that God hears you, that He loves you, and that He is acting in your best interest even if the answer to your prayer is no."

"Why do you think God set it up that way?"

Madison smiled. "I've often asked myself that same question."

"And what was your answer?"

"To challenge us maybe? To grow our faith? Or perhaps for reasons that only God Himself knows. Rather than trying to figure Him out, perhaps we should strive to trust Him more."

"That's easier said than done."

The conversation turned to other topics as we finished our breakfasts. By then, it was time for me to start my rounds and for Madison to report for work. As we bussed our trays, I said, "It doesn't feel like I've found the answers I was looking for."

"Then keep looking." Madison waved goodbye and hurried off.

When I arrived in the office after completing my rounds, I found an unpleasant surprise waiting for me. Jerry was pacing the hallway, obviously in a grim mood. He followed me into my office, and before I could even shed my sport coat, he said, "There is something I need to tell you, and you are not going to like it."

"Let me guess," I responded. "Mr. Wright's family is suing us for malpractice."

Jerry scowled. "I wish it were that simple." He sank down into one of the two armchairs that faced the desk. Without additional preamble, he announced, "I'm selling the practice to Flintridge Healthcare. It's the only reasonable solution to our dilemma."

About to hang my coat on the rack in the corner, I stopped and turned to face him. "You can't do that. We haven't discussed this."

"There is nothing to discuss. The decision has already been made."

"By whom?" I protested.

"By me."

"But we're partners. I have a vote too."

"You're the junior partner. I have seniority, and since there are only two of us, it really doesn't matter how you vote. Believe me, I wish there were some other way, but there isn't. I've already been in touch with Marcus Eldridge. He's having the hospital's lawyers draw up the purchase agreement."

"I won't sign it."

"You do remember that you're on probationary status. You're not yet a full member of this group. It doesn't matter whether you sign or not. The sale is going to occur with or without your permission."

"If Adam were here, you wouldn't get away with this."

"If Adam were here, this would never have become an issue. As it is, this is the only way we can raise the money to pay him off. I know you don't like this, and neither do I, but it is going to happen, and that's a fact. Now I have patients to see."

Jerry rose from his chair and stomped out of my office.

A short time later, Ellie McDonough, my nurse, appeared in my doorway, a chart in her hand. Most of the time she came across as being timid and unassuming, and yet she could stand her ground if challenged. I admired that about her.

"Did you know about this?" I barked.

Ellie seemed to withdraw into herself. "You mean selling the practice? We heard about it this morning."

"How does the staff feel about becoming employees of the hospital?"

"Honestly? There are some that like the idea and some that don't. The pay and the benefits will be a little better, but we won't get to choose where we work. That sucks." Ellie flushed slightly. "Personally, I would rather leave things the way they are, but it doesn't look like that's possible." She laid the chart on my desk. "Your first patient is ready."

I gathered up the chart and forced myself to temporarily banish the matter from my mind. I would deal with it later.

Friday, over the lunch hour, I was seated in the hospital's lecture hall, listening to a CME presentation on new advances in the treatment of inflammatory bowel disease given by Doctor Cecil Lowden, one of Flintridge Healthcare's three gastroenterologists. I was trying to pay attention, but my mind kept wandering.

Seated three rows in front of me and a couple of chairs to my left, Jerry Tucker was conversing with a colleague. Four days had passed since our confrontation in the office. During that time, we had hardly spoken despite the fact that I had taken his call day on Tuesday. He had claimed he was feeling stressed. Adding the extra day had put me on-call four days in a row. I had willingly agreed to cover the extra day despite my resentment for being excluded from the decision-making. It was the charitable thing to do. Had Jerry said thank you or expressed his appreciation? Not once. His apparent lack of gratitude still nettled me.

In addition, on Wednesday, Marcus Eldridge had tracked me down. In an officious display of power, he had condescendingly announced that he was canceling my directive that all pneumonia patients be maintained on strict respiratory isolation. His stated reason was that family members had begun complaining about the inconvenience and the medical staff had decided that I had exceeded my authority. He had refused to consider my argument that placing patients in quarantine effectively reduced the risk of an unknown pathogen invading the hospital.

Actually, the pathogen was no longer unknown. Rather, it was poorly understood. A human bocavirus (HBoV) had been found in sputum samples taken from both Mr. Goldstein, and Mr. Wright. Antibodies against the virus had also been found in the blood of both Billy Mitchel and Agnes Gilroy, indicating that they too had been infected by the virus. The circumstances by which the virus had come to sicken four unrelated patients was unknown.

Technically, bocaviruses were members of the parvovirus family. As such, they were small non-envelope single-stranded DNA viruses of about 5,300 nucleotides. First isolated ten years previously, four subspecies, HBoV1, HBoV2, HBoV3, and HBoV4 had thus far been identified. The virus was known to cause both acute respiratory infections and gastroenteritis, primarily in children ages six to twenty-four months. Adult infections were less common but not unheard of.

No antiviral therapies were known to be effective against HBoVs.

In discussions with Heather Oliver regarding these revelations, several anomalies had been identified. That four adults and no children had been infected had seemed strange. The rapid onset–rapid recovery presentation had not yet been mentioned in the literature. This suggested that if HBoVs were responsible for our patients' pneumonias, as we suspected, we were dealing with a new, more virulent version of the virus. The fact that Mr. Wright's clinical course had differed significantly from that of his predecessors was worrisome. It implied that the virus was still mutating and had become even more aggressive, although there was another possibility.

Mr. Wright already had a bacterial infection in his gallbladder when his pneumonia began to take hold. Perhaps the two infections had interacted in ways that bolstered the severity of each. Had he been afflicted with just the pneumonia, perhaps the outcome might have been different. That, of course, was pure speculation, but it seemed feasible. Dual infections would explain why he had failed to improve after twenty-four to forty-eight hours.

The lecture ended, and I rose to my feet. Jerry passed by as I stepped into the aisle. I should have kept my mouth shut, but I was frustrated and tired and more than a little apprehensive about my future with Pulmonary Associates. "You could have waited," I said to his retreating back loudly enough to be overheard by people standing nearby.

Jerry halted and turned to face me. "Waiting would have accomplished nothing."

"You don't know that. At least we would have had time to work the problem."

"To what end? Do you have a quarter of a million dollars to buy Adam out?"

I shook my head. "No, but—"

"Then what would be the point of discussing it further than we already have? Look, it's done," Jerry declared harshly. "You need to let this go."

As I glanced around, I saw that other physicians were starting to take notice. Even so, I wasn't about to back down. My ego had been bruised, and I felt compelled to make my point. "If you want me as a partner, you should respect me enough to include me in the decision-making."

"Why can't you understand?" Jerry countered. "We don't have a choice. If you are unhappy with the way things stand, perhaps you should make other arrangements."

"What are you saying?" I demanded.

"Go out and start your own practice. See what it's like, taking on a burden of debt. Maybe then you will understand what we're up against."

"Are you telling me you want me to leave?"

"I'm telling you that if you stay, you will have to accept that things are what they are."

Jerry turned away and started to leave. I thought about calling after him and continuing our disagreement, but what would be the point? Clearly his mind was made up.

Suddenly I realized that I had a monumental choice to make. Would I stay with a partner who didn't value my opinion, or would I branch out on my own and have to deal with all the headaches of starting my own practice? I would need time to think about my response. In an attempt to defuse the tension in the room, I said mildly, "Well, what partnership doesn't have its ups and downs?" Nobody laughed. Nobody even smiled.

Beginning to feel increasingly self-conscious, I hurriedly left the auditorium.

# A GRIEVOUS LOSS

Early Saturday morning, I was jarred awake by the ringing of my cell_phone as it lay on the nightstand beside my bed. My head ached as if I had been bludgeoned with a cudgel. Wearily I rubbed the sleep from my eyes. In luminous numerals, the clock on my dresser told me it was 3:00 a.m. My on-call shift wasn't supposed to start till 8:00. My first inclination was to roll over and go back to sleep. I had been dreaming about my run-in with Jerry the previous day. In my dream, we were on the verge of exchanging blows. When I thought about how I had behaved, petulantly challenging him in front of our colleagues, I felt a fresh rush of embarrassment. Discussing private matters in public was something you just shouldn't do—like airing your dirty laundry for all to see.

Abruptly, the phone quit ringing, and I thankfully closed my eyes, but then it started up again.

"Hello?" I said as I fumbled the phone to my ear.

"Doctor Sterling, this is Nancy in the Emergency Department. We just admitted a patient I think you will want to come evaluate."

"Call Doctor Tucker," I mumbled groggily. He's on call."

"Sir, it is Doctor Tucker. He's the patient, and he is not doing well."

Instantly I came fully awake. "What is his status?"

"We believe he has a pneumonia. His blood gases aren't looking so good."

"What are his levels?"

"His PaO2 is 61, his PaCO2 is 57, and his pH is 7.23."

"So he's hypoxic, and he probably has a respiratory acidosis."

"That's what Doctor Larson thinks."

I blinked several times to clear my vision and dispel the last vestiges of sleep. Before hanging up, I promised, "I'll be there as soon as I can."

My mind began to race as I threw on my clothes. *How had Jerry contracted pneumonia?* I wondered. There were the usual possibilities. Most were associated with some sort of community exposures: the febrile child, the coughing coworker, the wheezing clerk. Yet there was another scenario that was considerably more worrisome. Jerry had treated Mr. Wright during his on-call weekend. Although as physicians we take whatever precautions as we can, there was always the risk that we might be laid low by whatever infectious agent our patients were battling. *If Jerry has contracted a bocavirus infection, which clinical course would he follow? The rapid onset–rapid resolution variety or the progressive downhill calamity?*

When I finished dressing, without taking time to shave, I rushed to the Emergency Department. I would have shaved enroute to the hospital except I had again forgotten to charge the electric razor I kept in my car. Perhaps I should grow a beard.

I parked in the doctors' lot in front of the hospital and sprinted through the lobby, past the gift shop, and down the long corridor that gave access to radiology, to the hospital laboratory, and to the Emergency Department, which was surprisingly quiet when I keyed in the appropriate access code and entered through the double doors.

When she saw me, a portly nurse carrying what looked like an intubation tray exclaimed, "Doctor Sterling, it's good that you're here. Doctor Larson just got called to see an epileptic having a seizure. I'm not sure how long he will be. Your patient…that is, I mean Doctor Tucker is in room 4. I was just getting set up in case you need to…"

"Yes, thank you. Are you Nancy?"

"I am."

"It's good to meet you. I'm still learning people's names. Look, Nancy, I'll need a gown, a mask, gloves, and a stethoscope. I'd like a face shield too if any are available."

"You'll find most of what you need on a cart by the door. There is a stethoscope on the counter inside the room."

"Before I see him, I'd like to review his chest x-ray."

"Peggy, our ward secretary, can call it up for you. Let me take this into the room, and then I'll come see if there's anything else you need."

I turned to an older woman seated at the nursing station, her attention focused on the computer monitor in front of her. "Peggy?" I said, stepping up behind her.

"Can I help you?" With two fingers, she adjusted her tortoiseshell glasses as she turned her head to look at me.

"I'm Doctor Sterling. I wonder if you could retrieve Doctor Tucker's chest x-ray, if you wouldn't mind?"

"I think we can do that." She tapped a couple of keys on her keyboard, and an image appeared on the screen in front of her. I bent down to take a closer look. Large sections of both lungs were lighter in color than normal, indicating the presence of inflammatory changes— what we commonly refer to as multilobar pneumonia. Clearly his infection was more advanced than I had anticipated. This was not a good sign.

"Thank you," I said to Peggy.

"Not a problem. Let me know if there is anything else you need. We do hope Doctor Tucker will be all right. We have enjoyed working with him over the years." There was genuine concern in her voice.

"We will do what we can. By the way, has his wife been notified?"

"I believe she's on her way in. I'll check."

After suiting up, I went in to see my partner/patient. Jerry was lying on a hospital gurney, his upper torso propped up at a forty-five-degree angle. A nonrebreathing oxygen mask covered the lower half of his face. His skin was sallow. Beads of perspiration dotted his forehead. The worried look in his eyes bordered on panic, and he was laboring to take in each breath.

The change in appearance that had overtaken him in the last twenty-four hours left me momentarily speechless. After I recovered my composure, I quipped, "You know, we've got to stop meeting like this." When it became apparent that my attempt at humor had fallen pitifully flat, I said, "Sorry, my bad. When did this start?"

Between breaths, Jerry said in a hushed voice, "Yesterday…late."

"Any idea how this happened?"

"I did this. I'm…responsible."

It was clear that Jerry wanted to say more, but the effort required to get the words out lay beyond his capabilities. Instead, he pointed to the notepad and pencil lying on the countertop. I handed them to him, and he began to write. I could barely make out his scrawl. Squinting, I read, "It's my fault. I should have known."

His head lolled forward, and his eyes drifted shut. I reached out and shook his shoulder. "Jerry? Stay with me."

He aroused briefly and resumed writing. "Get the book. It's in—"

Then the pencil fell from his fingers, and he lost consciousness entirely. He did not respond when I again shook his shoulder.

I rushed to the door and called out, "Nancy, I could use some help in here."

The nurse stopped what she was doing and hurried over to see what I needed. Struggling to keep from sounding panicked, I called out more loudly, "Peggy, ask Respiratory Therapy to bring us a ventilator, would you."

I reentered the room. Nancy was already opening the intubation tray.

If it is anticipated that a patient may fight having a tube introduced into his or her windpipe, a sequence of drugs such as etomidate, ketamine, and propofol may be given in rapid order one after another. This is called rapid sequence intubation, or RSI. However, when I again attempted to rouse Jerry, he remained unresponsive. There was no need for additional sedation.

Stepping to the head of the bed, I accepted the laryngoscope and the ET tube that Nancy handed me and easily completed the intubation. We then took turns ventilating him with an Ambu bag until Respiratory Therapy arrived.

I was about to go ask Peggy to find out what was taking so long when the doors to the ED swung open. Tyler Wickham wheeled in the ventilator we were expecting. I caught his eye and signaled him to come to Jerry's room. Before entering, he paused to gown up. He then backed through the door, pulling the ventilator with him. When he turned and saw that the patient we were resuscitating was Doctor Tucker, he froze. The color drained from his face. "What the hell...?" he exclaimed under his breath. "How did he—" but then he startled, as if abruptly realizing he had just spoken aloud. "Sorry. I didn't know it was Doctor Tucker."

His reaction troubled me, but I didn't make much of it at the time.

When the ventilator had been configured with the desired settings, I sat down to write out my orders and prepare my patient for admission to the ICU. I found it hard to concentrate as my mind struggled to cope with questions that kept popping into my head. *How would this affect our partnership? What do I do if he doesn't survive? How can I handle the patient load by myself?*

"Dear God," I prayed silently. "Help me in my hour of need. Give me wisdom and sound judgment. Heal my partner, if it be Thy will. Afford me the skill to do what needs to be done. Amen."

It was a short prayer, but I have never believed that excess verbiage improves the odds of a favorable response.

In my orders, I specified my patient's diagnosis and activity level, the nursing care he was to receive, the diagnostic studies to be performed, the respiratory services to be administered, the medications to be given, his diet—including IV nutritional supplements—and other therapeutic considerations.

Having done all I could do to maximize Jerry's chances of recovery, I set out to begin my rounds. Before leaving, I tore the top sheet off the notepad upon which he had written. I folded it and slipped it into my shirt pocket. Although cryptic, Jerry's scribblings seemed important. Later I would try to puzzle out what he had been attempting to tell me.

Then it struck me. Not only would I be seeing my own patients for the foreseeable future, I would be seeing Jerry's patients and Adam's patients as well. My life as a private practice pulmonologist had suddenly become substantially more challenging.

Later that same evening, I was again back in the ICU. It had been a horrendous day, and I was exhausted. In the office, I had done my best to see as many patients as possible, but being one man covering three practices, I could not see everybody. I had prioritized the sickest patients to be seen first. The others I had trusted would be okay, but who knew what troubles were brewing in those who had not been seen.

Jerry's condition had not improved. In fact, it was a little worse. He was still unresponsive to both verbal and physical stimuli. Although his vital signs were stable, his respiratory parameters had deteriorated slightly. I had been forced to add a bit of positive pressure to his ventilator settings. Keeping a slight bit of pressure in his airways would prevent the tiny air sacs in his lungs—called alveoli—from collapsing between breaths, allowing him to exhale more completely.

One thing was certain. Managing my partner's medical therapy was sorely testing my critical care skills. There were so many factors to take into account, so many physiological parameters to balance that keeping them all straight was mind numbing. Not only were there fluid balances to consider, as measured by intake and output, there were electrolyte levels to adjust—including sodium, potassium, chloride, calcium, magnesium, phosphorus, and others. These all had to be maintained within discrete levels. Significant deviations from normal could have serious, perhaps fatal, consequences.

While treating the lungs, it was important not to place undue stress on other organs such as the heart, the liver, or the kidneys. Medication dosages had to be adjusted by matching clinical efficacy against observed side effects.

At times, it felt like I was walking on a tightrope with a long pole across my shoulders and leaking bags of sand tied to either end. Continuous adjustments were needed to keep from toppling over. When I thought about it, toppling over seemed a good metaphor for how I felt. I was in a continuous state of toppling over, constantly struggling to stay upright.

"Are you all right?" Madison said as she stepped up to join me. "You look done in."

"You should see me from the inside." I arched my back and rolled my shoulders. The morning's headache had become a dull throbbing.

Gently Madison said, "It's time for my break. Would you care to join me in the cafeteria for a cup of coffee and maybe relax for a few minutes?"

"Sure. For the moment, there's nothing more I can do here."

In the cafeteria, we chose a table away from the larger clusters of people. Madison gripped her coffee mug with both hands as if keeping her fingers warm. She leaned on her elbows braced against the table. "How is Doctor Tucker? Is he going to make it? Do you think?"

"It's too soon to tell, but I'm worried. He's slowly moving in the wrong direction."

"Do you know what he has, what's causing his pneumonia?"

"It's a bocavirus. His PCR was positive."

"PCR? Refresh my memory."

"Polymerase chain reaction—it's a test that looks for specific strands of abnormal DNA in a patient's blood. It's highly specific."

"So…do you think he has the same infection Mr. Wright and the others had?"

"I do. To prove it, I've ordered genetic mapping on the viruses we obtained from Jerry, Mr. Wright, and Mr. Goldstein. I would have included Billy Mitchell and Agnes Gilroy, but the lab doesn't have any samples of their blood from when they were ill."

"Tests like that have got to be expensive. Do you think their insurance companies will cover the cost?"

"Probably not."

"The patients are not going to like being responsible for the cost."

"I'm hoping the County Health Department will pick up the tab. After all, we are looking at a potentially serious community outbreak. We still don't know the source—where this virus came from—or how many others have been exposed. I've even sent bocavirus samples to a virologist Heather Oliver recommended. Maybe he's encountered this strain before."

"It sounds like you've got the bases covered."

"Then why am I so unsettled? I'm missing something. I can feel it."

Madison stared off into the distance. I could tell she was picturing what might happen if a mutated pathogen got loose in the community. It was not a pleasant scenario to consider. She shivered and said, "Will you be in church on Sunday?"

"I don't think so. It looks like from this point forward, I'm going to be on permanent call—unless Jerry turns around and starts getting better."

"What are the odds that he will survive do you think? Be honest."

I pondered her question for a moment and then responded, "Less than fifty-fifty. More like thirty-seventy. The next forty-eight hours will be crucial. I wish I could be more optimistic, but…" I shrugged. The uneasy feeling arose within me again. If only I could identify what was troubling me.

*Only time will tell*, I thought as I stared into the darkness outside the window.

Mansfield Park—ten acres of gently rolling lawns interrupted by occasional stands of mature oak, maple, and evergreen trees—was located on Flintridge's southern edge, four miles from the medical center. The parking lot was only a third full when Marcus pulled into an empty space and shut off his engine. Technically, he was on his lunch hour. Even so, he detested being away from work in the middle of the day. Saturdays were no exception. Who knew what unfortunate difficulty might flare into a minor emergency without him there to offer guidance?

An asphalt footpath circled the perimeter of the park. Wearing leather wingtip shoes with his suit and tie, Marcus stood out from the exercise enthusiasts who frequented the park. Even if he had noticed, he would not have cared. His attention was focused upon the meeting that was about to take place—a meeting he would have avoided if at all possible. However, circumstances had arisen that were impossible to ignore. He began walking the footpath in a counterclockwise direction.

On the side of the park opposite the parking lot, he came to a shallow pond dotted with lily pads and stocked with koi. Slender reeds and cattails grew around the shoreline. In the center of the pond, an aerating fountain sprayed a fan of water skyward. Marcus slowed his pace.

Shaded by the branches of a willow tree, a bench seat beside the path faced the pond. Seemingly lost in meditation, the man seated on the bench gazed out upon the water, its surface rippled by an autumn breeze.

Marcus cast a glance skyward. Dark clouds threatened rain. He sat down on the end of the bench opposite the man and tried not to look at him.

In a similar fashion, Captain Summers stared placidly ahead. Except for the splashing of the fountain, the cawing of a raven nearby, and the sound of children playing far off, the park was quiet.

"All right, what's so important that you'd force me to give up a round of golf?" Captain Summers's had spoken so softly that his words were inaudible more than a few feet away.

"Jerry Tucker is in a coma in the ICU. He presented to the Emergency Department early this morning complaining of difficulty breathing. The current diagnosis is that he has pneumonia. He's on a ventilator and in pretty bad shape. There's a good chance that he's not going to make it."

"Damn," Captain Summers swore under his breath. He continued to stare straight ahead. "Do they think our virus is the cause?"

"They suspect it might be. They are doing a bunch of diagnostic studies. Some are quite sophisticated." Marcus turned his head to look at the captain.

"Don't," Captain Summers snapped. "As far as you're concerned, I don't exist. You got that?"

Marcus could almost hear the word *soldier* spoken at the end of his sentence. He begrudgingly turned his head and faced forward. "What are we going to do?" he said with a quaver of uncertainty.

The captain ignored the question and instead asked, "Any idea how this happened?"

"None," Marcus said, reflexively shaking his head. "I would guess somebody must have screwed up somewhere, and it wasn't me."

"Did Doctor Tucker say anything? Before he got to the hospital, did he talk to anybody?"

"I don't know, but he's not talking now."

"Did he take the antiviral meds we sent with the specimen?

"I don't know."

"Where is the virus now? Did he have the specimen with him when he arrived in the Emergency Department?"

"Look, all I know is what I've already told you. There is no point in grilling me with questions about things for which I have no knowledge."

"Have you spoken with Tyler?"

"Briefly. He was pretty upset, as you might imagine. He and Jerry were close. I got the impression he's as much in the dark as I am. So… what are we going to do?"

"Let me think." For two long minutes, Captain Summers sat quietly, watching ripples on the water catch the afternoon sunlight. Still unmoving, he said, "Nothing. We are going to do nothing except you are now responsible for collecting the patient's medical records especially the results of the fancy test the doctors are running."

"How am I supposed to do that? They are access protected. I'd need a provider code to open the file."

"You are Flintridge's chief administrative officer. You figure it out. For now, everything stays the same—same timeline, same protocols."

"This is getting way too serious. One person has already died, and soon there may be a second. We need to stop."

"We're not going to stop." Captain Summers turned his head to glower directly at Marcus. The intensity of his stare sent a chill down Marcus's spine. "You've been paid, and you will do your job. Let me know when you're ready to give me the records." With that, the captain stood and without haste began strolling the asphalt path.

Marcus lingered briefly and then hurriedly walked back in the direction of the parking lot.

Monday, toward the middle of the morning, I was seated at my desk in my office. The patient I had been scheduled to see was a no-show, and I had been afforded a rare breather from the frenetic pace needed to singlehandedly cover three practices. It wasn't even noon yet, and I was already feeling the strain of being overworked.

To make matters worse, I could not stop thinking about Jerry Tucker's code blue. He had suffered a cardiac arrest in the wee hours of the morning. Since I was already in the hospital admitting another patient, it had fallen to me to manage the code team during his CPR.

I had tried everything I could think of to resuscitate him. I had defibrillated him twice then given him epinephrine and vasopressin, two medications intended to raise his blood pressure and strengthen his heart's contractions. When those meds had failed to do the job, I had defibrillated him a third time and then administered amiodarone, a drug used to normalize the heart's rhythm. When that had failed, I had given him two more doses of epinephrine and defibrillated him twice more.

None of the team's interventions had made a difference. After ninety minutes of resuscitation, Jerry had been pronounced dead at 5:27 a.m.

It had then fallen to me to notify Linda, his wife, that her husband of thirty-two years was gone. Likewise, upon arriving at the office, I had been obliged to tell the staff that the man whose medical practice they had served for the past ten years was dead. Those two notifications were among the most difficult duties I had ever performed in my medical career.

Not only was Jerry's code foremost in my thoughts, I was drawn to consider the course of his entire hospital stay, trying to imagine if there was anything more I might have done. I had covered him with both antiviral drugs and antibiotics. Neither had altered the course of his pneumonia. While on the respirator, he had received aerosolized medications to open his airways and improve his lungs' ventilation. I had carefully adjusted his fluid and electrolyte balances and had seen to his nutritional needs. In addition to treating his lungs, I had supported his other organ systems—anything to maximize his chances of recovery. He had not responded to any of those efforts.

Jerry had not regained consciousness after falling into a coma at the time of his admission. The neurologist I had consulted had suggested that we do a brain scan and an EEG. Both were essentially negative. No treatable cause for his coma was found, which was extremely frustrating. There were so many questions I had wanted to ask him. Did he know how he had contracted his infection? Had he been in contact with anyone manifesting similar symptoms? Was there anything else he could tell me about the nature of his illness? Most of all, I would have asked about the cryptic note he had scrawled in the Emergency Department.

What did he mean, "It was my fault—I should have known?" And what was this book he had mentioned? What did it contain, and where could I find it? Pressed flat, Jerry's note lay on my desk. I stared at it intently, as if fervent scrutiny might extract answers to my questions.

There were so many loose ends. The entire business left me frustrated and dissatisfied.

That morning, however, there was one bit of good news. I had tracked down a physician named Fred Spalding, who had just completed a year's fellowship in cardiopulmonary medicine. I had come across his name in a job-finder website for medical professionals. He had listed himself as being available to work as a locum tenens. When I spoke with him, he had agreed to help by sharing on-call duties. Regrettably, due to a prior commitment, the earliest he could start would be the following Saturday, five days hence. Until then, I would be holding down the fort by myself.

Ellie McDonough stepped into my office and placed a chart on my desk. "Mrs. Paxton is coughing up blood-tinged phlegm. She is of the opinion that her bronchiectasis is acting up."

"She's probably right." I regarded Ellie, whose features conveyed an attitude of sorrow. She seemed on the verge of tears. "Are you okay?" I asked with concern.

"I will be. Doctor Tucker could be difficult at times, but he was a good physician. We're going to miss him."

"I know. It won't be the same around here without him." Little did I know how true that statement would prove to be.

Friday evening, after a hectic week that was both mentally and physically grueling, Madison and I were having a late dinner at a small Italian restaurant not far from the medical center. Although I was still on call, we had decided to chance the possibility that I might make it through a meal without being summoned back to the hospital. Perpetual call is no fun, and I was eagerly looking forward to 8:00 a.m. Saturday morning when Doctor Spalding would begin his locum tenens. The thought of having an entire weekend off almost seemed too good to be true.

"I don't think he will go that far," Madison declared with conviction. We had been discussing the conflict between Russia and the Ukraine and Putin's threat to use nuclear weapons.

"He may be insane," Madison stabbed the air with her index finger. "But he's not stupid. He must know that if he were to launch, his country would be annihilated."

"Maybe," I replied. "But I think he's betting we won't respond. He's convinced the West is weak, that we lack the willpower to fight a nuclear war."

I was doing my best to keep the conversation going, and I hoped that my words were making sense. I was dead tired and very near falling asleep. I wondered, *How embarrassing would it be if I were to drift off and do a faceplant in my lasagna?*

Madison shuddered. "Can you imagine how horrible a nuclear war would be? How could anyone in their right mind even think of starting such a conflict?"

"Like you said, he may be insane."

"Was Doctor Tucker a believer? Do you know?" Madison said somewhat abstractly. "Sorry, I was just imagining all the people that would die in a nuclear conflict without having come to know the Lord."

"That would be an unfathomable tragedy. To answer your question, actually, I'm not sure. I'm inclined to think that Jerry was not a believer. No doubt, I should've asked. Too late now."

"Fighting a nuclear war would be horrific, but dying without any hope of redemption would be far worse."

"Speaking of Doctor Tucker, while I'm thinking about it, take a look at this." I fished his note out of my shirt pocket and passed it across the table.

Madison read the note and then responded with a quizzical look.

"What do you think?" I said. "Any idea what he was trying to tell me?"

"Not a clue. 'I did this. It was my fault. I should've known.' That could refer to almost anything. Was he blaming himself for not coming to the Emergency Department when he first began showing symptoms? Was he referring to the flareup you two had had over the future of the practice?"

"You heard about that, did you?"

Madison cocked her head at me. "Hospital grapevines, remember. In a hospital, nothing is private."

"True," I agreed.

"While we're thinking about Doctor Tucker, is there anything new with regards to the tests you ordered? Any idea of what killed him?"

"It was an odd variety of bocavirus. The genetic mapping we did showed some interesting anomalies. Between Mr. Goldstein's illness and Mr. Wright's, there was a shift in the virus' DNA, making it more lethal. The virologist Heather recommended reviewed the results. He believes the alteration might be man-made."

"What?" Madison exclaimed. "Man-made as in—"

"Bioengineered! He's of the opinion that we can't rule it out. It's either that or somehow the virus miraculously evolved on its own."

"Has anyone else contracted this virus that you know of?"

"Only Doctor Tucker, and I don't have his DNA mapping back yet."

"Have you reported this to anybody?"

"You mean like the CDC or the NIH?"

"I was thinking more along the lines of the County Health Department," Madison finished off her linguine. She put her fork down and blotted her mouth with her napkin.

"Not yet," I admitted. "There's not a whole lot to go on, and I'm still trying to puzzle out Jerry's note." I held out my hand, and Madison handed the note back to me. I refolded it and slid it back into my shirt pocket.

"So, where do we go from here?" Madison's facial expression registered apprehension.

"Home and to bed, I hope. Eh…I mean separately. You go to your home. I go to mine." I blushed.

"That's what I thought you meant." There was a twinkle in Madison's eye.

The waiter brought our bill. I noted with surprise that my lasagna was only half eaten. *Too fatigued to eat*, I thought. *That's not a good sign.*

As we were about to leave, my cell phone rang. When I answered it, there was a nurse on the line who informed me that I had a patient waiting in the Emergency Department. I groaned. It was promising to be another long night. *Doctor Spalding*, I said to myself. *You'd better be ready to go in the morning. Otherwise, I'm not sure I'll survive.*

When Captain Jack Summers crossed the threshold of the sprawling two-story mansion, he felt as if he had just stepped out of reality and into a Hollywood movie set. This was his first visit to The Angel's home, and he considered just being permitted to enter a high honor indeed. In truth, the text message he had received had read more like a summons than an invitation. Still no one he knew had ever been allowed anywhere near the place—certainly none of his subordinates in the militia.

After passing through the lavish entryway, Captain Summers entered a cavernous room that on one side gazed out through tall picture windows at the estate's manicured gardens. On the other side, five hallways radiated outward like spokes on a wheel or ribs on a fan. He assumed that each wing had a separate function. One would house the family's sleeping quarters. One would be richly appointed for entertaining guests. Another was probably reserved for business activities. Who knew what purpose the other two served.

*Why would anyone need this much space?* Captain Summers asked himself. *It would take the better part of a day just to move from room to room without stopping.*

"The master is expecting you," the butler at his elbow announced in a tone of voice that might appropriately herald either a coronation or an execution. "He's out by the pool. Exit onto the patio and then turn right. You can't miss it." Rather than leave, the butler stood waiting, probably to confirm that Captain Summers exited the building as instructed. His starched white uniform literally gleamed in the Sunday morning rays that poured in through an overhead skylight.

Captain Summers followed the paving stone path that led around the south end of the mansion to a pool that was not quite Olympic sized but close. Rows of folding wooden deck chairs lined the tiled edges of the pool on three sides. There had to be at least fifty of the recliners, but only one was occupied. The pool itself was empty. If guards were stationed nearby, they were out of sight. As far as Captain Summers could tell, he and The Angel would be alone together.

As he made his way to where The Angel was relaxing with his eyes closed, Captain Summers noted that the tiles he crossed were dry even near the ladders. It was a moderate autumn day with the temperature hovering around seventy. That suggested that no one had been swimming within the last hour or two.

Captain Summers had met The Angel on only one previous occasion—at a banquet hosted by a political action committee to honor a recently elected congressman. It had been a brief encounter, and nothing of substance had been discussed. Since then, The Angel had communicated with the militia only through its senior officers holding a rank of lieutenant colonel and above. Captain Summers had been receiving his orders second and third hand.

At the sound of Captain Summers's approach, The Angel opened his pale-blue eyes to peer directly at his guest. The gaunt man shifted in his lounger to bring his torso more upright. The white terrycloth robe he wore gaped open at the front, revealing a growth of white chest hairs. The tattoo of a winged serpent was noticeable on his right pectoral region. Those areas of skin not covered by the robe were tanned. A thin pale scar crossed his left cheek, much like a Prussian dueling scar. For a septuagenarian, he appeared to be in remarkably good condition.

"Aw, Jack, how good of you to come see me," The Angel said.

"It's an honor, sir," Captain Summers replied. "Considering all you've done for our cause."

"Would you care for a drink?" The Angel gestured toward a wheeled cart that sported a variety of liquors and nonalcoholic beverages. "Help yourself."

"No, thank you, sir. I'm fine." Rather than sit down on an adjacent recliner, Captain Summers remained standing at parade rest.

The Angel raised the back of his chair even further. "I'll come right to the point. I know you're a busy man, and I won't detain you any longer than necessary. The reason I asked for this meeting was so that I could get a first-hand assessment of the man running Ophis Pterotos. I can't begin to tell you how important this mission is. The uprising is coming, and it won't be long before it is upon us. The government is filled with decadence and decay. Every day more and more citizens realize how corrupt politicians are. They understand that the old order must be swept away. Otherwise, we will lose all our liberties.

"When the revolution begins, the government's forces will move against us in a significant way. We will be outmanned and outgunned. Our chances of succeeding will be slim. Our only hope will be to deploy a tactical surprise that our adversaries are not expecting. That's where you come in. The experiments you are conducting will largely determine the success or failure of our campaign. We must have a way to temporarily incapacitate our foe, or we will be overrun. The virus is the solution to that problem. Do you get what I'm telling you?"

"Yes, sir," Captain Summers declared smartly.

"Then why in the hell are you screwing this up? Not only did you manage to lose a complete printout of a patient's medical records in the mail, one of your soldiers has gotten himself killed. Such sloppiness is unacceptable. Fortunately, with a little pressure applied in the right places, we've managed to keep the man's death out of the media—so far.

"Now you hear what I'm telling you. We need three more runs to configure the virus properly, and we only have six weeks to get it done, so it's on your shoulders to get out there and make it happen. Am I making myself clear?"

"Yes, sir," Captain Summers responded meekly. "I understand."

"You damn well better be sure you do. You are dismissed. Charles will have the instructions for your next run."

"Charles…?"

"The man in white."

Captain Summers executed an about face and started to leave but then turned back. "Sir?"

"Yes," The Angel said with a tone of exasperation.

"I thought the original goal was to test the virus on seven patients. Is that not still the case?"

"It is. Why do you ask?"

"Because if that is so, we only need two more runs. Mr. Leland Wright was patient number four, and Doctor Tucker can be patient number five. I've already sent their medical records to your lab for evaluation."

"Very well. I stand corrected. Two runs."

The butler was waiting for Captain Summers when he reentered the cavernous main room. The butler handed over a thin well-sealed manila folder and a cigar-box-shaped package.

A short time later, Captain Summers was driving back toward Flintridge, his tail between his legs.

# OVERLOAD

At 7:30 a.m. Monday morning, the first Monday in October, I was leaving the hospital, having just finished my morning rounds. I should have been feeling refreshed, eager to embrace the day ahead. Doctor Fred Spalding, the locum tenens I had hired, had just taken call for me for the second weekend in a row; yet instead of feeling grateful for having had the time off, my thoughts were instead struggling with the realization that I would be on call for the next five days straight.

In the past, as a rule, I hadn't minded taking call, especially if I wasn't already following a number of seriously ill patients; but of course, the more calls you take, the greater the number of patients you're going to wind up following. Being available to respond to emergencies at any hour, day or night, for five days in a row can be quite taxing, and the workload was taking its toll.

As I strode toward my office, the northerly breeze bringing cold air down from Canada easily penetrated my lightweight sport coat, causing me to shiver and adding to my sour state of mind.

Rather than appreciate the opportunity to make a difference in patients' lives, I was beginning to resent their claims on my time and talents. It had evolved to the point that when a call would come in from the Emergency Department announcing another patient to be admitted, I would silently curse the intrusion into my day's routines. I tried to maintain a positive attitude, though I couldn't help feeling that the burdens of patient care were slowly sucking the life out of me. It was an unhappy, worrisome situation—one that could not be allowed to endure. What to do about it, however, I had no idea.

If I hadn't been so irritated, I might have prayed for God to intervene, but I was too pettishly disposed to converse with the Almighty.

That was why I was in no mood for surprises when I entered the Pulmonary Associates' offices through the back door, and yet surprises happen—that's why they are called surprises.

As soon as she saw me, Ellie stepped forward and announced, "There's someone here to see you. He's waiting in your office."

"Who is it?"

"You'll see."

Acting on the assumption that it was a patient that was waiting, I demanded, "Why put him in my office? Why not leave him in the waiting room?"

"You'll see," Ellie said again. This time she smiled.

I nearly growled something that, no doubt, I would have regretted later. Fortunately, I kept my peace as I went to see who had come calling.

Doctor Adam Richards sat in one of the two armchairs that faced my desk. He stood and stuck out his hand when I entered. "Good morning, Blake. How you doing this fine morning?"

I returned the handshake and studied his demeanor, curious as to why he was there. "I'm doing okay," I lied. "How about you? Sorry I didn't get a chance to visit with you at Jerry's funeral."

Adam nodded slowly. "It's all right. I noticed you left as soon as the service was over. I didn't stay much longer myself."

"I truly don't like funerals," I admitted. "They remind me of what we as physicians are up against—especially Jerry's funeral—but then I wasn't the only one in a bleak mood that day. Did you happen to notice the other people that were there?"

"You're referring to the group that kept to themselves, I presume."

"I didn't know Jerry had such rough-looking friends. Was it just me, or did you get the impression they were ready to go to war?"

"Now that you mention it, they did seem inordinately hostile. Guess I'd assumed it was their way of grieving."

"Anyway," I said more brightly. "It's good to see you again. How's retirement treating you?"

"That's why I've come. I wanted to talk to you…if you have a few minutes?"

I glanced at the printout of my morning's schedule lying on my desk. Every slot was full. "I can spare a few, I think, but only a few. What's on your mind?" After stepping around behind my desk, I shed my sport coat and hung it on the rack in the corner. I then put on the short white coat I wore in the office. We both sat down.

Adam nodded pensively. "Retirement isn't what I thought it would be. I've got entirely too much time on my hands. There isn't enough to keep me busy, and I'm bored. Worse, I'm driving Flo crazy. She is about ready to kick me out of the house."

"I'm sorry to hear that. How can I help?"

"I want to come back to work. I still have a few good years left in me, I think. Quitting practice was a bad idea. I need to be doing something productive, and I figured you could use the help now that Jerry is…"

"You want to practice medicine again," I declared with incredulity.

"I've only been gone two months. I still have my medical license, and the hospital hasn't terminated my privileges. I'm prepared to start today if you would like."

"Does that mean you'd be sharing call as before?"

"Absolutely."

"What about your buyout? Jerry had been meeting with the hospital, cutting a deal so we could get you your money. I'm not sure where those negotiations stand."

"Yeah, I couldn't believe it when I heard that he had decided to sell the practice. Bad idea. Look, if I'm not retired, there's no need to buy me out. Therefore, there's no mandate to sell. What do you say? Can I come back to work?" Adam regarded me with a look of expectant optimism.

It took me less than three seconds to make up my mind. "Hell yes," I nearly shouted. More mildly, I said, "I mean, it would be a privilege to work with you again."

"Excellent. I'll even start by taking call today."

"Thank you Lord Jesus," I breathed silently and then in a normal tone of voice added, "Only if you want to."

"I'm looking forward to it."

"Okay then. Let's go tell the staff and ask them to find you some patients to see."

As we set out to track down Lois and inform her of the good news, it occurred to me that my investigation into the bocavirus infections could now resume, having stalled for a lack of both time and energy.

The Flintridge Medical Center's Infection Control Committee was regularly scheduled to meet at 8:00 p.m. on the first Tuesday of every month. Having been appointed chairman, it fell to me to set the agenda and then oversee the proceedings. This being my first experience in such a role, I had felt uncertain as to how to proceed. Fortunately, Heather had stepped forward to help me out. She had walked me through how the meeting was supposed to progress according to Roberts Rules of Order. We had reviewed the minutes of previous meetings and identified old business that was still pending. Next we had decided on which items of new business to bring to the committee's attention. First and foremost in my mind was a discussion of the recent bocavirus infections.

The committee had assembled in a conference room in the hospital's administrative wing. The kitchen staff had set up a large urn of dark roast coffee and a tray of mugs on a sideboard. Presumably, the coffee was intended to help committee members stay awake, but it wasn't doing a very good job.

The committee was comprised of six members. In addition to Heather and myself, four physicians had been appointed from the medical staff. None gave the impression that they wanted to be there. Those who weren't nearly asleep looked bored to tears.

Finally, we came to the part of the meeting I was actually anticipating. I began by saying, "I realize it's late and you're tired and want to go home, but I would like to take a moment to discuss what I think might be a serious problem. Over the past two months, we've had five patients admitted to the ICU with viral pneumonia. Presumably, they all were infected with the same pathogen. They—"

Interrupting, Doctor Cecil Lowden, the gastroenterologist, said, "What do you mean presumably?" He was a small man with tortoiseshell glasses. He wore a polka-dot bowtie with a striped dress shirt.

I responded, "We collected viral cultures from the last three patients. The first two were not cultured, but their clinical presentations were similar to those that followed. Also, we found increased levels of antibodies against the virus in their blood, suggesting a recent infection."

"What sort of pathogen are we discussing?" said Doctor Kyle Larson, an emergency medicine physician. He was known to be an enthusiastic outdoorsman and had the suntan to prove it.

"A human bocavirus. First identified about a decade ago, the bocavirus is classified as a strain of parvovirus, it's a non-encapsulated virus containing a single DNA strand."

"In addition to pneumonia, the bocavirus can cause gastroenteritis," Doctor Larson added smugly.

I proceeded to draw a thumbnail sketch of each patient's history, clinical findings, and hospital course. I especially emphasized the fact that the virus seemed to be increasing in virulence with each new victim.

"You're telling us that this virus is becoming more lethal?" Doctor Sharon Kingston leaned forward and looked at me intently. She was a doughty middle-aged internist known to have a keen intellect.

"That is correct." I looked at Heather and nodded.

Heather cleared her throat and then said, "We sent samples of the virus obtained from the last three patients for genetic mapping. I then provided copies of the results to a friend of mine at Cornell, a world-renowned virologist. He believes he can document a gain of function when the last sample is compared with the first. He also believes that the changes are man-made."

"You're kidding," exclaimed Doctor Drew Thompson, the hospital's only rheumatologist. He was a younger man, perhaps a year or two older than me. Rather than a shirt and tie, he was wearing a gray hoodie and a pair of tan cargo pants. "Are you suggesting that someone is intentionally infecting these people? That seems rather outlandish, if you don't mind my saying so."

"You're right," I admitted. "It does sound far-fetched, and this could all be a coincidence. However, we are left with the fact that two patients have died from a virus that we haven't seen before, at least not around here." I felt a fresh surge of grief when I recalled that one of those patients have been a colleague and a friend.

"Which leads me to ask," Doctor Larson said. "Have you checked with other hospitals in the region to see what their experience has been?"

"I did," I said. "That is…we did." I again looked at Heather.

She sat up straighter and responded, "I spoke with my counterparts at Mercy, St. James, and Martin-Green Medical Center. They've had no cases that resemble ours."

Doctor Larson looked pensive. "What about other agencies. For instance, have you spoken with the County Health Department?"

"I did."

"And…what was their response?" Doctor Larson said.

"They weren't particularly interested. I suspect it's because they are overwhelmed with that other virus that's going around."

"What exactly did they say?"

"With so few cases and without having identified a common source, they felt there was too little evidence to justify the time and resources it would take to mount a full investigation. They told me to call back if additional infections are forthcoming."

"Well, there's your answer," Doctor Thompson declared. "If the Health Department doesn't see it as a problem, why should we?"

"I'm curious," Doctor Larson said, looking at Heather. "You indicated that you did genetic mapping. Did I hear you correctly?"

"Yes, sir, you did." Heather cast a quick look in my direction as if to say, "I told you this would be an issue."

"Is it common to do that sort of testing in cases of viral pneumonia?" Doctor Larson continued.

I replied, "No, but I needed to confirm that we were dealing with a single virus."

"How much did all that cost, if I might ask." Doctor Larson said.

"Two thousand dollars per test—approximately."

"Really? And who's going to pay for that?" Doctor Kingston demanded. "Surely not the insurance companies."

"I will," I announced. "I'll pay. I've already notified the lab that did the studies."

"That's a first," said Doctor Lowden with a look of amazement.

"Paying for the tests you order?" Doctor Thompson quipped. "Let's hope that idea never catches on." His fellow committee members chuckled.

"What is it you want from us?" Doctor Kingston said.

"I would ask for your guidance as to where to go from here." I spread my hands wide, palms up.

"I would say," Doctor Larson commented. "That the County Health Department has given you your answer. "Adopt an attitude of wait and see. If there is a problem, it will soon become apparent. That is usually the way it is in medicine. Nothing stays hidden forever."

I rocked back in my chair. Their response was not what I had expected. Resigned to the fact that nothing was to be done, I said, "Ladies and gentlemen, I thank you for your time and attention. Unless anyone has additional business to bring forward, this meeting stands adjourned."

*Well*, I thought to myself. *At least I managed to wake them up.*

In all honesty, I had expected more from the Infection Control Committee. What surprised me most was that the other committee members did not share my suspicions that something odd was afoot. To me, it seemed intuitively obvious that five patients presenting with pneumonia caused by a single strain of a relatively unknown virus was more than coincidence. There had to be an explanation, but for the life of me, I could not sort it out.

The committee was right about one thing, however. Without additional information to evaluate or new leads to follow, my investigation, such as it was, had come to a screeching halt. As much as it had nettled me to do so, I had been forced to adopt an attitude of wait and see. Still I could not shake the feeling that I was missing something. As much as it shamed me to admit it, I secretly hoped that another infected patient would provide the clues needed to solve the riddle.

Yet until that happened, all I could do was bide my time. As a result, life had begun to again flow in familiar patterns, one of which was that by unspoken agreement, Madison and I were spending Sundays together on a regular basis. The third Sunday in October might serve as an example.

That weekend, Adam was on-call, meaning I was free to relax without having to worry about being interrupted in whatever activity Madison and I chose to pursue.

After church, we had decided to do lunch and think about how we would spend the rest of our day together. Upon discussing where to eat, we had settled on a nationally franchised build-it-on-demand sandwich shop. Madison had ordered turkey and ham on Italian bread. I had gone for meatballs with marinara sauce and provolone cheese. We sat in a side booth next to a window that looked out on boulevard traffic.

"It's hard to tell how the vote will go," Madison said, continuing an ongoing conversation. Somehow we had gravitated to the topic of unionization, probably because the medical center's nurses were scheduled to decide the issue by the end of the month.

"How will you feel about joining a union?" I asked.

Madison pondered her response as she swallowed a bite of her sandwich. "I suppose, all things considered, I'd say it was a good thing. The way it stands now, the hospital can arbitrarily cut our hours and refuse to pay overtime, leaving us critically short-staffed—perilously so. There have been days when I've had seven ICU patients to care for by myself. Do you realize how dangerous that is? I'm sure you do. One of these days, a patient is going to die because the nurse was too busy to do his or her job properly."

"Can the hospital afford unionization?" I countered. "The lower the staffing ratios, the more it's going to cost, even excluding a pay raise. The hospital can pass on only so many expenses to its patients. Over time, if the cash shortfall is large enough, the hospital will have to file for bankruptcy. Imagine the havoc that would cause."

Madison eyed me suspiciously. "So you're opposed to unionization."

"Not necessarily, but there has to be a balance. It's not wise to solve one problem by creating a new potentially more serious problem."

"You do have a point," Madison admitted grudgingly. "Speaking of problems, how's it going with your virus quest?"

"Is that what we're calling it now?"

"You know what I mean."

"Everything's at a standstill. I'm missing something, but I can't figure out what. I keep coming back to the note Jerry wrote me in the Emergency Department. What did he mean, 'It's my fault'? And what book was he referring to? It's not at the office—I know that for sure."

"Have you talked to his wife?" Madison suggested.

"Actually, I haven't. I was going to approach her at Jerry's funeral, but I didn't want to intrude on her grief. Then I got busy, and it sort of slipped my mind."

"It's been a month. Maybe she's more settled now. You should go see her. She might know something."

"Would you go with me? She might feel more at ease if there was a woman present."

Madison paused as if considering her response. Then she brightened. "All right. I could do that. When did you want to go?"

I shrugged. "How about now? I mean, after we finish lunch. I'll call her and see if she's available." I pulled my cell phone out of my pocket and dialed the Tuckers' number. When I hung up, I announced, "She said to come on over—she'd be waiting."

Having never been to the Tucker's home, I wasn't sure what to expect. Even so, I never would have pictured them living in a two-story colonial house with dormer windows and a colonnaded front entrance.

When Linda opened the door, she was wearing a rose-colored pantsuit outfit with white tennis shoes and a patterned scarf around her neck. To me, she looked as if she had lost weight, but I elected not to comment in case I was wrong. She certainly didn't fit my mental image of a grieving widow, but then external appearances don't always tell the whole story.

"Hello, Linda." I gently took hold of her hand. "Thank you for agreeing to see us. You remember Madison Lane, don't you?"

"Of course. We met at your barbecue."

I let go of her hand, and Linda turned to greet Madison with a warm smile. "It's nice to see you again, dear. Come in." She led the way into the living room.

"Mrs. Tucker, you have a beautiful home," Madison said.

"Honey, call me Linda. Everybody else does. Can I get you all something? Coffee, tea—a bloody Mary?"

"Nothing for me, thank you," I replied. "We just had lunch."

"I'm fine," Madison agreed.

We both sat on the couch. Linda chose the claw-footed armchair. Looking around, I saw that the house was immaculate. I've heard it said that cleaning house can be quite therapeutic for grieving widows and widowers.

Another surprise caught my eye. On the mantle above the fireplace stood a picture of Jerry, obviously taken years before. He was wearing an Army uniform with two bars on his shoulders. I said, "I didn't know your husband served in the military."

Linda smiled with a faraway look in her eyes. "Army Medical Corps. He joined up during operation Desert Shield. It sounds odd when you think about it, but he used to claim those were some of the best days of his life. He regularly kept in touch with a few of the men he served with. Several even came to his funeral. Perhaps you saw them there."

I nodded. "I did, but I didn't realize who they were."

Linda sat back in her chair and crossed her legs. "So…what brings you to my home?"

"First of all," I said. "We wanted to check on you and see how you're doing—see if there's anything you need?"

"I'm doing well, I think. It's been difficult, but I feel like I'm coping."

"That's good," I said. "You look like you're doing well."

"Also," Madison added. "We're curious about a brief note your husband jotted down in the Emergency Department the morning he was admitted. We're hoping you could help us understand what he was trying to say."

Linda responded with a look of uncertainty. "What note?"

I took the slip of paper from my pocket, unfolded it, and handed it to her. She read it through several times and then looked up. "I don't have any idea what this means. Jerry was in pretty rough shape when the ambulance picked him up. Are you sure he wasn't delusional?"

"He didn't seem so," I said. "But then he was awake for only a short time before he lapsed into a coma. We are particularly interested in this instruction to 'Get the book.' Do you have any notion as to what he might have been thinking? Is there a particular book he might've had in mind—a journal or a diary perhaps?"

"Not that I know of. I've been gathering his things together and storing them in the guest bedroom. You're welcome to go through them if you'd like."

"Thank you. We would," Madison said. "As long as it won't upset you."

"It won't. My husband is gone, but I have years of wonderful memories. His things are just things. They don't have any special meaning for me, but thank you for asking." Linda hesitated, looking away. She then looked back. "What did he mean, 'It's my fault. I should have known'?"

"We don't know," I said. "We were hoping you could tell us."

Linda shook her head. "I can't imagine what he was thinking." She seemed to gather her resolve and said, "Come. I'll show you the way." She led us to a room at the back of the house

En route, I said as I trailed behind Linda, "Did Jerry have other places where he might have kept some of his things?"

Linda said over her shoulder, "I'm not sure what you mean. Such as…?"

"A storage locker. A safe-deposit box at a bank. What about a friend's house? Could he have given the book to somebody for safekeeping?"

"Oh, I don't think so. I'm sure I would have known. No, I don't believe he had any of those things."

Linda ushered us into the guest bedroom and then left to attend to other interests. When we were alone, I whispered to Madison, "What do you think? Is she being honest with us?"

"I believe so," Madison said. "I watched her body language when she read the note. She truly had no idea what it was about. She's as much in the dark as we are."

Madison and I spent twenty minutes rummaging through Jerry's possessions. When we were done, we were no closer to understanding his cryptic communication than we had been. Before leaving, we tracked Linda down to say goodbye. We found her in the arboretum, tending to her African violets. We again expressed our sympathy and assured her that she could call any time there was a need.

As we drove away, I couldn't help but wonder if she was truly coping as well as she seemed or if her apparent equanimity was a brave front put on for our benefit. It was hard to judge, but I assumed that over time, her true state of mind would become apparent.

As we drove back toward the center of town, Madison sat quietly, staring through the windshield at the road ahead. She seemed melancholy and drawn in upon herself. I could tell she had been sorely affected by Linda's plight.

"Are you okay?" I asked.

"I was just thinking about how capricious life can be. One minute you're happily married. The next minute you're alone. You casually say goodbye to your spouse in the morning, not realizing you will never see them again."

Her demeanor gave the impression that she was speaking from experience. "You know someone that happened to?"

"My brother. He said goodbye to his wife in the morning when he went to work. That was the last time he saw her alive. She was carrying a basket of dirty clothes downstairs to the laundry room when she tripped and fell. She broke her neck. It took him a long time to recover from his loss. Why do you think God allows tragedies like that to happen?"

"What you're really asking, I think, is a variant of the age-old question: Why is there evil in the world? Why does God permit evil to exist?"

"Claudia's death wasn't evil. It was an accident."

"Maybe, but I don't believe in accidents. I believe that events derive from a synthesis of forces—some forces are good, some are evil. The cause-and-effect relationships may not be obvious, and to us they appear to be random events, but they're not. Everything that is exists by design."

Madison looked perplexed. "Perhaps. So what's the answer? Why does God allow evil to exist?"

"I can only tell you what I believe. Of course, there is no guarantee that I'm right."

"Go on."

"It has to do with free will." The light ahead turned red, and I stopped the car. I angled my body to look at Madison. "God endowed man with the right to choose. We can choose to do good, or we can choose to do evil. We can choose to love God and draw near to Him, or we can reject Him and turn away. However, for our choices to be legitimate, we must have legitimate alternatives to choose between. In order to choose good and have that choice mean something, we must at the same time be able to choose evil. Otherwise, there is no choice.

"You see, bad things happen because evil exists, and evil exists so that we can know what good is and make it the cornerstone of our existence. You can't fully understand light unless you first understand darkness."

The light turned green, and I drove on. Madison said, "I get what you're saying—sort of, but why must we suffer so?"

"Our sufferings, or tribulations, to be precise, build character, and character produces faith, which leads to salvation. Experiencing travail trains us to trust God, and that trust then enables God to bestow upon us eternal life. It's all part of His divine plan."

"Why does it have to be so complicated?" It was easy to see that Madison was becoming upset.

"Death does that," I said gently. "It makes us angry. All I can tell you is that as far as I see, it all boils down to choice. God is glorified when we choose to love Him. He can't force us to love Him. If he did, it wouldn't be love, it would be something else—compulsion, coercion, not genuine love. Man was created so that he might choose to develop a close, personal relationship with his creator. That, in fact, is the purpose of life. It's why we exist. The concept is simple. It's the implementation that's complex."

Madison fell silent for a time and then said, "It's not easy…that's for certain."

"No, it's not," I agreed, then changing the subject, I said, "Say, are you in a hurry to get home? If you have the time, there's something I'd like to show you."

"I'm free. What do you want me to see?"

"It will be better if I show you rather than tell you."

I drove for another ten minutes and then turned off on a residential side street about a mile from the medical center. Halfway down the block, I pulled over and parked in front of a modern two-story farmhouse-style dwelling with large picture windows and an attached garage. A FOR SALE sign was prominently displayed near the front entrance.

"What are we doing here?" Madison said.

"I found this place yesterday while I was driving around. I called the realtor, and she said I could stop by and take a look at it. There is a key in the lockbox. She trusted me with the combination. Come on. Let's have a look inside."

"I like its curbside appeal," Madison stated as we started up the front walkway.

As we crossed the threshold, I was pleased with what I saw. An abbreviated entryway opened into a spacious living room that connected with the dining area which then flowed into a roomy kitchen with a central island. The home was unfurnished. A family room and a room that could serve as a home office were located on the side of the house opposite the garage. The downstairs bathroom stood between them. Upstairs was a second bathroom and three bedrooms— the master bedroom being positioned toward the back of the house.

"Three bedrooms, two bathrooms, and an acre of ground for $325,000," I said as we continued our tour. "Can you believe it? This house came on the market yesterday. In fact, I'm not sure it's in the MLS database yet. The kitchen was recently refurbished. The appliances are almost brand-new. The basement is only partially finished, but it wouldn't take much to turn it into a rec room or a man cave. So…what do you think?"

Madison stood in the dining area, arms akimbo. "I like it. It has an open welcoming feeling, and it looks to have been well maintained. I really like the hardwood floors. Is $325,000 a good price? I'm not as well versed on the value of real estate as I should be."

"It's probably low-to-mid-range. If I decide to go for it, I might start with a bid of $295,000."

"You're really thinking of buying it then?"

"I am. I like living in Washington State. I like the work I'm doing. I like the people I work with."

"You haven't endured one of our winters yet."

"Other people survive them. I don't see why I can't."

Madison chuckled. "Spoken like a true adventurer. Well, if it suits you, you should make an offer."

"I think I will." I declared with a finality that surprised even me.

After driving Madison back to the church so she could retrieve her car, I called the real estate broker handling the listing. She had promised she would be available even though it was Sunday. When I presented my offer, she assured me that she would let me know the seller's response as soon as possible. At nine o'clock that night, my counter offer of $310,000 was accepted, and we tentatively agreed to close escrow in ten days.

As I said goodbye to the broker and hung up the phone, I was reminded of the adage adapted from chaos theory: Big changes happen all at once.

*How true, how true*, I told myself. I was feeling good about the transaction, but then I began to wonder. *Am I doing the right thing? It had all happened so precipitously. I guess only time will tell.*

Tuesday evening, during the third week in October, I was at home, sorting through my stuff. I had moved into the apartment only eleven weeks before, and many of the possessions I had brought with me from Los Angeles were still in boxes. One advantage of being a bachelor is that you can leave things lying around for weeks on end, and no one is going to nag at you.

Earlier that afternoon, I had spoken with my real estate agent. She had just received my policy from the title insurance company certifying that the deed to the house I was purchasing was clear and unencumbered. Also, the home inspector had just filed his report. Except for a leaky bathroom faucet and the fact that the air ducts in the central heating unit needed cleaning, there were no significant deficiencies. The house, as Madison had noted, had been exceedingly well maintained, which was a comfort.

In anticipation of closing escrow and moving in, I was going through my belongings to see what I should take and what I could ditch. Limited by time constraints during my previous move, I hadn't been able to weed through my junk, and a good cleanout was overdue.

As a first-time homebuyer, my eagerness to own my own home was balanced by my apprehension that I was making a mistake by taking on such a hefty mortgage. The loan officer at the bank had assured me that as a physician, I should be more than capable of making my monthly payments. Still there is something daunting about being encumbered by such a large debt.

*No risk, no reward*, I told myself. Almost everything in life boils down to the choices we make, as my conversation with Madison had reminded me. In truth, all I could do was pray that my judgment was sound and that all would work out for the best in the long run.

I had just opened another storage carton when the phone rang. It was Nancy in the Emergency Department. A patient had just come in with what appeared to be pneumonia and was in need of admission. I had almost forgotten that I was on call. I assured her that I would be in as soon as possible.

As I hung up the phone, I wondered, *Would this be the case that answers my lingering questions surrounding the bocavirus patients? Would I finally learn how they had contracted their infections?* I quickly changed out of my grubby work clothes and into a clean shirt and a pair of gabardine slacks.

When I arrived in the Emergency Department, Nancy introduced me to Mrs. Ruby Lackland, a fifty-two-year-old Black woman who had been ill for less than forty-eight hours. Her history was somewhat atypical for a bocavirus infection in that her symptoms had been getting worse gradually rather than precipitously, as with previous patients. Also, her chest x-ray showed a limited lobar pneumonia rather than diffuse involvement of both lungs.

Despite the discrepancies, my initial impression was that she could be another bocavirus victim; and for that reason, I took an exhaustive history, looking for points of congruence with her predecessors. By the time I finished, Mrs. Lackland was worn out. Regrettably, her answers failed to explain how she or the others had come down with their illnesses.

As part of the initial workup, I had ordered a Gram stain of her sputum, looking for identifiable pathogens. As we were preparing her to be transferred to the ICU, I received a phone call from the lab. They had identified Gram-positive, lancet-shaped cocci in pairs and short chains. Mrs. Lackland had an ordinary pneumococcal pneumonia, not a bocavirus infection.

I should have been pleased for my patient. Her bacterial infection would be easier to treat and, therefore, would carry a better prognosis. However, deep down I was disappointed. I had sincerely hoped that she would provide the key to solving my bocavirus conundrum.

I immediately started Mrs. Lackland on ceftriaxone, a powerful, broad-spectrum antibiotic effective against the pneumococcus bacterium. Rather than admit her to the ICU, I asked the nurses to get her a bed on the medical ward.

By the time I finished admitting my new patient, it was already a little after 2:00 a.m. I was just finishing up recording my admission history and physical when I heard a voice behind me say, "Working late, are we? No rest for the wicked. Is it wicked, or is it weary? I can never remember."

I glanced up from the tablet computer to find Sam Duncan standing a few feet off, watching me with bleary eyes. He looked as tired as I felt. "Are you lost?" I said teasingly. "This is the medical ward. The surgical ward is that way." I pointed down the corridor to the east.

"I got called in to see a patient with an empyema." Empyema is a collection of infected fluid between the lung and the interior surface of the chest. "I may need to do an open drainage. What are you up to?"

"A garden-variety pneumococcal pneumonia."

Sam stepped forward and sat down beside me at the counter. "Not your virus then? I heard about your Infection Control Committee meeting. I gather it didn't quite go as you had planned."

"What did you hear?"

"Only that you were seeking other lines of investigation to pursue and the committee recommended that you wait. Actually, the person I talked to was impressed with your presentation of the case histories. He said you were fairly convincing."

"Not convincing enough, apparently. I still feel there is a community health risk. I just wish I could get someone to listen."

"I'm listening," Sam said mildly. "Tell me, if you could do anything you wanted to shed light on the problem, what would it be?"

"That's the point. I don't know where to go from here. It's clear that the patients didn't spread the virus one to another. They all developed their pneumonias independently. Therefore, there has to be a point of origin, a common source from which they contracted their infections, but I'll be damned if I can find it."

"So maybe the best thing to do is to wait and see—like the committee recommended."

"Yeah, maybe, but it certainly is frustrating."

"By the way, just to let you know. Mr. Wright's family has been complaining about receiving bills for lab studies ordered after he died."

"Sorry about that. I thought I had it worked out. I'll check with the lab and see if I can get it sorted."

"That would be appreciated. It's hard to justify doing a diagnostic workup on a dead man."

"I hear you." I handed the tablet computer to the ward secretary so she could transcribe my orders. "Don't work too hard," I called back to Sam as I headed down the main corridor. I was about to exit the hospital's front entrance when I stopped and checked the time on my phone. It had occurred to me that by the time I got home and climbed into bed, it would almost be time to get up again. I decided instead to check out the on-call rooms and see if one of them was vacant.

The medical center maintained three rooms where physicians who were working late could catch some shuteye. They were available on a first-come first-served basis. Housekeeping monitored the rooms periodically and changed the sheets and towels as needed.

I was in luck. One of the rooms was vacant. I called the hospital operator to inform her where I would be for the next four hours.

As soon as my head hit the pillow, I was asleep.

# OVERHEARD

Three and a half hours after falling asleep in the on-call room, I awoke to the chiming of my phone's alarm. I was groggy from too little sleep, and I felt grungy, having slept in my clothes. My teeth were wrapped in tiny fur overcoats. I would have to wait till I got to the office to brush them. For just such occasions, I kept a ditty bag of personal toiletries in the bottom drawer of my desk.

Before heading out to start my rounds, I used my pocket comb to impart some semblance of order to my unruly hair. In several spots, errant locks refused to cooperate. It was working up to be another really bad hair day.

I started rounding on the medical ward. I especially wanted to know how Mrs. Lackland was faring. Before the age of antibiotics, pneumococcal pneumonias were usually fatal, and the lungs of those who survived were often severely damaged. That was why I was pleased to note that Mrs. Lackland was already showing signs of improvement. Her temperature had fallen into a normal range, and her breathing was less labored.

Ever since medical school, I've been struck by a sense of amazement when I prescribe a therapy and it actually works. It always seems like wizardry when I administer a compound and a patient's physiology improves—sometimes dramatically. Of course, I'm aware that such healings are a direct consequence of the science that pertains. Cures are simply a matter of selecting the right molecule to interact with the targeted metabolic pathway to produce the proper result. Still, such remedies often feel like magic.

After rounding on my third and final patient for the morning, I was about to leave the hospital and walk to my office when a severe stabbing pain jabbed me in the back and nearly dropped me to my knees. My first impression was that I had been knifed. The pain was so intense that it triggered a wave of nausea, and I thought I might be sick. I recognized immediately the source of the pain. I was trying to pass a kidney stone. I'd had them before, and believe me, they are no fun.

Rather than continue on to my office, I switched directions and made my way to the Emergency Department. Instead of checking in, I look to see which member of the emergency medicine group was working that day. Fortunately, it was Doctor Kyle Larson, one of the physicians who served on the Infection Control Committee. I caught him as he was coming out of a patient's room. "Hey, Kyle, got a second?"

"What's up?" Kyle said with a look of solicitude. Clearly he could tell I was in distress even though I was trying not to let my anguish show.

I described my plight and shared my medical history, which I felt supported my self-diagnosis. I finished up by saying, "So you see, there really is no need to undertake a full-scale workup. Just write me a script for ketorolac, and I'll be good to go."

Kyle nodded thoughtfully. "At least let's confirm your diagnosis. How about we collect a urine specimen and see if you are passing any red blood cells."

"I can't hang around. I've got to get to the office. I've got patients waiting."

"How about this," Kyle suggested. "I'll write you a script, and you pee in a cup before you go back to your office. I'll call you when I get the results. If your urine is positive for blood, you can start the ketorolac then. How does that sound?"

"Sounds like a plan." I groaned as another surge of pain stabbed me in the back. This time, it radiated down my left flank toward my groin. The stone was moving.

After submitting a urine specimen, I collected my prescription from Kyle and headed straight for the pharmacy to get it filled. As soon as the pharmacist handed me a bottle that contained a dozen 10 mg tablets, I opened it and took one, dry-swallowing the pill with only modest difficulty. To my way of thinking, there was no need to wait for the report on the urinalysis. It would simply confirm what I already knew.

As I was walking to my office, the pain in my flank began to subside significantly. It's been said that ketorolac is so effective against renal colic that a strong response is very nearly diagnostic of a kidney stone. In any event, I was relieved that the pain was becoming endurable. Now if that damn stone would pass, I would be right as rain.

Adam snagged me just as I finished with my last patient of the morning. "How are you doing?" We stood in the hallway just outside my office.

"I'm hanging in there," I declared. I had taken a second ketorolac not an hour before. Again it had brought prompt relief, though not as dramatically as with the first dose. There is a phenomenon in pharmacology known as tolerance. This occurs when subsequent doses of a drug produce less of an effect than the initial doses. The corollary is that to produce the same effect each time, you need increasing doses of the drug.

Adam laid a hand on my shoulder. "What's your pain level?"

"Somewhere between a two and a three. It's not so bad that I can't stand it."

"Good. Do you think you are comfortable enough to go with me to the hospital?"

"Probably. What's up?"

"I thought we could grab a quick bite of lunch, and then we need to meet with the medical center's Legal Department."

"The Legal Department? Is there a problem?"

"They have a sales contract they want us to sign. It's the deal Jerry negotiated for the hospital to take over the practice. We need to talk about what we're going to do. Do you feel like you are up for that?"

"I think so," I said optimistically. The pain in my left flank had shifted more toward my groin. That meant the stone was continuing to move. My hope was that it would travel down the ureter until it passed into the bladder before leaving the body.

In the cafeteria, Adam and I made our way through the serving line and then selected a table that was set apart from the congested center of the room. Instead of a regular lunch, I had selected a small dish of peaches and a carton of milk. The nausea wasn't bad, but it wasn't gone either.

Adam, on the other hand, had chosen a serving of stew, a slice of garlic bread, and a helping of green beans. For dessert, he had included a wedge of chocolate cake.

"So," Adam said. "Here's the story. Apparently, Jerry negotiated a pretty good deal. The hospital is willing to pay us $500,000 to take over our practice. They would own our equipment. They would take over the lease on our office space. Our employees would become their employees. Our patients would become their patients. We would continue treating them, but instead of earning income based upon productivity, we would be paid a salary. The projections are that when the dust settles, we'd be taking home approximately the same amounts as what we earn now. The downside is that we would lose our autonomy."

"The $500,000? How would that be divided?" I asked.

Adam smiled. "Theoretically, 99 percent of that money should go to me since you really haven't worked here long enough to build up any equity. However, when you joined us, you had no idea that this transition was on the horizon, and in all fairness, you should be compensated for your good-faith efforts to become a full partner. With that in mind, I would be willing to see that you get $75,000. The rest would come to me."

"What about Jerry? Isn't his widow entitled to his share?"

"She's already been paid," Adam said flatly.

"How can that be?"

"You didn't know? When a partner completes his probationary period, the practice purchases a renewable term life insurance policy large enough to cover his buyout. It doesn't apply to retirement, but the monies are available in the event of an untimely demise."

"How much did Linda receive?"

"Two hundred fifty thousand dollars. That's what she would have received if Jerry hadn't died. So, what are your thoughts? What do you believe we should do?" Seventy-five thousand dollars would make a decent dent in the new mortgage I was about to assume. Even so, I didn't feature becoming someone else's employee. I especially did not want to work for an impersonal institution like the Flintridge Medical Center."

"What happens if we don't sign the contract?"

"Things would stay as they are."

"Is that an option?"

"I don't see how they can force us to sign."

"Then that's what I think we should do—leave things the way they are."

Adam grinned broadly. "I was hoping that would be your response. I am in total agreement. Let's go talk to the lawyers."

Before bussing my tray, I downed another ketorolac with a swig of milk.

"You can't refuse to sign," Marcus Eldridge shrilled. He had rushed to the Legal Department as soon as he had been informed that we were declining to endorse the contract. "We have a good-faith agreement. Signing is just a formality."

"The agreement wasn't with us," Adam countered. "The partner with whom you negotiated is dead, and now so is this agreement."

"You can't back out. We will sue you." Marcus gestured toward the hospital's two lawyers who looked as if they would much rather be someplace else.

"Sue us? For what—breach of contract? Except there is no contract."

"What's the matter," Marcus sneered. "Are we not offering you enough? Is it more money you're after?"

I started to respond, but Adam spoke first, "I'd say your offer is fair."

Marcus looked toward the lead attorney and gestured as if to say, "Help me out here."

In response, the man shrugged.

Still seated at the conference table, Adam steepled his fingers in front of his chin. "The issue is autonomy. You're asking us to give ours up, but our independence is not for sale."

Instead of continuing to stand, Marcus sank into a chair opposite Adam. "You will still be able to practice as you do now. That will not change."

"Maybe not initially," Adam declared. "But eventually, when the bean counters have had their say, subtle pressures will be applied to have us cut back on diagnostic testing or to restrict our services. The criteria used to decide which studies to order would no longer be, 'Are they medically appropriate?' Instead, they would become, 'Do they maximize profit?' Drugs would be added to or removed from the formulary depending upon how much they cost, not how well they work. Surgeries would be farmed out to the lowest bidder rather than to the most qualified surgeon. Rather than continuing as a healing art, medicine would become a profit-oriented business, pure and simple. No, sir. We will not endorse your corporate greed."

Having grown red-faced during Adam's denunciation, Marcus surged to his feet. Angrily he pointed across the table at me. "This is your fault, meddling where you shouldn't." Then he seemed to catch himself. Sputtering, he's spun on his heel and stormed from the room.

"What was that all about?" Adam said, looking at me wide-eyed.

"I have no idea."

"You must've done something to piss him off."

"You saw me. I was just sitting here." A renewed rush of pain punched me in the left flank. I grit my teeth and tried not to groan as I thought about the long afternoon that lay ahead.

A little before seven o'clock that evening, I was on my way to Madison's house. I had been invited for dinner. I had been to her home several times, but this was only the second time I had been invited for a meal. Her call had rung through in the early afternoon while I was still battling my kidney stone, and I had very nearly declined her invitation. The ketorolac was helping but not as dramatically as in the beginning, and the pain was holding steady at a level of four to five.

When I started to explain why I didn't think I could make it, Madison had interrupted by announcing that it was to be a special occasion, an opportunity that might not come around again for quite some time. When I had asked what the opportunity might be, she had teasingly announced that I would have to show up to find out.

My yearning to be with her, plus the fact that she had piqued my curiosity, had persuaded me to accept her invitation.

I was at home preparing for my date when my flank pain suddenly eased. Cautiously I tried flexing my back in several directions to see if the pain would return. It did not. Then I tried jumping up and down. When after fifteen minutes I was still pain-free, I allowed myself to hope that the kidney stone had passed. The only lingering symptoms were a faint ache in my groin and a dull malaise, as if I had just run a long distance or struggled through a hard exercise session in the gym.

When Madison opened the door, she was wearing a pale-blue knee-length party dress with a white belt and white pumps. Her auburn hair was drawn into a curl at the back of her head. What little makeup she wore had been carefully applied, and she looked spectacular.

I was about to compliment her on her appearance when she reached out. Taking hold of my hand, she tugged me inside. "Come with me," she said happily. "There are people I'd like you to meet." Still holding my hand, she guided me toward the living room.

A demure couple sat quietly on the couch. They both looked to be in their early to mid-fifties. The man was wearing dark-blue slacks, a white dress shirt, and a tan cardigan. The woman had on a lime green pantsuit outfit with black accessories. She too had auburn hair and light-blue eyes.

With a joyful lilt to her voice, Madison said, "Mom, Dad, this is Blake Sterling, the man I've been telling you about." She looked at me.

"Blake, these are my parents, Albert and Margaret Lane. They just flew in from Kansas to surprise me."

The man rose to his feet and extended his hand. He was lean and wiry and stood near to my own height of five feet eleven inches. His skin was suntanned.

I returned the handshake. "It's a pleasure to meet you, sir." His grip was firm, and I felt the calluses on his palm. It was the hand of a man who worked for a living.

"Call me Al. You are a doctor, I understand." He sat down again.

"Yes, sir…eh, Al. A pulmonologist—lung specialist."

Madison's mother remained seated. She did, however, extend her hand. I reached down and gently touched it in lieu of a full handshake. "Ma'am, it's a pleasure to meet you."

"Likewise, but please call me Margaret. *Ma'am* makes me feel ten years older, and who needs that."

Madison glanced at me and said, "What can I get you? I was just about to open a bottle of white wine. Would you like some?"

"I don't think I should." As I sat down in the padded easy chair, I explained about my kidney stone and the ketorolac I had been taking. I finished up by saying, "So for now, maybe I'll just stick with ice water."

"Ice water coming up." Madison disappeared into the kitchen and promptly reappeared with a glass. She then disappeared back into the kitchen—I presumed to see about dinner.

When I looked back at Madison's parents, they both were eying me intently, as if deciding whether or not to bid on a prize heifer at a 4-H auction. I smiled and said, "So, Al, I remember Madison mentioning that you're a farmer."

"A wheat farmer, yes. That's right. My spread's a little over a thousand acres. We're ninety miles southeast of Wichita. It's table-top land, flat as a bureaucrat's backside."

"Albert," Margaret exclaimed disapprovingly. Looking at me, she said, "You had a kidney stone? I thought doctors were supposed to be immune to those kinds of problems."

"That's right. We are," I replied, completely deadpan. "It's in our contract. I've been trying to decide who I should sue." Then I smiled, and Madison's parents chuckled. For a time, we engaged in small talk until Madison emerged from the kitchen and announced that dinner was ready.

After dinner, the women were in the kitchen cleaning up. Al and I had returned to the living room. Seated with his legs crossed, he trailed his right arm along the back of the couch. Our conversation had touched upon several topics including the state of the economy, how things stood in Washington DC, and what it was like farming wheat for a living.

When the dialogue paused momentarily, Al looked at me and said, "Madison told me what you'd said about good versus evil. If I understood her correctly, you believe that God allows evil in order to give man legitimate choices. Did I get that right?"

"In a nutshell, yes." I rested my arms on my chair's padded armrests. "We were discussing how your son's fiancé died—"

"Claudia. That was a tragedy. She was a fine girl…would have made a good wife." Al shook his head. "I've been thinking about your point of view, and I'm not sure I agree. I believe evil flows from the hearts of men, that the choices we make are responsible for the evil in the world rather than thinking that evil exists on its own."

"Actually," I corrected. "We'd been considering why God allows evil to exist in the first place. My premise was that when evil stands in opposition to good, man is presented with valid alternatives to choose between. It doesn't necessarily matter whether the evil is external or internal."

"It matters if you're discussing the nature of man. If evil is external, then we can presume men's hearts can be inherently good. However, if evil is internal, then men's hearts are, by definition, incurably wicked, just as the Scriptures say. Besides, I'm not sure evil can even exist as an entity unto itself. Perhaps the only way it comes into being is through the actions of men."

"You make a good point," I declared with the nod in Al's direction. I had been impressed by his arguments. Clearly he had thought about his theology before, which explained his daughter's interest in the subject. "What about a bomb?" I suggested. "Its only reason for being is to explode and damage something."

Al countered, "What if the bomb is used to fracture rock and create ore for mining? Mankind is benefited by the minerals that will be harvested."

"A bullet then. A bullet's only job is to kill something."

"Not necessarily. A bullet used for target practice can bring enjoyment to the shooter with no harm being done."

After a long period of thought, I suggested, "A book—a book that induces its readers to commit malicious acts."

"Interesting," Al sat forward and braced his elbows on his knees. "I suppose you could use the book as a paperweight or a doorstop. Those uses wouldn't be made evil just because the book is evil, but they would be a distortion of the book's reason for being. I'm going to have to think about this one."

"What are you two talking about?" Margaret said as she entered from the kitchen.

"The price of a bushel of wheat," Al said casually. He obviously did not wish to pursue an ethical discussion with his wife. I suspected he probably got his fill of her chatter at home.

Madison followed her mother into the room. She sat down in the armchair that completed the conversation group. I couldn't help but admire the grace with which she moved.

"That was a delicious roast you prepared," I said. "In fact, the whole meal was outstanding."

Al and Margaret added their agreement.

We chatted for another hour, and then it was time for me to leave. As I was preparing to depart, Al stepped closer and said, "I've been thinking about this book you proposed. It occurs to me that a book is a special case. Books encapsulate the thoughts of men in written form. As such, they enable communication between individuals separated by space and time. The impact on the reader is a function of the author's perspective. If the book espouses malicious actions, it's actually the author that's culpable. The evil message flows through the book, not from the book. The book itself isn't evil. The heart of the author is the wellspring from which evil flows."

"I do believe you're right," I said with genuine admiration. "Well done."

Al beamed proudly. "You as well. It was a good discussion. I can see why my daughter likes you. Just remember to treat her well. She's a special person."

"I couldn't agree more."

As I was driving home, I reviewed the evening in my mind and how enjoyable it had been. I also thought about how grateful I was that my flank pain had not returned.

The hospital's auditorium was filling with physicians and other medical professionals who had come to hear me speak. It was Friday noon, and my turn to deliver the weekly CME conference had finally come. It would be wrong to say that I was nervous when, in fact, I was terrified. I've heard it said that of all the things people dread, public speaking is right up there with dying in an airplane crash and drowning. As I stood at the front of the auditorium and gazed out at the faces of my colleagues, at that moment, drowning didn't sound all that bad.

The topic I had chosen for my continuing medical education lecture was severe bocavirus pneumonia. In addition to reviewing the world's literature, I had drawn heavily on the case histories of the five patients my partners and I had treated at the medical center. My goal was not only to educate my audience about bocavirus infections, but also to raise awareness of what I considered to be a looming public health risk.

Seated in the front row, Heather Oliver smiled at me encouragingly. As infection control nurse, she had helped organize the data and distill it into a presentable format. She had even arranged for the hospital's Audiovisual Department to summarize the information I would be sharing into a series of slides.

As I watched the audience assemble, I saw Marcus Eldridge enter the auditorium. *What's he doing here?* I wondered. *He doesn't usually attend our noon conferences.* When he looked at me, he glowered with unmistakable hostility. Clearly he was still angry that Adam and I had refused to sell our practice to the hospital. In that moment, I suddenly appreciated why he was so irritated. Not only had we challenged his authority, we had set a precedent. We had declared our opposition to the hospital's plans to take over all aspects of medical care in the community. Marcus was worried that other groups might follow our lead.

With difficulty, I put the hospital's chief administrative officer out of my mind and strove to focus on my lecture instead. One point of concern was that a coworker's medical history was included in the database. Doctor Jerry Tucker had died as the result of a severe bocavirus pneumonia. One reason physicians are able to deal with death and dying to the extent they do is because they tend to compartmentalize their sensibilities. Early in their medical careers, most doctors learn to avoid becoming emotionally attached to their patients. However, remaining dispassionate might prove difficult if the patient being discussed was a colleague. I would have to be mindful to strike a balance between objectively presenting a cut-and-dried case history and lamenting the death of a partner and a friend.

As people finished taking their seats, I looked out at the crowd and began, "Human bocavirus infections are an uncommon cause of severe pneumonia. First identified in 2005, a series of recent articles have suggested that the virus's virulence may be increasing. I intend to present the case reports of five patients recently admitted to this institution that tend to substantiate that supposition."

When I concluded my lecture forty-five minutes later, a round of applause arose from the audience. It was hard to tell if it represented an expression of sincere appreciation or merely a polite courtesy offered to the lecturer. One thing for which I was grateful was that by my count, only two people had fallen asleep. I assumed that was par for the course—or maybe a little better than par.

In any event, I was glad it was over. All things considered, I felt that I had accomplished my goal. I had made the medical community aware of the possibility that we were on the cusp of a new viral endemic that could put the community's health at risk.

"Well done," Heather said as she joined me at the front of the lecture hall.

I responded, "It felt dry. Was there too much data, do you think—boring statistics?"

"I think you did well. I wouldn't have wanted more, though. I thought your emphasis on diminished transmissibility was an important point. Imagine the damage this virus could do if it becomes highly contagious."

"Don't even speak of that. What we absolutely do not need is a pandemic with a virus that runs a 50 percent mortality."

"We are a long way from that scenario," Heather said.

"True, but we've already seen how the virus is evolving. We need to be alert, and we need to be careful. Anyone dealing with a bocavirus pneumonia must be aware of the harm that would result if it's allowed to spread."

"I think you got that point across just fine. Have you had lunch?"

"No. I was too nervous to eat."

"Me too. Want to join me in the cafeteria?"

"Thank you. I would, but there is a stop I need to make before heading back to the office."

"In that case, I'll talk at you later."

I said goodbye and headed for the Respiratory Therapy Department.

In preparing my lecture, I had done a lot of thinking about my encounter with Jerry in the Emergency Department in the wee hours of the morning on the day he had been admitted. I had especially struggled to understand his meaning when he had said, "I did this. I'm responsible," and when he had written, "It's my fault."

My first assumption had been that he was feeling guilty for having contracted the virus, perhaps by letting his guard down and ignoring strict isolation protocols when he should have known better. Then it had occurred to me that perhaps there might be another explanation, one I had not yet considered. The more I dwelled upon the subject, the more convinced I became that the book Jerry had referenced was the key. I had to find the book, and maybe it would tell me what was on his mind.

One place where I had not yet looked for the book was in the Respiratory Therapy Department. Pulmonologists, due to the nature of their practices, are frequently called upon to interact with respiratory therapists. In delivering patient care, it's like we are two sides of one coin. As a consequence, we spend a lot of time in their department. It would not be unheard of for a doctor whose professional responsibilities tie him to a particular location to maintain a private space where he might store reference materials and items pertinent to his medical practice—perhaps on a cupboard shelf, or in a desk drawer. At least it was worth having a look.

The department was vacant when I entered from the corridor. Glancing around, I noted that there were any number of spaces Jerry might have appropriated for his own use. I began systematically opening cupboards, cabinets, and drawers as I worked my way around the room. When my search of the large front space turned up nothing, I was left with two choices. I could continue by looking in the office reserved for the head of the department, or I could move to the back storage room. I decided to save the department head's office for last.

I had worked my way through half the room when I heard voices outside in the corridor. They were growing louder. Instinctively, I sprang forward and switched off the lights in the storage room. After partially closing the door, I retreated into the darkness. When I considered what I had just done, I decided that I probably had not made the wisest decision. Justifying loitering in a darkened storage area would be more problematic than simply admitting what I was seeking, but it was too late to correct my mistake. Hopefully, whoever it was would complete whatever business they needed to complete and leave.

To my surprise, Tyler Wickham and Marcus Eldridge entered together. They were engaged in an animated discussion, and from the sound of their voices, both men were troubled. By shifting my head back and forth, I could make out their profiles through the crack in the door. They stood toward the center of the room facing each other.

"I told you I don't know where they are," Tyler declared with a scowl. "I gave them to Jerry, and that's the last I saw of them. What he did with them, he never said."

"You do understand what this means," Marcus said.

"Of course I understand. I'm not stupid."

Marcus threw his hands up in a gesture of frustration. "This entire business is getting out of hand. I don't care what the captain says. I want to be done. What can he do to me anyway?"

Tyler stabbed an index finger into the center of Marcus's chest. "It's not the captain you need to worry about. It's The Angel. One word from him, and they will never find your corpse."

I could tell by the look on Marcus's face that he was frightened. His voice quavered when he said, "I should never have gotten involved in this project. I knew it was a bad idea from the beginning."

"But you did get involved. Look, if we keep our heads, this can still turn out all right, but first we've got to find Jerry's stuff."

Tyler's cell phone chirped. He dug it out of his pocket to read a text message. "I've got to go," he announced. "A patient on the surgical floor is crashing."

When Tyler started to leave, Marcus said, "And what am I supposed to do now?"

"For a chief administrator, you're not very bright. Use your contacts on the medical staff. Maybe Jerry confided in someone. Ask around. Just stay away from his partners. Blake is suspicious enough already." With that, Tyler promptly left the room. Marcus was not far behind him.

I waited until I was sure they were gone. Then I stepped forward and turned on the lights. I had entered the department with a handful of questions in mind. I now had a dozen more. What was it that Tyler had given to Jerry? Who was the captain, and who was The Angel? What project were Marcus and Tyler involved in, and why were they working together? When they talked about Jerry's stuff, were they after the same thing I was after? Most puzzling of all, I wondered why a respiratory therapist was able to talk to the hospital's chief administrator as he had, pointing out that he was not very bright.

Whatever was going on, I now had the unsettling feeling that it was bigger than I had first imagined.

One thing I knew for certain—I no longer needed to search the department. Obviously, those two would have gone over it inch by inch. Jerry's stuff had to be somewhere else.

As in previous years, Flintridge Healthcare's annual picnic was scheduled for the third Saturday in October, the day after my continuing education lecture. Mansfield Park had been reserved in its entirety for the event, and well over a thousand people were expected to attend.

Flintridge Healthcare was the parent company of Flintridge Medical Center, Flintridge Extended Care Facility, Flintridge Pharmacy, and numerous other medical entities including more than a dozen doctors' offices. The board of directors for Flintridge Healthcare touted the picnic as an employee appreciation function. Any employee, their family members, and guests could attend for free. Members of the community were also invited, though they would be charged a twenty-dollar entrance fee.

The medical center's dietitians, with the support of the cafeteria staff, oversaw the food service. A catering company out of Kennewick had been hired to barbecue half a steer and a whole hog. In addition, other vendors provided hamburgers, hot dogs, chili, fried chicken, stir-fry noodles, and a selection of vegetarian entrées. The culinary team's motto was "If you went home hungry, it was your own fault."

A variety of events had been planned to allow both children and adults to participate. Included were competitions such as three-legged races, water balloon tosses, tug-of-war rope pulls, a cornhole tournament, and a putting green. For the older kids and the adults, there was a karaoke contest and for the younger kids a treasure hunt as well as a pony ride.

Noise and commotion prevailed throughout the park. In that it was my turn on call, I had been obliged to first complete my rounds at the hospital, and by the time I arrived a little after noon, the festivities were well underway. The first thing I did was set off in search of Madison. She had promised to wait and have lunch with me. I finally found her by the Dunk-A-Clown venue. She was selling tickets and inviting people to come and try their luck.

The object of the attraction was to pitch a softball at a small target. A direct hit would trigger the release of the seat upon which a volunteer dressed as a circus clown was sitting, dumping him into a shallow pool of water. As luck would have it, when I arrived, it was Marcus Eldridge's turn to volunteer. With his multicolor wig, face paint, bulbous red nose, garish clown suit, and oversized shoes, he played his part well. His clothes were dry. I regarded his predicament as an opportunity too good to pass up.

"Excuse me, sir." Madison greeted me with a smile as I stepped forward. "Could I interest you in giving it a try? Three chances for a dollar."

"How can I resist?" I responded as I dug my wallet out of my pocket. I took out a dollar and gave it to her. In return, she handed me the first of three softballs.

Although it had been a while since I had thrown a softball, I felt reasonably confident in my abilities. For three years, I had pitched for our high school baseball team, and we had come close to winning the regional championship.

"Well, look who's up next," Marcus said, seated on his perch above the pool. "Come on, hotshot, let's see what you've got."

I rotated my shoulder several times in a full circle to limber up. Drawing back my arm, I hurled the softball at the target but missed by a couple of inches, which actually wasn't that poor of a performance. The target was hardly larger than the softball itself. Any umpire would have called my throw a strike. Madison handed me another softball.

"Is that the best you can do, hotshot?" Marcus chided. "My sister can pitch better than that."

I wound up again and hurled the second ball. It clipped the edge of the target but not with enough force to trigger the release mechanism.

"*Steeerike* two," Marcus bellowed. He waved his arms and wiggled his feet gleefully as he sat on his perch. "You can do better than that— or maybe not. Loser." He laughed.

"Don't let him rattle you." Madison handed me the third softball. "Take your time."

"Maybe you should let her pitch," Marcus sneered. "Look, I'm still dry."

"Not for long," I commented under my breath. Then I did as Madison had suggested. I took my time. Holding the softball in my hand, I made sure I had the proper grip. I imagined myself back in high school, standing on the pitcher's mound, staring down the batter. When I felt I was ready, I drew back my arm and let the softball fly. It struck the target with a loud metallic thunk. All of a sudden, the seat beneath Marcus gave way, and he dropped into the pool with a plop. He emerged sputtering, his multicolor wig dripping water onto his face and shoulders.

"You're not dry anymore, are you?"

"Lucky shot," Marcus protested as he reset the seat and climbed back aboard.

I considered spending another dollar just for the fun of it but then looked at Madison and remembered that she must be hungry, having waited to eat lunch.

Madison signaled the girl she had been helping sell tickets that she was leaving. Arm in arm, we sauntered off.

I chuckled at the memory of Marcus splashing into the pool. "I must admit that was fun."

"Yes it was," Madison agreed as we made our way to the food pavilion.

As we joined the serving line, I noticed Tyler Wickham standing not far off. I had been thinking about the conversation I had overheard, and I had decided that if the opportunity arose, there were several questions I intended to ask the respiratory therapist. Now seemed as good a time as any. "You go on ahead," I said to Madison. "I'll catch up with you in a little bit."

Tyler stood by the dessert table, facing away from me. I was able to approach unseen. When I touched him on the shoulder, he flinched, nearly dropping the plate he held in his hand. On the plate was a slice of apple pie.

"Sorry," I said. "Didn't mean to startle you. It's quite a shindig, isn't it?"

"I suppose." Tyler cut into the pie with his fork and took a bite.

"You sound as if you don't appreciate the board's attempt to improve employee relations." I gestured to encompass the park and the many activities that were underway.

"I would rather that they take the money they're spending on this picnic and put it in our paychecks."

"I'm sure there are those who would agree with you," I said pleasantly.

"These events get more extravagant every year."

"How long have you worked for the medical center?"

"A little over four years, why?"

"As you may know, I've been trying to determine how Doctor Tucker came by his infection. I think it's vital that we understand what happened. I'd only known the man for a couple months. You, on the other hand, had worked with him for years. Were you aware of anything that was distressing him in the days and weeks leading up to his death?"

"Such as?"

"I'm not sure. I was hoping you could tell me. Did he seem troubled or bothered by something? Might there have been an issue in his life that was weighing on his conscience?"

"Not that I'm aware." Tyler looked away. I had the distinct impression that he wasn't telling the truth.

It wouldn't do to flat out call the man a liar—not without proof. I would have to work with him at the hospital, and it would be unwise to sabotage our relationship without a very good reason; and yet, I could not allow his denial to stand unchallenged. "Are you sure? Perhaps there was something that didn't seem important at the time but now could be significant."

"I have no idea what that might be," Tyler declared defensively. Clearly I was making him uncomfortable.

I decided to try a different tact. "Tell me about the man. How would you describe him?"

"I don't see how that's relevant. The man is dead. Let him rest in peace."

"Doctor Tucker might be gone, but the bocavirus that killed him isn't. It's out there somewhere, waiting to infect another victim. I can feel it. All I'm asking is if there is something in Doctor Tucker's history that might help us understand what happened?"

"You're asking the wrong guy. I can't help you. Yes, Doctor Tucker was a friend, but as to what was going on inside his head, I can't say. Now if you'll excuse me…" Tyler set down his half-eaten slice of pie on the dessert table and walked away.

I thought about Tyler and his evasive responses as I moved off to catch up with Madison. The respiratory therapist knew far more than he was letting on, but confronting him directly wasn't the answer. I would have to come up with a different ploy.

For the time being, I put the matter out of my mind. Instead, I focused on the good news that I would share with Madison. The seller had accepted my offer on the property we had visited. For the first time in my life, I would soon become a genuine homeowner.

Tyler found Marcus in the tent next to the Dunk-A-Clown venue where volunteers could change out of their wet costumes and back into their street clothes. They were alone.

"I'm telling you. I think he knows something," Tyler declared with conviction.

"What exactly did he say that gave you that impression?" Marcus used a towel to dry his hair.

"It was more the way he said it. He kept asking about Jerry and if there was something bothering him—something on his conscience. I'm certain he suspects us."

"Don't be paranoid." Marcus pulled on his pants and then put on a clean striped shirt with an open collar. He folded the wet clown suit in a bundle as best he could and then wrapped it in a towel. He would drop it off at the hospital laundry to be cleaned, then the maintenance staff would store the outfit and the Dunk-A-Clown venue for next year. "Besides, suspicions aren't evidence."

Tyler paused and looked at Marcus. There was apprehension in his eyes. "What if he's looking for the stuff Jerry was holding onto, same as we are? What if he finds it first?"

"That would be a problem."

"You're damn right it would be a problem. We need to do something to make sure it doesn't happen."

Marcus finished dressing and turned around. He looked straight at Tyler. "What are you suggesting? No, I don't want to know. Whatever it is, you need to back off. I'm supposed to meet the captain this afternoon to pick up the next batch of virus. I'll tell him what you told me. We'll let them deal with it. In the meantime, you need to chill."

"What? I'm just supposed to sit on my hands? If someone finds out what we've done…"

"I'm telling you that isn't going to happen. Just be sure that when I give you this latest sample, you're ready to do your part. This next patient and one more and then we're done. Just don't screw it up, and we'll be home free."

Tyler seemed unconvinced. "I hope The Angel knows what he's about and this will all be worth it."

"One more thing," Marcus cautioned. "Stay away from Blake. In the hospital, have as little to do with him as possible. Outside the hospital, avoid him completely."

"Fine, but I'm telling you he knows."

"All right. Here's what we'll do. I'll tell the captain we need two weeks to let things quiet down. In the meantime, we will wait and watch. If nothing has changed in two weeks, then we will go ahead. Agreed?"

Reluctantly, Tyler nodded. "Agreed."

# AN ACT OF MALICE

The first Sunday in November, in the middle of the afternoon, I had just finished rounding on one of Adam's patients on the medical ward, a middle-aged woman with COPD—chronic obstructive pulmonary disease, also known as emphysema. A heavy smoker for most of her life, she was slowly dying from end-stage lung failure. Other than keeping her as comfortable as possible, there was nothing we could do to help. Her plight made me want to scream and throw things or pound my fist against the wall.

My anger must have been evident because Sam Duncan, who was seated at the nursing station, startled when I dropped my tablet computer on the counter. He looked up and said, "Whoa, what got you so riled up?"

"That woman." I pointed toward the room I had just exited. "How can people not know that every time they put a cigarette in their mouth, they are committing slow suicide? She's on high-flow oxygen, her sats are in the mid-80s, and the first thing she asks when I enter the room is 'When can I go outside and smoke?' Unbelievable."

"Tell me about it." He aimed a thumb at a patient's room down the hall. "This guy I'm seeing has an aortic aneurysm. He's going to need a surgical repair, but he's a chronic alcoholic. His liver is shot. I'm not sure he can survive an operation."

I heaved a deep sigh. "Imagine how much lighter our workload would be if people would stop harming themselves. It's not rational. There is nothing glorious about making yourself ill."

"I totally agree." Sam sat back and laced his fingers behind his head. Smiling up at me, he said, "Say, did you hear the results? They tabulated the vote. The nurses have chosen not to unionize."

"That's a good thing, right?"

"I think so," Sam said with an edge of uncertainty. "At least it means that some overpaid union boss can't tell them when to strike and for how long. Now the hospital just has to bargain in good faith and offer them a decent wage."

"Do you think that will happen? I don't. If Marcus Eldridge has his way, the nurses will take a pay cut rather than get a pay raise."

"I suspect you're right," Sam agreed. "Let's hope he's not involved in the negotiations." Sam rocked forward. "I also heard that you closed escrow on a new home. Is that true?"

"It is. I've even moved in already. I am now officially a native of Flintridge."

"Congratulations, and welcome to the community. I guess this means you'll be hanging around a while?"

"That's the plan. It was a big decision, but I think it was the right choice. I guess from this point forward, it will depend on what real estate values do."

"And what Medicare and insurance companies have in store for us. I don't know about your practice, but they have a major impact on what I take home every month. If they keep cutting back, pretty soon I'll have to pay them if I want to keep seeing geriatric patients."

"It's a shame they didn't teach us about this kind of stuff in medical school."

Sam laughed. "If they had, a large portion of the student body probably would have dropped out."

"You have to love this job to do it—that's for sure." I stifled a yawn. "Look, I've had a rough morning. I need a nap. I'm going to see if I can find an empty on-call room and catch a few hours of shut-eye."

"Sleep tight." Sam touched two fingers to his forehead in a farewell salute as I turned away.

Sam was one of the good guys. I liked him a lot, and so did other people. Perhaps that's why he was chief of staff.

Thankfully, one of the on-call rooms was unoccupied. I let the hospital operator know where I would be for the next couple of hours.

After slipping off my shoes, I fell asleep on top of the bed without bothering to climb under the covers.

Tyler Wickham just happened to be strolling down the corridor when he noticed Blake disappear into an on-call room. It took a moment for the significance of what he was seeing to register. Medical professionals, especially physicians with hospital-based practices, often learned to sleep whenever an opportunity would present itself. Aware that their services might be required at any hour day or night, they became adept at sneaking in power naps. How long any given nap might last was entirely unpredictable.

A strange set of emotions overtook Tyler as he contemplated the strategy taking shape inside his skull. He understood that he was being presented with an opening that might never come around again. He also understood that what he was considering entailed great risk. Discovery would ensure his incarceration for an extended period of time.

Tyler made his decision with surprising swiftness. He turned and walked briskly back to the Respiratory Therapy Department. In the equipment storage room, he opened the door to a cabinet that had his name on it. Having his own storage space was one of the perks of being assistant department head. From the second shelf, he took down a metal thermos and a nondescript cardboard box containing a small atomizer. After snagging a pair of disposable gloves and a clean surgical mask, he carried both the thermos and the atomizer to the men's room just down the hall.

In the restroom, Tyler entered the farthest stall from the door and set the latch. He deposited the thermos and the box containing the atomizer on the toilet's tank. He then put on the gloves and the mask.

Taking the thermos, he unscrewed its lid and removed a long slender metal cylinder with a screw-on cap, which he slipped into his pants pocket before removing the atomizer from its packaging. The thermos with its lid, he set back down on the toilet's tank. After unscrewing the atomizer's reservoir, he set the top part of the atomizer down on the toilet's lid. However, when he placed the reservoir on the toilet's lid, it began to slide off. He caught it just in time. The glass reservoir would have shattered against the tile floor. With greater caution, he tried again. This time, the reservoir stayed where he put it.

Tyler retrieved the cylinder from his pants pocket. Gently he unscrewed the cylinder's cap which he placed on the toilet's lid. Then with great care, he extracted a glass test tube from the cylinder. The test tube was half-full of amber liquid. The empty cylinder he set down beside its cap.

Slowly and with deliberate attentiveness, Tyler pulled the stopper from the test tube. Holding the stopper in his left hand and the test tube in his right hand, he squatted down and very, very carefully poured approximately two milliliters of amber liquid from the test tube into the atomizer's reservoir. After replacing the stopper in the test tube and returning the test tube to its metal cylinder, he tightly screwed on the cylinder's cap. He then slid the cylinder back into the thermos and screwed on its cap as well.

Next, with equally deliberate caution, he attached the reservoir to the atomizer's top. The reassembled atomizer he returned to its cardboard box. After pulling off the gloves and the mask, he flushed them down the toilet. He then washed his hands at the sink before carrying the thermos and the cardboard box with the loaded atomizer inside back to the Respiratory Therapy Department.

The thermos and the empty cardboard box he returned to the cabinet shelf. The atomizer with the amber liquid inside, he carried with him as he made his way back to the on-call room where Blake was sleeping.

Holding the atomizer in his hand like a weapon, Tyler walked slowly down the corridor toward the room Blake had entered. Along the way, he confirmed that no one else was around. The on-call rooms were in a part of the hospital where there was very little foot traffic. Having encountered no one, he stopped and put his ear to the door. He thought he heard the sound of breathing, but he wasn't sure.

Guarding the atomizer in his hand, he reached for the doorknob with his opposite hand. As he did so, Tyler felt a sense of panic arise within him. He very nearly turned and fled back in the direction from which he had come. *Courage,* he counseled himself. *This must be done. It will solve two problems. It will rid us of a serious threat to our operation, and it will give the captain more of the data he needs.*

Tyler held his breath as he opened the door very slowly, millimeters at a time. When he again paused to listen, he heard the sound of rhythmic breathing. Exhaling slowly, he opened the door just enough to slip inside. Rather than close the door completely, he left it partially ajar so that he could exit in a hurry.

The room was dark except for the faint glow that seeped in from the corridor. Tyler paused to allow his eyes to grow accustomed to the darkness. A peculiar human scent hung in the air, like in the boys' locker room when he had played high school football.

With the atomizer held in front of him, Tyler crept to the bedside. In the dim light, he confirmed that it was Doctor Blake Sterling who was asleep in the bed. He advanced the atomizer until its tip hovered mere inches in front of Blake's face.

Steeling himself, Tyler drew in a deep breath and held it. He squeezed the atomizer bulb twice, expelling a faint mist from the tip. Then for good measure, he squeezed once more and hastily turned and tiptoed out of the room. He did not release his breath until the door was securely shut behind him.

Carrying the atomizer carefully so as not to touch the tip or the bulb, he returned to the Respiratory Therapy Department. There he wrapped the atomizer in a hand towel and double bagged it. At the housekeeping station, he would stuff his bundle into a bag of trash, waiting to be incinerated.

As Tyler was about to leave the department, he realized that in his haste, he had forgotten to suit up. He should have put on a paper gown, face mask, shoe covers, and gloves. He immediately shed his lab coat and tossed it into a laundry bag. At the deep sink in a corner of the department, he began vigorously scrubbing his face and hands, knowing that if he had come in contact with the virus, it was already too late.

After drying his hands and face, Tyler studied his reflection in a glass-fronted cabinet. Was he about to display symptoms of a bocavirus infection? Was his life now in jeopardy? Only time would tell.

When I awoke from my nap, I immediately sensed that I was in trouble. My body felt stiff and lethargic, and I was conscious of my breathing, as if I had to worry about taking each breath. I felt warm, but when I touched my forehead, my skin was cool and clammy. I tried sitting up. The act seemed to require twice as much effort as usual, and when I managed to sit on the edge of the bed, a worrisome lightheadedness made me wobbly.

As best I could, I steadied myself and tried to reason out what was happening. I remembered entering the on-call room and falling asleep on top of the bed. None of the symptoms I was now experiencing had been present at that time. Whatever was wrong, it was progressing rapidly.

My first thought was that I had been food poisoned. I remembered eating a light lunch in the cafeteria at around noon. I checked my watch. It was now a quarter past four. Although plausible, the food poisoning scenario seemed unlikely. The timing was right, but that theory failed to explain my heaviness of breathing.

A word came into my mind that sent a shiver racing through me: bocavirus. I was experiencing the same symptoms that Jerry and Mr. Wright had described in the early stages of their infections. Had I somehow contracted the virus? *How could it have occurred?* I wondered, dumbfounded. Although implausible, the possibility seemed the only reasonable explanation I could imagine. Then another even more ominous thought struck me. *Had I unwittingly come in contact with a carrier?* Or even more worrisome, *Had someone infected me deliberately? Could I be the victim of malicious intent?* The idea seemed so preposterous that I put it out of my mind. At that moment, I had more urgent concerns with which to contend. I needed help, and I needed it now.

My first instinct was to get to the Emergency Department. Had I been more clearheaded, I might have chosen to call the operator and summon assistance to the on-call room. Instead, I set out on my own.

When I bent down to tie my shoes, The room began spinning around me. It made me nauseated, and when I stood up, I nearly blacked out. In halting steps, I crossed to the door and stumbled into the corridor. Even such a little bit of exertion took my breath away. Bracing myself with an arm against the walls as I went, I slowly made my way to the Emergency Department. Each step was a struggle, and at times, I was forced to stop and rest. My respirations were labored—as if I was underwater breathing through a straw. I simply could not take in enough air. By the time I reached my destination, my heart was pounding in my chest, and my muscles were weak. I wasn't sure that my legs would continue to support me.

With a shaky hand, I keyed in the code to open the electronic lock and then staggered into the department. I nearly made it to the nurses' station before collapsing on the floor. The nurse who saw me go down rushed over to help. She and other members of the ED staff soon had me on a gurney and were wheeling me into an exam room. In virtually no time at all, I was on supplemental oxygen. An infusion of 5 percent dextrose with half normal saline was dripping into a vein. My shirt off, my vital signs were recorded, and the leads of a cardiac monitor were pasted to my chest.

The oxygen helped a little, but each breath was becoming progressively more difficult.

When Kyle Larson—the emergency medicine physician covering the department that day—bent over to listen to my chest with his stethoscope, I gripped his arm. In a voice barely above a whisper, I pleaded, "Call Adam Richards. Let him know I have the virus and I want him to be my admitting physician. He'll understand. Tell him to give me high-dose steroids. He'll argue against it, but tell him I insist that he give it a try. Look, I'm soon going to need to be intubated. You might as well set up for it now." With that, I lay my head back and drifted off for a while.

Prescribing steroids to treat a viral pneumonia seemed counterintuitive, even dangerous. The current thinking was that because steroids would suppress the host's immune system, the virus would be allowed to replicate unopposed. In other words, steroids would make the pneumonia worse and were, therefore, contraindicated. However, I had been reading a discussion in the literature that suggested that it was the immune system itself that caused much of the damage to the lungs and that steroids might mitigate the inflammatory component of a viral infection. It was a high-risk strategy. Of that, I was well aware, but hopefully Adam would be willing to take a chance.

The rest of my time in the Emergency Department passed as a blur. I remember being positioned for a portable chest x-ray. I remember Adam slipping an endotracheal tube into my windpipe—a memory I would have forsaken if I could. I remember watching overhead lights glide by as they wheeled me from the ED to the ICU, and finally, I remember Madison peering down at me, a look of grave concern furrowing her brow.

In the ICU, time passes differently than it does in the real world. Rather than its normal ebb and flow, time stutters by in chunks. In the unit, there is little to distinguish night from day. The lighting, the ambient noise levels, and the bustle of activity remain pretty much the same day and night. In critical care units, patients are periodically interrupted for various reasons—a vital sign check, medications to be administered, a meal, a bath, a test to be performed, a treatment to be given, or a physician's interrogation to be endured. The net result is there are no extended periods when a patient can simply rest. Cumulatively, such a schedule can lead to sleep deprivation, which in turn can cause depression and a low-grade cognitive impairment— sometimes referred to as Sundowner syndrome because affected patients tend to become a tad goofy in the evenings.

Admittedly, lack of sleep wasn't my problem. My problem was precisely the opposite, too much sleep. In fact, for the first forty-eight hours, I was completely unresponsive to external stimuli, a polite way of saying I was in a coma. I have no memories from this period of time.

On the third day, my condition began to improve. That is to say I would now react when challenged either verbally or with physical stimulation. Of the next few days, I have several truncated memories.

Most involve Madison hovering over me, tending to my medical needs. As I began to improve, the worried look on her face began to fade as well. I also remember Adam monitoring my progress and supervising the therapies I was receiving. Only later, when I was more alert, did I appreciate the fact that he was singlehandedly covering his practice and mine, as I had done after Jerry had died. No wonder he was looking so haggard.

It was during this time frame that something extraordinary happened. I began to experience the practice of medicine from a patient's point of view. Until then, I had assumed I was doing my job if a patient's condition improved as the result of the therapies I prescribed. It never occurred to me that I also had an obligation to meet their psychological needs—to ease the burden of worry they carried and dispel the uncertainties that clouded their future. I'd never given serious thought to my duty to offer words of encouragement or give reassurances that there was hope for what lay ahead. The bottom line was I was learning to care about patients as people—to recognize their afflictions as multidimensional rather than purely physiological.

Perhaps this is another way of saying I was becoming more human.

On Thursday, the fifth day after my admission, I was transferred to the medical ward to continue my recovery. From a pulmonary standpoint, I was still significantly impaired, but I was alive, and I was slowly getting better. My chest was tight, and it was difficult to draw in a deep breath. My exertional capacity was severely limited. I fatigued easily, and I often had to stop and rest when active. On the other hand, I could talk in full sentences without gasping for air, and I could sleep lying flat in bed without having to elevate my head and shoulders.

Although Madison was no longer my primary nurse, she managed to visit me several times a day, and she made sure the nurses on the medical ward were paying me the attention she felt I deserved. The way she mothered me was almost embarrassing, but I sincerely appreciated her concern.

Late in the afternoon on the day I was transferred to the medical ward, Heather Oliver stopped by to see me. "Are you decent?" she said, poking her head into my room.

"My modesty is protected, if that's what you mean," I wheezed, my throat still sore from having been intubated.

Heather came partway into the room. "You seem better. How do you feel?"

"Like my get up and go got up and went." I thought I detected an edge of anxiety in Heather's normally cheerful demeanor. "What's wrong?" I said with a sense of foreboding.

Heather moved closer to stand beside my bed. "I've been looking into your activities for the week before you showed up in the Emergency Department. I've interviewed the patients you treated. I've spoken with members of the medical staff with whom you came in contact. I've tried to retrace your steps as best I could, and I have nothing to report. For the life of me, I cannot figure out how you came by your infection."

I pressed the button to raise the head of my bed so I could sit up straighter. "I've also come to a dead end. I've been racking my brain, trying to think of someone I might have contacted, someone showing signs of a viral infection, or maybe there is a carrier out there, someone shedding the virus but asymptomatic."

Heather shook her head. "If that were the case, wouldn't we expect more infected patients to start turning up?"

"That would depend upon how socially connected the carrier might be?"

"You mean we need to be looking for a Typhoid Mary type of hermit? Hey, at this point, I'm willing to consider anything."

"Yeah. You're right. It's a silly idea. Forget I said anything."

Heather's dimples deepened as she smiled. "I spoke with Doctor Richards. He thinks that when you recover, there will be very little residual scarring in the lungs. He admitted that he never would have prescribed steroids if you hadn't suggested the idea. In retrospect, it makes perfect sense. By limiting the body's inflammatory response to the virus, the steroids protect the lungs from immune mediated injury. That was a good call on your part."

I nodded an acknowledgment and then frowned at Heather. "How is Adam? Is he holding up okay? When he stops in to see how I'm progressing, he's always wearing his white coat and maintaining an air of professionalism. When I ask, he tells me he's fine. Is he?"

"He seems to be coping well. He did mention that he spoke with Doctor Spalding, who has agreed to return as a locum tenens. He'll be taking call this coming weekend."

"Oh, good. I'm so glad to hear that." A tickle in the back of my throat caused a paroxysm of coughing. When it ended, I closed my eyes and lay my head back on the pillow, suddenly fatigued. Apparently my recovery still had a ways to go.

"Look," Heather said. "I'm going to split. You need your rest. I just wanted to stop by and tell you how things stand. I wish there was more to report, but..." She shrugged.

Madison appeared in the corridor outside my door as Heather was leaving. The two women stood talking for a moment, then Heather departed, and Madison came in to see me.

"I brought you something." Madison reached into the pocket of her scrubs and drew out a package that looked like a bag of candy. She handed it to me.

I read the label. "Eucalyptus cough drops. Great. I can sure use these." I opened the bag and put a cough drop in my mouth.

Madison said, "I checked with Doctor Richards. He said it would be okay for me to give these to you."

"Thank you," I said with sincerity. "In fact, it would appear that I owe you a great deal of thanks. I've been hearing how devoted you were during those first few days when I was in a coma. Is it true you took extra shifts just so you could take care of me?"

"I wanted to make sure you got the best possible nursing care."

"Is that why you've been supervising the nurses on this floor as well?"

"Just making sure they're doing their jobs."

"Why would you go to all that trouble?"

Madison gave me an odd look that declared, "You figure it out."

Humbled, I said, "When I get out of here, hopefully I'll find a way to pay you back."

"There's no need," Madison said dismissively. "Just glad to be of help."

"No, I mean I want to. I want to show you how much I care for you as well."

Madison blushed. "We'll talk about it when you're stronger. For now, you need to rest." She bent down and kissed me on the cheek—a clear violation of respiratory isolation protocols. "Get well soon," she called back as she slipped out of the room.

"Thanks again for the cough drops," I called after her as her footsteps trailed down the hall.

The second Sunday in November, I was discharged from the hospital. I wasn't completely recovered, but I was well enough that I could continue my convalescence at home. Although Fred Spalding was taking weekend call, Adam made a special trip to the hospital to make sure I was fit enough to be turned loose and to deliver my discharge instructions in person. With sincere gratitude, I thanked him for the care I had received during my hospitalization and especially for having honored my request that I be treated with steroids. I was strongly inclined to believe that the drug had most likely saved my life.

"I truly appreciate that you were willing to take a risk," I said to Adam as he stood beside my wheelchair. Hospital policy was that all patients being discharged were to be transported in a wheelchair rather than being allowed to walk out on their own. It was a liability issue. The hospital was afraid of being sued if someone were to trip and fall or suddenly black out. I had protested that I was strong enough not to need the wheelchair, but neither Adam nor Madison had been willing to listen.

Adam laid a hand on my shoulder. "When I thought about giving you steroids, it seemed a reasonable treatment option. I'm very glad you suggested it. You know, it's always refreshing when a patient recovers from their illness, but in this case, it's especially gratifying. Don't hesitate to call me if there is a problem."

"Don't worry, I will, but I doubt it will be necessary. I'm feeling stronger every day."

Adam looked at Madison, who was about to wheel me out of the room. "Take good care of him. Make sure he takes it easy for a while." He shifted his attention back to me. "Remember, you're not as strong as you think you are."

"Don't worry, Doctor Richards," Madison said as she wheeled me toward the door. "We'll see that he behaves."

As we emerged through the hospital's front entrance, I said to Madison, "I can drive myself."

"Nonsense. You're not ready yet."

"My car is still in the parking lot. If I ride with you, I'll be stuck at home without transportation."

"Let's see how you do tonight. If you are well enough tomorrow, maybe I will bring you back, and you can pick up your car then."

By the time I had finished transferring into the passenger seat of Madison's Dodge Charger, I knew she was probably right. Even such a small amount of exertion had started me breathing hard. I felt weak as a kitten. My rehabilitation would be slow-going, but at least I was alive.

"Welcome home," Madison said as she parked in the driveway of the home I had owned for precisely eighteen days. Of those eighteen days, I had actually only lived in the house for eleven days; the other seven days I had spent in the hospital. Still, as I shuffled up the walkway, leaning on Madison for support, it felt like a genuine homecoming.

Madison used the key I had given her to unlock the front door. She helped me cross the threshold and then guided me into the living room. What few possessions I owned had already been brought over from the apartment I had rented upon joining Pulmonary Associates. Most of my things were still in cardboard boxes.

Supporting my arm at the elbow, Madison steadied me as I sank down in the recliner in the corner. It was one of only a handful of items of furniture I had acquired after closing escrow—a bed, a chest of drawers, a couch, a microwave, a small dining room table with four chairs, a rolltop desk, and a winged armchair. With so few pieces of furniture, the house still looked empty. Eventually, I would have to find the time to do some proper shopping.

Madison stood with her hands on her hips. She looked around, an expression of uncertainty on her face. "Are you sure you're going to be okay here alone?"

"I'll be fine," I said with more bravado than I felt. "It may look chaotic, but there is a method to the clutter. The essentials have already been unpacked. Anything else I might need, I'll know where to look."

"Well, if you're sure..." Madison seemed dubious, then she brightened a bit. "I went grocery shopping this morning. Your larder is reasonably well stocked. There are TV dinners in the freezer and the ingredients of easy-to-prepare meals in the fridge. If there is something you need that you don't have, call me, and I will bring it over the next time I come."

I looked at Madison with a deep sense of appreciation. "I can't begin to tell you how grateful I am for all you've done for me. I wish there were better words to convey how I feel. All I can say is thank you."

"It was a privilege," Madison replied. "I am ever so grateful that you are improving. I just wish we knew how you came by your infection."

"Me too," I admitted.

Madison frowned. "The last time I spoke with Heather, we again went over the possibilities, all of which, for the most part, have been ruled out. The only scenario we couldn't eliminate is that you were deliberately targeted as an act of malice. Why someone would seek to harm you like that was beyond us. Do you know of any enemies that harbor that much ill will?"

"None. I've also considered the possibility that my exposure was intentional, but remember I wasn't the only one infected, nor was I the first. If someone was out to do me harm, why infect the others? It makes no sense. What could possibly be their motive?"

"Maybe it wasn't you they were after. Maybe the attacks were random."

"That would be even more bizarre."

"You're right. It would seem we're back to square one. Look, I'm going to go. Let me give you your key back—"

"You keep it. You're welcome to drop by anytime."

"Are you sure?"

"I am."

When Madison looked at me, I saw the sympathy in her eyes. She said, "May I pray with you before I go?"

"Most certainly."

Madison moved closer and took hold of both my hands. We both closed our eyes. "Dear Lord…Father…Abba. Hallowed be Your name. Thank You for watching over Blake and protecting him during his recent illness. We pray that You will continue to strengthen his body and restore him to excellent health. Father, we also pray for wisdom and discernment. Help us determine where this virus came from so that we may prevent others from being infected. These blessings we ask in the name of our Savior, Jesus Christ. Amen."

"Amen," I added with a nod of agreement. I gave Madison's hand a gentle squeeze before releasing it. I then realized that I would need to remember to add my own name to the prayer notebook.

I looked at Madison as she prepared to leave. "When will I see you again?"

"Probably tomorrow after work. I'm scheduled for a short shift. I can stop by and fix you dinner…if you'd like."

"That would be splendid. I will look forward to it."

After Madison had gone, I leaned back in the recliner and put my feet up. I felt exhausted, but I was glad to be in my own home. *Tomorrow*, I promised myself. *I'll get up and start exercising. For now, maybe I'll just rest a bit.* I picked up the lap blanket lying on the floor beside the recliner and covered my feet and legs before drifting off to sleep. The last thought that crossed my mind before slumber overtook me was *If someone was out to do me harm, who would it be? Who has been openly hostile toward me?*

Two faces came to mind: Marcus Eldridge and Tyler Wickham. *Why them?* I wondered. *What possible reason could they have?* It was a question for which I had no answer.

Two days later, I tried going back to work. I probably should have known that I wasn't ready. The spirit was willing, but the flesh needed more time to recover. Even so, it was good to visit with the office staff and learn the status of several of my more severely afflicted patients. I even managed to make a few phone calls to inquire as to how they were progressing and wish them well. The heightened levels of empathy that had emerged after my coma seem to be holding. Beyond my desire to practice superior medicine, I discovered that I actually cared about my patients' well-being. It was a unique feeling, and I sincerely hoped it would last.

While touching base with Lois Carlton, our office manager, I learned of another change implemented during my absence. Fred Spalding had agreed to treat office patients in addition to taking call on alternate weekends at the hospital. In essence, he was functioning as the group's newest partner, though he was still a locum tenens. When I asked him how he felt about his expanded role, he seemed quite pleased to have the opportunity. I knew Adam was grateful to have his help, and I told him as much. What I didn't mention, because I wasn't 100 percent certain as to where things stood, was what Fred's role would be after I returned to work full-time. That was a topic Adam and I would have to sort out later.

There was one issue that bothered me during my visit. Several times, I was asked about my hospitalization. In general, the staff wanted to know what had occurred—the reasons for my admission. I had been able to explain what had happened but not the how or the why of it. Those essential details were still a mystery—a mystery I was absolutely committed to solve.

Captain Summers had already arrived by the time Marcus entered the Scrubbed Clean Laundromat, a half-full laundry bag in one hand.

The thought of washing his dirty clothes in a machine used by the public at large made Marcus's skin crawl, but his instructions had been explicit. Feeding in a stack of quarters, he started his load of wash and then sat down at the far end of a line of chairs backed up against the rear wall.

Captain Summers stood up, checked his own wash, and then sat down next to Marcus. "How dare you infect a member of the medical staff without my permission," Captain Summers hissed. "Whose bright idea was that anyway?"

"It was Tyler's," Marcus protested softly, relieved that he wasn't required to take responsibility for that decision. "He acted on his own volition."

"Idiot," Captain Summers spat like it was a curse. "I'll deal with him later."

"But sir," Marcus protested. "He did get Doctor Sterling off our backs for a while, and we have the data we need for patient number six." Marcus reached into his nearly empty laundry bag and took out a thick manila envelope which he handed to Captain Summers.

In return, Captain Summers handed Marcus a plainly wrapped cigar-box-shaped container and his own manila envelope, which was substantially thinner.

"Your instructions are in there," Captain Summers said, indicating the envelope. "There is one thing I want to emphasize. This time, you are to administer a dose of antiviral medication before the subject is infected. A bottle of pills is included with the specimen."

"How am I supposed to do that?" Marcus protested with alarm. "We no longer have a physician who can prescribe medications."

Captain Summers sighed. "As I think I have pointed out before, you are the chief administrative officer. Make it happen. How you get it done is up to you. Just do it."

"Fine," Marcus said with a grunt of resignation. "But after this run, I'm done with this whole business. I will have completed my side of the bargain, and I'm out. Is that clear?"

"Agreed."

The two men sat side by side and ignored each other while waiting for their washing machines to signal that the rinse cycles were completed. Neither man spoke again.

When Marcus's machine chimed that it had finished, he stood up and began stuffing wet clothes into his laundry bag. He would wash them again when he got home. Hefting the laundry bag in one hand and carrying the package and folder under his other arm, he strode from the laundromat without looking back.

# NO CHANCE AT ALL

The call from the Emergency Department rang through to my house at 9:57 p.m. I had just fallen into bed and was almost asleep. When I answered the phone, the nurse who had placed the call said, "Doctor Sterling, please hold for Doctor Ramsey." Then the line fell silent.

While I waited for the hospitalist to pick up the phone, I fought to come fully awake. I had been back at work for five days, and Adam and I had returned to our regular call rotation, meaning it was supposed to be my night off.

Although I had improved substantially in the sixteen days since developing pneumonia, some of the effects of the bocavirus infection lingered. I fatigued easily, and strenuous activities left me short of breath. Also, deep breaths often triggered paroxysms of a dry, hacking cough.

"Hello, Blake?" Doctor Ramsey said when he picked up the phone.

"Hey, Peter, what's up?"

"I'm admitting a patient I need you to see."

"I appreciate the referral, but the consult should go to Adam. He's on call tonight."

"I spoke with your partner. He told me to call you. Apparently he's tied up with an asthmatic on the pediatric ward. From the sound of it, the kid's not doing well. Look, I need somebody now. I think this woman has the same virus you had, and I'm worried because she's rapidly moving in the wrong direction. Can you help me out here?"

"Sure. I'll be in as soon as I can, but tell me, how confident are you that she has a bocavirus pneumonia?"

"Fairly confident. She fits the criteria you presented in your CME lecture."

A small surge of gratification swept through me. At least one person had been paying attention.

Normally, I'm guided by the precept that first you examine the patient and then order whatever tests may be necessary to establish the diagnosis. Finally, you prescribe the appropriate therapy. Treating a patient without first seeing them is considered malpractice by some. On the other hand, I knew from first-hand experience that if the patient did have a bocavirus pneumonia, any delay in initiating treatment might have serious, perhaps fatal, consequences.

Although it made me uncomfortable to do so, I suggested, "How would you feel about hitting her with a bolus of steroids?"

I expected Peter to agree wholeheartedly, having paid attention during my lecture, but to my surprise, he objected. "I don't think we should do that."

"Why not? I'm living proof that they're effective."

"Yes, you are, but you didn't have a wound infection. Two days ago, this woman was camping at Potholes State Park. She stepped on a broken bottle but didn't do anything about it at the time. Now she's developing what looks like gangrene. I'm afraid if we suppress her immune system, she could lose her foot...or worse."

"Damn! That does complicate things. I'll be in as soon as I can."

"I'll see you when you get here." Peter ended the call.

The solution to this conundrum would be to let the patient decide: save the lungs and maybe lose the foot or save the foot and maybe lose her life. It should be a straightforward choice, but sometimes patients can surprise you when it comes to the risks they are willing to take.

I rushed through getting dressed and was out the door in near record time.

Very early the next morning, I was still at the hospital. Although dead tired, I had shied away from bedding down in one of the on-call rooms, considering what had happened the last time. Instead, I had catnapped by resting my head on the work counter at the nurses' station.

My newest patient, Mrs. Hazel Marsh, was faring poorly. There was evidence that her wound infection had penetrated the plantar fascia, the thick, fibrous band on the bottom of the foot that stretches like a bowstring on a bow between the toes and the heel. Had that been her only problem, it would have been difficult enough to treat. Combined with an aggressive viral pneumonia, she would be fortunate to survive.

When I had presented the option of adding steroids to her regimen, Mrs. Marsh had refused. As a single mom with four young children, she had decided she could not risk losing her foot. I did not agree with her decision, but I could sympathize with her point of view.

Other than steroids, I had prescribed every therapy that I thought might make a difference. She was intubated and on a ventilator. I had added antivirals even though they had failed to help the other bocavirus patients. I had prescribed bronchodilators to open the airways. I had also ordered a sedative to help her relax and, thereby, reduce her work of breathing. Even so, we were steadily losing ground.

Despite Mrs. Marsh's refusal, as her condition deteriorated, I had considered using steroids but had decided against adding them to her regimen. Prescribing them would have been both unethical and illegal—treating people without their permission is assault. Besides, it was probably too late for them to have much benefit. The inflammatory damage was already done.

Having exhausted other options, it seemed there was only one thing left to do—pray. When I looked around, it occurred to me that I could recruit the nurses and invite their participation. To my dismay, when I passed the word, less than half the nurses responded. Had Madison been on duty, she probably would have orchestrated a much more enthusiastic response. Perhaps I should've waited for her to start her shift.

In any event, those of us who were willing gathered at the nursing station. Forming a circle, we joined hands, and I began, "Heavenly

Father, we pray for Your healing grace this morning. Be with Mrs. Marsh and all the other patients in this unit who so desperately need healing. We pray for mercy, Father. Strengthen these patients. Watch over them. Mend their bodies, and cure their afflictions. Comfort them and bring them peace and bless us, Father, that we may deliver the best possible medical care. All these things we ask in the name of Your son, Jesus, our Savior. Amen."

A chorus of quiet amens arose as the circle broke up. Just then, the alarm on Mrs. Marsh's cardiac monitor began chirping, signaling that she was in full cardiac arrest. Her resuscitation lasted almost an hour and was ultimately unsuccessful. She was pronounced dead at 6:43 a.m. In truth, she never had any chance at all.

It then fell to me to inform her sister that her sibling had passed on. This was hard enough, but when I had to watch the sister try to explain to Mrs. Marsh's four small children that their mother was gone, I lost it. For a time, it seemed the tears would never stop flowing.

In the corridor outside the unit, Marcus caught up with Tyler, who was just leaving, having responded to the code blue summons. He fell in stride beside him.

"I gather she didn't make it?" Marcus said in a muted but accusatory tone of voice.

Tyler did not react.

"You were supposed to wait." Marcus snarled under his breath. "My instructions were to give her the medication before you infected her. Now what are we going to tell the captain?"

"We're not going to tell him anything," Tyler replied nonchalantly. "He doesn't need to know about this. We will find somebody else."

Marcus halted in the middle of the corridor and glowered at Tyler. "Are you out of your mind? You can't just go around killing people." Clearly Marcus was having trouble controlling his rage. "Enough of this. I'm done."

"You can't quit. We have a job to finish."

"Oh yeah? Watch me." Marcus spun on his heel and stalked off.

Blake, who had just emerged from the unit, just happened to catch the last part of this exchange. *Those two are up to something,* he thought, not for the first time. *I can feel it. I need to speak with Tyler—find out what he's got going on.*

Tyler flushed when he noticed Blake watching him. He too turned and scurried off.

Fifteen minutes later, I entered the Respiratory Therapy Department, expecting to find Tyler there, but the department was vacant. I started to sit down to wait but then decided to have a look around. As I was poking about in the equipment room where the machines were kept, I noticed Tyler's name on a storage cabinet. I hadn't paid it any heed when I had gone through the department seeking Jerry's book. Curious, I opened the unlocked cabinet door and peeked inside. The shelves were bare except for a beat-up thermos and a pill bottle with an encrypted label.

*That's totally strange,* I thought. *Why would anyone encrypt the instructions for pills they are supposed to take?*

I was about to open the pill bottle when the sound of someone entering the department filtered in from the front room. I hastily shoved the pill bottle into my pants pocket and quietly closed the cabinet door. I turned away and stood as if inspecting the far wall just as Tyler entered the storage room.

"What do you want?" Tyler said as if issuing a challenge.

I turned to face him. "To speak with you."

Tyler scowled. "Oh yeah? Why?"

"I see you and Marcus together. You're always skulking about. I know you're up to something. I want to know what's going on."

"I think your pneumonia has made you paranoid," Tyler quipped. "Nothing is going on. Mr. Eldridge is my boss. He likes to keep abreast of what's happening in his hospital, so I keep him informed. Now go away, and let me do my job."

I was about to pose another question when it occurred to me that Tyler wasn't about to divulge any useful information. In confronting him, what had I expected would happen? Perhaps Mrs. Marsh's death had rattled me, causing me to act precipitously and without thinking. Unable to conceive of a way to exit gracefully, I declared, "Fine. Be that way. Just be aware, I'll be watching you."

As I left the department, I shoved my hand into my pants pocket to muffle the sound of the pills rattling around in the plastic bottle. My next stop was the hospital pharmacy where I turned the bottle of pills in and requested that they be analyzed. I explicitly asked that the results be released to me and to me alone. The pharmacy tech assured me that that would not be a problem. Pharmacy rules specified that all requests to confirm the identity and dispensing of medications were to be kept confidential.

Madison sat on the corner of my couch, her legs drawn up and tucked beneath her. She had on a pair of denim jeans and a flannel shirt. They were warmer than the scrubs she usually wore. It was late November, and the winds were turning chilly. Winter would not be far off. Snow was expected to begin falling at any time.

Rather than settle into the recliner in the corner, I sat in the winged armchair facing Madison. It had been a brutal day, and my emotions were still frazzled. I was having a hard time letting go of Hazel Marsh's death. I kept seeing the faces of her children as their aunt tried to explain what had happened to their mother. Not only was I distressed by the children's plight, I was growing increasingly angry as we reviewed what we knew about the bocavirus patients I had treated.

In particular, I was seeking threads of commonality, trying to discern patterns in their medical histories that might offer a clue as to how they had acquired their infections.

Madison gave me a look of encouragement and suggested, "Perhaps you should simply state the things they shared in common." She sipped her coffee from the mug she balanced on the arm of the couch. I made a mental note that perhaps an end table should be one of my next furniture purchases.

For dinner, I had served a small salad and a premade lasagna. Together with the garlic bread Madison had prepared, it had proven to be a decent meal—not elegant but filling.

"Well, let's see," I said. "They were all middle-aged adults." I fell silent as I tried to think of other points of commonality. "I can tell you lots of ways they were different. So far, we know of seven patients who had the virus. Three were women. Five were men. Five were married, one was widowed, and one divorced. They all had different occupations. They traveled in different social circles. They shopped in different stores. Six had children. One had none. They were of various ethnicities. Three attended church on a regular basis. The others did not. Should I go on?"

"Try to focus on how they were the same. There has to be something they shared in common. Think. What ties them together?"

"Believe me, over the last four-and-a-half months, I've thought about little else."

"Try harder. Even name things that might seem blatantly obvious."

I leaned forward and rested my elbows on my knees. "They all breathe air. They all eat food. They all—"

"Maybe not that obvious."

"Okay. They were all hospitalized at the Flintridge Medical Center. They were all admitted through the Emergency Department."

"Good. Go on."

"Except for Jerry and myself. When admitted, they all had a secondary medical problem, although none of their problems were the same."

"Keep going."

I sat up straight and looked at Madison. "None of the patients came to the hospital because they had pneumonia. They all developed their respiratory symptoms after they arrived." I stood up and began pacing the floor. "I've been focused on the notion that we were dealing with a community-acquired infection. What if it wasn't community acquired? What if it was hospital acquired?"

Madison nodded. "I see what you're saying. You mean like something in the Emergency Department."

"Exactly."

"But if it is something in the Emergency Department, how come we aren't seeing more infections? A hundred or more people, both patients and hospital employees, pass through the ED every day."

"That's true, but what if it's not something? What if it's someone?"

"You mean like a carrier? If that were the case, wouldn't you expect the nurses and MDs, people most likely to come in contact with a carrier, to be infected?"

"That is a consideration. Still, we we're looking for points of commonality, and one of those points is that each of the patients first began showing signs of pneumonia after arriving in the Emergency Department."

"Except for you and Doctor Tucker."

"Yes, but we were both in the hospital when we got sick."

I stopped pacing and looked directly at Madison. "If someone in the hospital is the source of the infection, and if other employees are not getting infected by being around that person, as we might expect, maybe it's because that person isn't spreading the virus. Maybe it's because that person is distributing the virus."

"You mean on purpose?"

"It would fit the pattern we're seeing."

Madison scoffed. "We've been over this. Are you now suggesting that someone is intentionally infecting people with a lethal virus?"

"As Sherlock once said, if you eliminate the impossible, whatever is left, no matter how improbable, it must be the truth."

"Who would do such a thing? And why? What could they possibly stand to gain?"

"Right. We don't have a motive."

Madison gestured for emphasis. "Nor do we have means. Remember means, motive, and opportunity. We have no idea how people are getting infected."

"You'd have to assume it's by direct exposure—perhaps handling something contaminated with the virus or by aerosol."

"Assumptions aren't proof of anything,"

"I agree, but so far, the only explanation that fits the facts is that someone is deliberately infecting selected patients being admitted through the Emergency Department.

Madison shook her head. "I find that nearly impossible to believe."

"Maybe that's why we haven't considered the possibility before."

Lines of small wrinkles appeared on Madison's forehead. I had seen the look before. They signaled that she was troubled by what she was hearing. "What are you going to do now?"

"I've been thinking. The key to this whole business is going to be Jerry's book. I remember the look in his eyes when he wrote the note. He knew he was in bad shape and he needed to tell someone, but he couldn't hang on long enough."

"You don't really believe he was involved? Tell me you don't."

"All I know is I need to find that book."

The day after Hazel Marsh's passing, Marcus Eldridge prowled the aisles of a regional department store two blocks from the Flintridge Medical Center. He wasn't shopping, although he did his best to make it appear that he was. Earlier that afternoon, Tyler Wickham had phoned him and had demanded that they meet. Mutually they had agreed that it was no longer wise to be seen together at the hospital. That was why Marcus was poking through hand towels as if trying to decide which color would best compliment his bathroom decor. He startled when he felt a tap on his shoulder.

"You need to be more situationally aware," Tyler chided. "You would know that if you had any military training."

"Playing weekend soldier with your buddies in the militia doesn't count as military training. What's so urgent that you insisted I leave work early?"

"Do you remember when I warned you that Doctor Sterling was getting suspicious and that we would need to do something about him?"

"If my memory serves me correctly, you did something about him. You nearly killed him."

"And I truly wish I had." Tyler used his thumb and index finger to smooth his full mustache, a nervous habit that signaled the stress he was feeling. "Yesterday, after the code, I confronted him in the Respiratory Therapy Department. He challenged me and wanted to know why you and I were working together."

"Did he now? What did you tell him?"

"That you like to stay abreast of what's going on at the hospital, and it was my job to keep you informed."

"That sounds reasonable. How did he respond?"

"He got pissed off, then he left in a huff."

"Did he say anything?"

"He claimed he would be watching us."

"Did he say anything else? Anything specific?"

"No, but that's not the worst of it. Yesterday, when I confronted him, he was standing in the equipment room, trying to look nonchalant. That's where my storage cabinet is located. This morning, when I checked my cabinet, the antiviral pills I had placed there were gone. I think it's almost certain that he took them."

"I presume that this cabinet he got into wasn't locked?"

"No, it wasn't. There's never been a need."

"Until now. Why, for heaven's sake"—Marcus growled harshly—"would you keep the project's antiviral tablets in an unlocked cabinet?"

"I had to put them somewhere. Remember, Jerry is no longer here to deal with them. Normally, I would have given him the pills and the viral sample to hang onto until they could be destroyed, but he went and got himself infected."

"Sterling didn't get the viral sample, did he?" Marcus asked with genuine alarm.

"No, it's safe."

The chief administrator exhaled a sigh of relief. "Thank goodness for that. Your fingerprints are probably all over that vial. You need to be more careful—much more careful."

"What about you?" Tyler demanded. "What are you going to do about this? After all, this sort of problem is exactly the reason you were brought on board. You need to figure out some way to make Sterling and his suspicions go away."

"I'm working on it. I have an idea that should suffice. It will take a few days to set it up, but if it works, the good doctor will no longer be in a position to trouble us."

"What do you have in mind?"

Marcus formed a malign smile. "You're just going to have to wait and see. In the meantime, act as if nothing has happened. Go about your normal routines, and for goodness' sake, don't get into a pissing contest with Doctor Sterling. Just leave him to me."

# SLINGS AND ARROWS

A somber mood pervaded the hospital's conference room as I entered and looked around. That morning, I had received a cryptic text message inviting me to attend a special meeting of the Quality Improvement Committee that very day and to make certain that I arrived no later than 1:00 p.m. The message had failed to explain the reason my attendance was being requested. I had tried calling several people to find out what was going on, but they either didn't know or they wouldn't say. Lacking evidence to the contrary, I concluded that I was probably being summoned to give testimony in a case pending before the committee. *That must be why the QIC Committee is meeting on the last Wednesday of the month rather than the second Thursday.*

Fortunately, my office schedule for that afternoon was relatively light. Only a handful of patients had needed to be rebooked. Because I was unsure how long the proceedings might last, I had freed up the entire rest of my day, though it had troubled me to do so; and since it was Adam's turn to take call, I probably wouldn't be interrupted by a consultation request.

When I stepped into the conference room, I immediately noticed several things that I found worrisome. First, the furniture had been rearranged. A large conference table with its surrounding chairs generally dominated the center of the space. That table had been replaced by a slightly smaller table positioned transversely at the far end of the room. An even smaller table with a single chair faced the head table from five feet away. At the near end of the room, four rows of chairs were lined up facing both tables. Many of the chairs were already occupied, as were the chairs at the head table where the five members of the QIC Committee had assembled, which was the next thing I noticed.

Doctor Sam Duncan occupied the middle seat. As chief of staff, it would be his duty to preside over the committee's meetings. To his left sat Doctor Jose Rodriguez, nephrologist and medical director of the dialysis unit. To José's left sat a petite woman I did not recognize. The name tag on the table in front of her read Judith Purdue. I suspected she was a member of Ridgecrest Healthcare's board of directors and was serving as the QIC Committee's civilian representative. To Sam's immediate right sat Nancy Cockrell, RN. I recognized her as a nurse who worked in the Emergency Department. To her right sat another person I also recognized. Marcus Eldridge averted his eyes and refused to make eye contact when I glowered at him.

Last and most distressing was the way people looked at me when I entered the conference room. I noted a range of facial expressions. The majority were without emotion. Several people seemed antagonistic— even hostile. A few, like Madison, seated in the second row of the gallery, actually looked worried. The thing that troubled me was that there were no smiles, no expressions of good cheer or encouragement.

Suddenly apprehensive, I halted just inside the door. "What's going on?" I said in a quiet voice, not really expecting an answer.

"Doctor Sterling," Sam called out in an official tone of voice. "Please step forward and take a seat." He gestured toward an empty chair backed up against a side wall, midway between the head table and the small table that faced it.

"What is this?" I demanded more loudly. "What's going on?"

Sam declared, "We're here to judge the validity of the charges that have been brought against you."

"What charges?" I said with increasing trepidation.

"The ones that were spelled out in the notice you received."

"Notice? I haven't received any notice."

"A detailed notice of the pending charges was mailed to your office." Sam sounded a tad uncertain.

"If it was, I never got it. The only reason I'm here is because a text message popped up on my phone this morning inviting me to this meeting. I can show it to you if you'd like."

"Notice was to have been given." Sam cast a questioning glance at Marcus.

The hospital's chief administrator shrugged.

"So, no notice was given," Sam said with an exasperated huff. "Well, this does present a problem. Please, Doctor Sterling, take a seat while we discuss this." He again motioned toward the solitary chair by the side wall.

Reluctantly, I crossed the room and sat down. The five members of the QIC Committee huddled together behind the head table. After a couple of minutes of quiet collaboration, they returned to their places.

Sam looked from me to the audience and back again. "The fact that the defendant has not been advised of the charges brought against him constitutes an unfortunate breach of protocol. However, this oversight is not sufficient reason to delay these proceedings. The chair is perfectly capable of taking into account the fact that the defendant has not had time to prepare a defense, and the chair is both willing and capable of making allowances in that regard. Let me remind you that we are not a court of law, and this committee is not bound by the rules of jurisprudence.

"Our sole function is to determine whether or not the standard of medical care has been breached to the extent that the defendant's hospital privileges should be revoked. To this end, we will now begin.

"Doctor Blake Augustus Sterling, accusations have been brought against you that you did wrongly commit malpractice resulting in the death of a patient and that you then willfully and illegally sought to cover up your misdeed. In pursuing this cover-up, you resorted to blackmail and intimidation. How do you plead?"

Stunned by what I was hearing, I sat unmoving for a moment; but when the implications registered, I sprang to my feet. Loudly I protested, "What are you talking about? This is outrageous. These charges are preposterous. Who says I did these things? Is this some kind of sick joke—stick it to the new guy."

Sam frowned. "I can assure you this is no joke. The chair will record your plea as not guilty. Please, Doctor Sterling, take your seat. You will be given a chance to speak soon enough."

Rather than sit down, I advanced toward the head table. "These charges are absurd. I've never heard anything so ludicrous. I must protest in the strongest possible terms."

Sam remained placid. "We understand that this must come as a tremendous surprise since you weren't notified in advance." He cast another glance at Marcus, who again looked away. "However, we do have a format that we need to follow. You will have your chance to respond. Until then, I must ask you to take your seat and allow us to get on with these proceedings."

"You expect me to sit mutely and listen to lies?"

"If you hope to clear your name, yes."

I threw my hands up in disgust and petulantly took my seat.

Sam gave me a grateful nod. "It appears we are now ready to begin. The chair would ask Doctor Morton Stone to step forward."

Doctor Stone was an elderly family practitioner, well past the age when many in our profession opt for retirement. Dressed in blue jeans, a white shirt, and a gray vest with gold accents, he fit my mental image of an old-time country doctor. I had spoken with the man several times on the phone but had never met him in person.

"Please, Doctor Stone, have a seat." Sam motioned toward the chair at the small table.

"Aren't you going to swear me in or something?" Doctor Stone hesitantly sat down in the chair that had been indicated.

"This isn't a court of law," Sam said. "The rules regarding perjury don't apply. However, we will expect you to tell the truth."

"Of course," Doctor Stone said.

Sam continued, "Tell me, sir, did you have occasion to treat a patient by the name of Leland Wright?"

Doctor Stone nodded sharply. "I did."

"Could you please tell this committee the circumstances that caused him to seek your care."

"He came to me with acute right upper quadrant abdominal pain. My diagnosis was that he had acute cholecystitis. I referred him to the Emergency Department for admission."

"Did Mr. Wright have any other medical issues that you were aware of?"

"He was significantly overweight. He was known to be hypertensive, and he had a history of coronary artery disease."

"By coronary artery disease, what do you mean precisely?"

"He had suffered a moderate-sized heart attack about a year ago."

"Would you say that when he was admitted to the hospital, he was at risk for having another heart attack?"

"He had multiple risk factors. Yes."

"I presume his hypertension was one of them. Is that correct?"

"It is. I'd been after Leland for years to try and get his blood pressure under control."

"Did you communicate your concerns with the physicians who treated Mr. Wright in the hospital?"

"I spoke with Doctor Ramsey and Doctor Sterling both. I told them that Leland's blood pressure had a tendency to spike when he got distressed and to keep an eye on it."

"Thank you Doctor Stone." Sam looked to the other members of the committee. "Does anybody have other questions for this witness?"

Nobody spoke up.

Sam looked back at Doctor Stone. "If not, then you are excused." He then waited for the witness to return to his seat before announcing, "The committee would request that Doctor Rodney Gardner step forward."

*Who is Rodney Gardner?* I wondered. I wasn't aware of anyone on the medical staff by that name. A tall gentleman with a slight limp arose from the gallery and came up to stand beside the small table. I could not recall having ever seen the man before. After a moment, he sat down.

Sam consulted his notes arrayed on the table in front of the room. "Doctor Gardner, correct me if I'm wrong, but my understanding is that you are a doctor of pharmacy and one of five pharmacists employed by Flintridge Healthcare to work at the Flintridge Medical Center."

"That is correct."

"In early September, did you have occasion to dispense medication prescribed for a hospitalized patient by the name of Leland Wright?"

"Yes, I did."

Sam stood up and retrieved a tablet computer off the table in front of him. He stepped around the head table to stand in front of the witness. He tapped several keys on the tablet and then showed its display to the witness. "Would you please note the physician's order highlighted there and tell this committee what it is."

Doctor Gardner glanced at each of the committee members. "The order is for hydralazine 50mg to be given orally four times a day."

"In whose chart is that order written?"

The pharmacist again checked the tablet's display. "Mr. Leland Wright's chart."

"And who wrote that order?"

"Doctor Blake Sterling."

"That's not true," I blurted out. "I never wrote such an order."

"Doctor Sterling, please," Sam said. "You will have your chance to respond in due course." He turned back to the witness. "Doctor Gardner, do you remember filling that order?"

"I do, mainly because it was such a high dose—five times what is usually prescribed. I even called the patient's nurse to confirm that the order was valid. She verified that it was."

Sam paused for a moment and then said, "Doctor Gardner, in your opinion, what would be the effect if a patient were to take that much hydralazine?"

"Hydralazine is a vasodilator. It opens up blood vessels. It is used as an antihypertensive medication. The patient would experience a substantial drop in their blood pressure."

"Enough to cause the circulation to collapse?"

"Very possibly."

"Thank you. You may return to your seat." Sam put back the tablet computer and returned to his place at the head table.

A sense of unreality welled up within me. I felt as if I was living a nightmare from which I could not wake up. One minute I'm in my office, going about my daily routine. The next, I'm defending myself against outlandish charges that have absolutely no basis; in fact, I knew for certain they were lies because I remembered the medications I had prescribed for Mr. Wright, and they did not include an antihypertensive. There had been no need to lower his blood pressure. With his pneumonia and his gallbladder infection, his blood pressure was already on the low side.

Sam consulted his notes again and then said, "Next, the committee would like to hear from Doctor Peter Ramsey."

Toward the back of the gallery, Peter rose to his feet and stepped forward to the witness table. As he sat down, he cast a look in my direction that proclaimed, "I'm sorry about this, but I don't have a choice."

"Doctor Ramsey," Sam began. "You were Leland Wright's admitting physician?"

"That is correct."

"For the record, could you please present an overview of his medical history and describe what happened to him in the hospital."

Upon hearing the word *record* spoken, I looked around and for the first time noticed a woman seated behind the head table taking shorthand. She did not look up as Peter presented a straightforward account of Mr. Wright's hospitalization.

Peter finished by saying, "We were unable to restore a heartbeat. There was nothing more we could do."

"Doctor Ramsey," Sam said. "Did you prescribe hydralazine for Mr. Wright?"

"No, I did not."

"Were you aware that Doctor Sterling had prescribed hydralazine?"

"Not until I reviewed the patient's chart in preparation for this meeting."

"So, during Mr. Wright's resuscitation, you did not know that his blood pressure had plummeted because he was given hydralazine?"

Once more, I interrupted, "His blood pressure was low because he was septic. It was his infection that made him hypotensive."

Rather than reprimand me again, Sam turned to the witness. "Is that your opinion?"

Peter hesitated. "I'd say it's possible, but if he did indeed receive 50 mg of hydralazine, I would think that would be a more likely cause." Again Peter looked at me with a mixture of embarrassment and regret.

After Peter was dismissed, Sam called his next witness, a nurse by the name of Gretchen Smith. I halfway recalled having seen her in the hospital, but I could not bring to mind where or when. She was an attractive woman with blonde hair and nice legs; rather than scrubs, she wore a knee-length dress. She made a point of smiling at each of the committee members.

Sam cleared his throat and began, "Ms. Smith—"

"Mrs. Smith," the witness said. "I'm married."

"Yes, of course," Sam corrected himself. "Mrs. Smith, you are a nurse employed by the Flintridge Medical Center. Is that right?"

"It is."

"And you are what's called a float—a nurse that can be assigned to different patient care areas when there is an acute need."

"Yes, sir."

"Do you remember to which area you were assigned on Tuesday, September 5th, of this year?"

"I was working the night shift in the ICU."

Sam looked slightly surprised. "You must work lots of places in the hospital. How can you be certain about a single shift you worked almost three months ago?"

"Because of what happened around dawn that morning. I don't think I will ever forget it."

Sam spread his hands to indicate the others seated at the head table. "Could you please tell the committee exactly what did happen."

"At around 3:30 a.m., Mr. Wright coded. He had been losing ground, and he went into full cardiac arrest. Doctor Ramsey was in the hospital and responded immediately when we called him. He began CPR, which lasted about forty-five minutes, but it was unsuccessful. The patient did not survive."

"I see," Sam said. "Thank you. Now could you tell us what happened next?"

"Doctor Sterling had been notified that his patient was being resuscitated. He arrived at the hospital a short time later, but Mr. Wright had just died. He and Doctor Ramsey discussed the case briefly. Then Doctor Sterling sat down to review the chart. That's when he noticed the order for the hydralazine."

"What do you mean he noticed the order?"

"I mean that's when he realized he had made a serious error and had prescribed the wrong medication."

I heard murmurs emanating from the gallery.

Sam said, "How do you know he was thinking he had made a serious error?"

"Because he told me. He was really upset. He said it had to be a mistake because he was sure he had ordered hydroxyzine 50mg, not hydralazine. Hydroxyzine is used to reduce anxiety, and in Mr. Wright's case, it would have been intended to make him more comfortable."

Sam became very serious. "I see. What happened then?"

Mrs. Smith hesitated.

"It's all right," Sam said. "Take your time and just tell us what came next."

"Doctor Sterling told me to change the record. He wanted it to show that it was hydroxyzine, not hydralazine, that had been given."

More grumblings arose from the onlookers.

"What was your response?" Sam said.

"I told him I couldn't do it. It would be unethical."

"And what did he say?"

Mrs. Smith seemed disinclined to continue. She blushed and looked away.

"I realize this is difficult," Sam said soothingly. "But please tell us what Doctor Sterling told you."

Mrs. Smith squared her shoulders and declared, "He told me that if I didn't alter the record, he would let my husband know that we had been seeing each other."

"You and Doctor Sterling had been having an affair?"

"Yes."

I heard a gasp coming from the direction of the gallery.

"How long had this affair been going on?"

"About a month, maybe five weeks."

"So…Doctor Sterling threatened to expose your relationship. What did you tell him?"

"I told him I still wouldn't do it, that I could lose my license if the truth ever came out."

"You refused to alter the medical record. Did Doctor Sterling inform your husband about your affair?"

"No. I did. I felt extremely ashamed and embarrassed, but I thought it would be best if my husband heard it from me."

Sam nodded thoughtfully. "Let me summarize, if I may, and correct me if I'm wrong. Mr. Wright suffered a circulatory collapse that led to his cardiac arrest. After his unsuccessful CPR, Doctor Sterling told you that he had mistakenly ordered hydralazine rather than hydroxyzine. He then demanded that you alter Mr. Wright's medical record, but you refused even though Doctor Sterling threatened to tell your husband about your affair. Is that the essence of what you have told us?"

"It is?"

"Thank you. This is been quite difficult for you, I'm sure, but we appreciate your willingness to come forward. I have no further questions." Sam looked at the committee. "Does anybody else have questions?" The other members shook their heads.

Mrs. Smith got up and returned to her seat in the gallery. She did not look in my direction as she passed by.

I sat in shocked silence. The tapestry of lies had rendered me speechless. I could not believe that people would proffer so many blatant falsehoods with impunity. *Dear God,* I thought. *This can't be happening. False witnesses are bearing their testimony against me. Give me the words I need to defend myself against these untruths. Help me, please.*

Sam drummed his fingers on the table while he scanned the pages in front of him. He then looked up and said, "There is one more witness we should hear from. I would ask Mr. Tyler Wickham to step forward."

As Tyler made his way to the small table, he too refused to look at me. When he was seated, Sam said, "It is my understanding that you have information that you think might be relevant to these proceedings. Would you please tell us what it is that you want us to know."

"Sure. Well, it was back in August of this year. I was returning from the administration wing of the hospital and going past that area where the on-call rooms are located. That's where I noticed Doctor Sterling and that nurse, Mrs. Smith, coming out of one of the rooms. They didn't see me, but I saw them clearly."

"What exactly did you see?" Sam said.

"They were hugging each other and kissing. He had a hand on her…well, let's just say that it was a very personal place. It was obvious to me that they were involved with each other."

"By involved you mean…?"

"You know—getting it on, having sex."

"And you could tell this because…?"

"Because of the way they acted toward each other. It was obvious."

Sam frowned. "So…tell me, Mr. Wickham, why did you think it necessary to bring this information to our attention?"

"When I heard about this committee's investigation, it occurred to me that it was going to wind up being her word against his, and in all probability, he would claim that the affair never happened. It seemed only right that y'all should know the truth."

"Thank you," Sam said. "You may return to your seat." He sat back in his chair and slowly turned his head to look at me. "I assume you're going to speak in your own defense. What say we take a ten-minute break, and then you can have your turn. We will reconvene at 2:00 p.m."

People began to filter out of the room. I turned to look at Madison for the first time since the proceedings had begun. She sat with tears in her eyes and a horrified expression on her face. I was about to proclaim my innocence when she broke eye contact and looked away. She rose from her chair and hurriedly left the room.

Ten minutes later, I stood in front of the head table. I had elected to remain standing rather than sit in the witness chair. Before beginning, I scanned the gallery. Madison had not returned. I could only imagine how betrayed she must be feeling. I remembered the care and loving-kindness she had shown me during my bout of pneumonia, and then for her to think that while dating her, I had been with another woman—no wonder she had fled.

During the interlude, I had mulled over the defense I would mount. In reviewing the testimonies I had been forced to endure, it occurred to me that without proof there was very little I could say to refute the charges. Whoever had instituted these proceedings had crafted a strong case against me. At least three witnesses had been induced to lie, and a medical record had been falsified. I had a strong premonition that the outcome of this kangaroo court had already been decided. Still, I would give it my best shot.

Standing tall, I said, "Ladies and gentlemen of the committee, you have listened to multiple testimonies this afternoon that are blatantly false. I can only guess why these outrageous lies are being told, but let me assure you I never ordered hydralazine or hydroxyzine for Mr. Wright. I did not tell Mrs. Smith to falsify the patient's medical record, and I never had an affair with that woman. These things are simply not true.

"If you would ask me, 'Where is your proof?', I would be forced to admit that I don't have any—yet. If you would ask me, 'Why would someone do this to you?', I would have to say I don't know—yet. Rest assured, however, one day I will find out, and I will clear my name. The truth will not stay hidden forever."

Having said my piece, I returned to the chair by the wall and sat down. A deafening silence filled the conference room.

Sam heaved a sigh of disappointment. I got the impression that he had expected more. With an air of reluctance, he announced, "The committee will retire to consider its decision."

The members rose to their feet and filed out of the room.

While I and the spectators waited for their return, I thought about what would happen going forward. My presumption was that I would be found guilty of the charges brought against me. Given the evidence, had I been on the committee, I too would have been forced to vote guilty.

As to what penalty the committee would impose, I would just have to wait and see.

It took the five members of the QIC Committee barely fifteen minutes to reach a decision. With somber faces, they filed back into the conference room.

Without preamble, Sam read from a slip of paper he cupped in his hand. In a flat voice devoid of emotion, he announced, "It is the judgment of this committee that Doctor Blake Sterling violated the standard of care by committing an act of malpractice that resulted in the death of a patient. He then unethically sought to cover up his misdeed using blackmail and intimidation. As a consequence, his hospital admitting privileges are to be suspended indefinitely, pending additional review. Furthermore, there will be a detailed evaluation of the hospital records of every patient he has treated at Flintridge since joining the medical staff in early July. This meeting is adjourned."

The committee's decision was right in line with what I had expected. One thing about QIC judgments—there would be no recourse. There was no avenue for appeal. Any action taken against a defendant had to be certified by the administration. However, with Marcus Eldridge smugly gloating like the victor in a prize fight, the administration's approval was a foregone conclusion.

Bottom line, I was barred from having anything to do with patients admitted to Flintridge Medical Center even if I had been their treating physician beforehand. I could still see patients in the office and I could accept outpatient referrals, but if hospitalization was required, I would have to turn the patient over to someone else.

All this led to another devastating consequence. Since I could no longer round on inpatients, I could no longer participate in the on-call rotation. For the foreseeable future, Adam would be back to taking call by himself.

An additional result of the committee's decision was that my income was about to take a tremendous hit. The majority of a pulmonary specialist's earnings derive from hospital consultations. With these no longer available to me, I wasn't sure that my earnings would pay my bills especially considering the new mortgage I had recently acquired.

As I walked back to the office, I thought about what I would tell the staff. Of course, I would present my side of the story, but people tend to believe salacious accusations over placid denials. My only hope was that they would take my word for what had happened.

The other thing I thought about was my relationship with Madison. I desperately wanted to call her and set things right, but I knew that option was currently out of the question. She would need time for the shock of the accusations to wear off so that she could soberly search for the truth. In the meantime, I would have to force myself to stay away, regardless of how much I wanted to be with her.

As I climbed the back stairs to my office, I began to formulate a plan as to how I would deal with this catastrophe, though I had no clear idea where to begin. One thing was certain. Some days just don't turn out the way that you expect they will.

In the middle of the afternoon, I sat alone in my office, mulling over the QIC Committee meeting which was still fresh in my thoughts. The full weight of the judgment that had been rendered against me was beginning to sink in, and I was growing increasingly dispirited and angry. I wondered, *How could God allow those people to brazenly lie about me like that? Their testimonies were deliberate, well-rehearsed falsehoods. Why hadn't He stifled their words while they were still in their mouths?* I felt I was do an explanation. A thought came to me that made me acutely apprehensive because it felt like I was challenging God. *What good is my faith if it can't protect me when evil men conspire against me?*

Then I remembered Jesus when he was brought before Pontius Pilate and was falsely accused by the Pharisees and the Sadducees. He offered no defense though he was innocent of the charges leveled against him. Then it occurred to me that Jesus, during his trial, was looking ahead to his crucifixion and subsequent resurrection. His humiliation at the hands of Pilate was necessary to accomplish a greater good.

*Would any good come of my humiliation?*

Abruptly I pictured the passage from Romans chapter 5 that I had referenced to Madison. It tells us that suffering brings perseverance and perseverance builds character and character produces hope, which is faith. Another saying I had heard years before came to mind: God is more interested in our character than our comfort.

*Is that what this is all about*? I wondered. *Is He working on my character? Is this a test of some sort or an object lesson intended to lead me to some fundamental truth*? If so, I wished He would just get on with it and tell me what I was supposed to do next.

A knock sounded at my open door, and Ellie, my nurse, stepped into my office.

"Yes, what is it?"

"The pharmacy called and left a message. They said the pills you gave them to evaluate are an unknown compound."

"Unknown? Really?"

"That's what they said. They also said they're running additional tests to narrow down what they do."

"That's interesting." *Why would Tyler keep an unknown drug in a pill bottle with an encrypted label*? It was frustrating, having so many questions and so few answers.

Ellie hesitated. She seemed on the verge of speaking up.

"Was there something else?"

"We heard what happened. I just wanted to say…that is, I don't believe what they said about you. You are a good doctor. You wouldn't do what they claim. I just wanted you to know how we felt."

"Thank you. That means a lot."

Adam appeared in the doorway behind Ellie. When she realized he was there, she said, "If there is anything we can do to help, just let us know." Then she turned and, slipping past Adam, left my office.

"They all feel that way." Adam sat down in one of the two armchairs that faced my desk.

"Yeah? And how do you feel?"

"Same as them. I have no idea what's behind the allegations made against you, but I know you are incapable of doing what they said. Even if you had prescribed the wrong medication, which I strongly doubt, you would never try to cover it up. You're not that kind of person."

"That's quite a vote of confidence."

"I've been in this business a long time, and I'm a fairly good judge of character. I never would have invited you to join this practice if I'd had any doubts about your integrity."

I leaned forward and looked at my partner. "You do realize that my suspension is going to create a real problem for the practice."

Adam nodded solemnly. "I imagine it will."

"What do you propose we do about it?

"First off, I think we should invite Fred Spalding to come work with us again. He can take call and see patients in the hospital. You can work the office and take over his patients when they are discharged. I'm quite sure he will agree to that. Beyond that, we look for a way to clear your name. I know Gretchen Smith—not well, but maybe I can talk to her, find out why she lied. In addition, I'll keep my ears open and see if I can discover who is behind this charade."

"I'm pretty sure I already know who is responsible. Did you see the expression on Marcus Eldridge's face when the verdict was announced? He was practically orgasmic."

"You think he orchestrated this inquisition to weaken our resolve to remain independent?"

"I think it goes deeper than that, much deeper, but like you said, keep your ears open. Maybe you'll pick up something we can use."

"Can do." Adam stood up. "I've got to get back to work. I have a patient waiting."

"And I've got to get to the hospital. There's someone I need to talk to. By the way, you never asked if I was guilty."

"I didn't need to. Like I said, you have integrity."

Heather Oliver was doing paperwork at her desk in the infection control office when I stopped by. She looked up in surprise when I entered. "Are you supposed to be here?"

"They suspended my privileges to treat patients. They didn't ban me from the building. I can still visit people if I choose."

"I'll buy that. What can I do for you?"

"Did you have a chance to speak with Madison like I ask you to?"

Heather sat back and seemed to withdraw into herself. "I did as you requested."

"What did she say?"

"She's pretty upset. She's going to need time to sort things out."

"How can she believe the lies they told about me? She must know me better than that."

"I got the impression she's not sure what to believe. The testimonies she listened to at the hearing hurt her—probably more than you know. For the time being, I'd recommend that you give her some space. The truth will come out eventually. It can't stay hidden forever."

"What do you believe? Do you think I'm responsible for Mr. Wright's death and that I had an affair with that nurse and then tried to blackmail her into falsifying a patient's record? Is that what you believe?"

"I don't want to believe it, but the evidence was compelling."

I had expected a more forceful proclamation of my innocence, but in all honesty, I could not fault Heather for having her doubts. Like she said, taken as a whole, the lies were compelling.

I raised an index finger to emphasize the point I was making, "I don't know how yet, but I'm going to prove the charges against me are false. This injustice will not be allowed to stand."

"Oh, I do so hope that is true." Heather seemed sincere. "In the meantime, do yourself a favor—leave Madison alone. If you push her, she will shut down entirely."

I considered Heather's advice for a bit and then agreed, "All right. I'll stay away, but it feels wrong. It feels like we should be communicating—working things out."

"You will in time…if it's meant to be."

"Maybe." I started to leave and then turned back. "While I'm here, is there anything new on the bocavirus patients?"

"No. Nothing."

"If there was, would you tell me?"

"Perhaps. I'd have to think about it."

With nothing waiting for me back in the office, I bid Heather farewell and headed home.

The next morning, I intercepted Marcus Eldridge as he was arriving at the hospital. Aware that he liked to start his day early, I had been waiting since 5:00 a.m. to make sure I didn't miss him. In fact,

I had been awake since midnight, struggling with what I knew I had to do.

God's commands are not optional. If you call yourself a Christian, you are obligated to obey his precepts to the best of your ability. This is true even if compliance conflicts with the very essence of your being, as was the case with Marcus and his transgressions against me.

Marcus startled and nearly dropped the briefcase he was carrying when I approached him as he was getting out of his car.

"Got a moment?" I positioned myself to block him from slipping past me.

"Actually, no. I have an important meeting this morning, and I don't want to be late." He tried to ease around me, but I moved to cut him off.

"What I have to say won't take long. I know you're responsible. I know that because of you, my privileges were suspended. This was your doing. You either bribed, coerced, or threatened the people who testified against me. Somehow you got them to lie, and I'm pretty sure I know why you did it."

"You're insane. If you don't get out of my way, I'm going to call security and have you arrested."

"Hear me out. I've given this a great deal of thought."

More than anything, I wanted to punch him in the face. It took every ounce of willpower I could muster to speak the words that next came out of my mouth. "What I came here to tell you is I forgive you. As a Christian, I am compelled to forgive those who transgress against us, and I take my faith seriously. From this point forward, the debt of retribution you owe me is set aside. There is nothing I need from you. My prayer for you is that one day you will learn to forgive yourself— although I'm not sure that will happen…at least not until you confess what you've done. That's all I have to say." I turned and started to walk away.

Marcus called out after me, "You think that's the end of it? It isn't."

I halted and looked back.

Marcus continued smugly, "I've been in touch with Leland Wright's family. They are preparing a malpractice suit against you. Also, I've spoken with Washington State's Medical Board. I sent them a transcript of the QIC Committee meeting. They're opening an inquiry into your misdeeds. They're going to revoke your license to practice medicine. You're finished. When all is said and done, you won't have a pot to piss in. You think you can forgive me and walk away? We'll see about that."

I smiled at Marcus and then, without saying another word, I turned again and put the hospital's chief administrator behind me. I had done my duty. Technically, I had forgiven my enemy. How long it would take for me to release the anger I felt—that was another matter.

# CONSEQUENCES

Three days later, I found myself in church during the second service. It was the first Sunday in December, and winter had finally arrived. Snow had fallen during the night, leaving an inch on the ground. It was debatable whether or not this new snowfall would stick or whether it would melt before winter settled in for real. Being from Southern California and, therefore, unaccustomed to coping with winter weather, I had almost decided not to chance driving on slick streets, but my need for spiritual comfort was too strong.

The Resurrection Bible Church was nearly full when I entered the sanctuary. I found an empty seat in a pew toward the back of the nave and quietly slipped in, trying not to step on people's toes as I worked my way down the row. Assisted by the choir, we sang three songs. As was customary, we stood while we sang. I have always assumed that the tradition of standing was initially adopted to honor God, but if so, why were we allowed to sit during the rest of the service?

The morning's sermon was taken from 1 Peter chapter 2 wherein he exhorts his readers to lead godly lives and to abstain from all malice, deceit, hypocrisy, envy, and slander. Reverend Thomas's delivery made me wonder if the message was being recorded. If it was, I thought about obtaining copies and sending them to the people who had lied at my hearing—not that it would do any good.

Madison sat four rows ahead of me, next to a female friend. They exchanged comments periodically during the service. Once Madison had turned her head to scan the audience, but I don't think she saw me.

I noted the dark circles under her eyes. She seemed sadder than I had ever seen her. I yearned to talk with her, but Heather had been right. She needed time to bring her emotions under control. I thought about how I would feel had the shoe been on the other foot and I had been the one jilted. It was an unpleasant thought, and I chose not to dwell on it for long.

After the service, I caught up with Reverend Thomas as he was concluding his conversation with a pair of young newlyweds. After bidding them farewell, he turned to me. "I understand you've been going through some tough times recently." His comment made me wonder if all of Flintridge had learned of my embarrassment. News travels fast in rural communities even when they are nestled up against a larger city.

I ignored the sense of shame rising up inside me and said, "It's been a rough few days, and that's what I'd like to talk to you about. I'm afraid this ordeal has irreparably damaged my faith, and I'm not sure what to do about it."

"I gather that means you want to talk?"

"If you have the time. It doesn't have to be today."

The reverend smiled. "Today is fine. My heavy lifting is done. Let me finish up a couple things first, and I will meet you in my office in thirty minutes. How does that sound?"

"Thirty minutes works for me. I'll be there."

The reverend strode away, leaving me standing alone in the reception area outside the nave. To my surprise, Madison and her female friend had also remained behind and were chatting approximately ten yards away—too far to overhear what they were saying. She again stood with her back to me. Whether or not she knew I was there, I couldn't tell. I had to restrain myself from stepping up and saying hello. I very much wanted to, but I had committed to letting her work through her issues without interference.

I turned and headed toward the kitchen. I had skipped breakfast, and sometimes the ladies auxiliary served pastries and coffee after the Sunday services. I figured it wouldn't hurt to see if there were any goodies left.

Reverend Elijah Thomas was a sturdily built man. His broad shoulders and muscular arms would have marked him as a laborer of some sort, perhaps a longshoreman, had his profession been unknown. He invited me in when I knocked on the door to his office. His light-brown eyes, the color of milk chocolate, carried a haunted look, as if he had witnessed his share of the world's sorrows.

The reverend stood by a coat closet in the far corner of the room. "So...we're experiencing a crisis of faith, are we?" He shed the suit coat he had worn during the morning's services. After draping it over a hanger, he hung it in the closet. He then tugged on a cardigan sweater and loosened his tie. Turning toward me, he gestured toward a conversation group in the near corner of the room. I sat down in a padded armchair, and the reverend sat down, facing me. He then waited for me to begin.

Rather than jump in with both feet, I said, "You are aware, I presume, of my recent difficulties?"

Reverend Thomas cocked his head to peer at me. "Recent difficulties? That's how you choose to describe what happened to you? The way I heard it, your troubles were far more than a minor inconvenience. I was told that you were found guilty of committing malpractice that caused the death of a patient, that your hospital privileges were suspended, and that you were deemed to have engaged in blackmail, not to mention being an adulterer. I also heard that you claim you're innocent."

"You are surprisingly well-informed."

"I like to keep up with what's happening to members of my congregation. Are you innocent?"

"If I was guilty, do you think I would admit it?"

"Maybe not, but I would know if you were lying."

"As God is my witness, the accusations against me are false. Yes. I am innocent."

"So what is it you think I can do for you?" Reverend Thomas laced his fingers together in front of him.

"I'm not sure. I just know that I have to talk to somebody."

"Fair enough. Go ahead."

"That's part of the problem. I'm not sure what to say."

"Then tell me what you're feeling. What's going on inside of you?"

I hesitated while I tried to sift through my jumbled emotions. "I'm wounded, and I'm angry. I feel like I want to lash out and break stuff. I want to hurt somebody the same way I've been hurt."

"Is that all?"

Again I paused to consider my response. "It's not easy admitting this, but I'm scared. I don't know if I can undo what has been done to me. I'm afraid that my career as a physician might be over."

Reverend Thomas eyed me sharply. "Anything else?"

"Isn't that enough?"

"I don't know. Is that all there is?"

"What are you asking?"

"Earlier, you had mentioned that you were losing your faith. Do you want to talk about that?"

Abruptly, a dark void seemed to open up inside of me. It sent a shiver racing through me. Then the words started coming in a rush, as if a floodgate had been opened. "I've been a follower of Jesus since I was seventeen. I've always thought that Jesus and I had a close relationship. I've trusted him as my Savior and my Lord. I read the Scriptures and pray regularly. I go to church when I can. I've tried to live a good life and to love God and to love others as commanded. More than that, to the best of my ability, I've tried to forgive, though it's nearly impossible. I'm not sure what more I can do."

"So…what is it that's troubling you?"

"It feels like God has turned His back on me. I no longer feel close to Him. When I cast my prayers to heaven, they never make it past the ceiling. I feel alone, and it terrifies me." This admission had come unbidden, and I suddenly understood what had been distressing my soul. I felt tears welling up in my eyes. "For some reason, God has abandoned me, and I don't know why. Why won't He tell me what He wants from me? What have I done wrong?"

Reverend Thomas picked up a box of facial tissues from the table beside his chair and handed it to me. I used a tissue to dab my eyes as he said, "Do you remember when Christ was in the garden of Gethsemane and He prayed three times that if there was any way that the cup from which He was about to drink should be taken from Him? In other words, He was asking His Heavenly Father if He could avoid the agony that was about to befall Him, but then he prayed, 'Not My will but Thine be done.'

"And then later, as He hung on the cross, He cried out, 'Eloi, Eloi, lama sabachthani?'—'My God, My God, why hast Thou forsaken <e?' In that moment, He too felt abandoned, but then what happened next?"

"He died and was buried."

"And then? "

"He was resurrected to eternal life."

"Precisely. God hadn't turned His back on Jesus. He was allowed to feel abandoned, but because of the resurrection, we know that everything He experienced was part of God's plan of salvation. Paul reminds us in his letter to the Corinthians that we are hard pressed on every side but not crushed, perplexed but not in despair, persecuted but not abandoned, struck down but not destroyed.

"In other words, there are going to be difficult times when it feels like God has withdrawn His favor, but He hasn't. God is always with us whether we sense His presence or not. In those times of darkness, that's when we need to draw upon our faith and trust that God will see us through whatever difficulties confront us. We need to believe that God's plan for our lives will play out just as it's supposed to.

"I don't know how your struggles are going to turn out, but I do know that whatever happens, it will be according to God's will for your life, and in the end, God will be glorified."

I sat quietly while I pondered what Reverend Thomas had said. As the message behind his words began to unfold in my consciousness, the darkness inside of me seemed a little less distressing.

Three days later, I was at home. It was late in the evening, and I was busy doing a whole lot of nothing. The void inside me hadn't gone away entirely. I was still having a hard time sensing God's presence in my life, but it was getting easier to trust that He was still with me.

As I lay back in the recliner and looked around, I noted the boxes scattered throughout the living room, the dining room, and the kitchen. I had suspended my unpacking activities. Having reviewed my financial situation, I'd concluded that unless a new source of revenue were to open up in the near future, I would no longer be able to afford my mortgage. It was a depressing admission, but I had gone over the numbers several times. My outpatient office practice simply wasn't bringing in enough revenue. I had to do something, but what that something might be, I hadn't a clue.

The front doorbell rang. I climbed out of the recliner to see who might be calling at nine o'clock at night.

Adam stood on my front porch. He carried a sixpack of beer in his hand. "Sorry I missed touching base with you at the office. I got called to the hospital for an admission. I had wanted to check with you and see how you're doing."

"I'm not suicidal if that's what's worrying you." I stood aside and allowed Adam to enter.

"That's good to know. I'd hate to have to bury another partner." He held up the sixpack. "Want one?"

"Sure, why not."

We gravitated to the kitchen. I popped the top on a can of beer. So did Adam. "So…how are you really?" he said. "Be honest with me."

I gestured toward my small dining room table, and we sat down. "I'm okay—sort of. Actually, I'm a bunch of things. I'm trying to remain calm, but I'm furious inside. I want to stay busy and do stuff, but I can't seem to find anything productive to do. I'm trying to stay optimistic, but I worry about the future. Worst of all, I want to fight back against the injustice that was done to me, but I feel totally helpless. I guess all of this is a sad way of saying I'm frustrated. Aren't you sorry you asked?"

Adam shook his head. "Nope. Speaking of fighting back, have you come up with a way to refute the charges against you?"

"Not a thing. Their damn lies are tight. So far, I can't poke a hole in any of them."

"I may know a way," Adam declared optimistically. "Or maybe not. It's too soon to tell."

"What have you got?" I asked hopefully.

"It's not much, but do you remember Rodney Gardner, the pharmacist who testified against you?"

"Of course. How could I forget him?"

"Well, Flo is friends with his wife, Patricia. They're in a book club together, and they got to talking. The subject of your hearing came up, and Patricia was surprised to learn that her husband had testified against you. Apparently, he hadn't told her that he was going to. When Flo mentioned that we were convinced that he hadn't told the truth, Patricia got really upset. Flo had the impression that it was because something serious was going on in their marriage, though she refused to talk about it. Flo came away thinking that Patricia intended to speak with her husband and confront him about not being truthful. Maybe she'll convince him to come clean and recant his testimony against you. I know it's not much, but it's all I've got."

"Hey, at this point, I'll take any help I can get."

"Tell me something," Adam said casually. "What will you do if we can't clear your name?"

"I've been giving that scenario some thought. Assuming that the medical board will vote to pull my license, I'll have to find another line of work. As things stand, I have no idea what that might entail. The only thing I'm qualified to do is practice medicine. The only thing I ever wanted to be is a physician. If I'm forced to choose another profession, in all probability, I'd have to go back to school for additional training."

Adam polished off his beer but didn't reach for another. I could tell he was disturbed by what I'd said. However, rather than echo my pessimism, he commented, "There is something else I wanted to talk to you about. I'm thinking we should offer Fred Spalding a position as an associate. Assuming that in the near future you will be reinstated, it would mean there will be three of us again. I've reviewed his charts. He does good work, and I get the feeling that he's tired of hiring out as a locum tenens. With three of us, it would be the same as when Jerry was alive. What do you think?"

"Off the top of my head, I'd say it's a good idea. I like Fred…and you're right. He practices good medicine. Go for it. See what he says."

The doorbell rang. I got up to see who was calling.

Madison stood on my front porch. She held a bottle of wine in her hand. "I was in the neighborhood, and I thought I would drop by and see how you're doing." I noticed that there were snowflakes on the shoulders of her winter jacket.

"It's good to see you. Please, come in." I held the door open wide. After I hung her coat up in the hall closet, we made our way into the dining room.

"Oh," Madison exclaimed when she saw Adam. "Doctor Richards, I didn't know you were here. Excuse me if I'm interrupting. If you'd like me to leave, I will."

"Not at all," Adam said as he rose to his feet. "Blake and I were just chatting, but we're done and it's time for me to get on home." He turned to me and said, "Partner, you hang in there and keep the faith. This is going to turn out all right. I can feel it."

"I appreciate your stopping by, and let Fred know that he has my support."

I bid Adam farewell and then returned to visit with Madison. When I saw that he had left the remnants of his sixpack, I said, "It looks like we have a choice."

Madison caught my drift and replied, "You know, a beer does sound pretty good. I think that's what I'll have. We can save the wine for later."

"Later?"

"For another occasion."

"Oh. Sure."

"Look," Madison began, her mood becoming serious. "I owe you an apology. I should have allowed you to present your side of the story. I was wrong to react the way I did. I'm sorry."

"It's all right. I've thought about it, and it occurred to me that I might have done the same thing—under the circumstances."

Madison inhaled a deep breath and took hold of my hand. Looking straight at me, she said solemnly, "I've searched my heart, and you need to know that I trust you. I cannot believe that you were capable of doing the things they said you did. More than that, Doctor Blake Augustus Sterling, I want you to know that I love you, and I plan to stand by you, whatever comes."

Without having to think about my response, I exclaimed. "Madison Rose Lane, I love you too. I have missed you so much. You have no idea how happy I am that you are here." For the first time since my ordeal began, I could sense a growing optimism—an emergent hope for the future. In that moment I knew that, as Adam had predicted, everything was going to turn out all right.

Madison and I chatted until just after midnight when we both agreed that she should go home. By the time she departed, the void that had threatened to consume my soul was gone.

# THE VALUE OF EXERCISE

I find it amazing how my emotions can shift one day to the next. In a lull between patients, I sat at the desk in my office, trying not to think about the mess my life had become. The optimism that had lifted my spirits after Madison's visit had begun to fade. I was having a hard time accepting that the harm done to my career was permanent and an even harder time believing that the trials yet to come were real. I kept expecting a phone call from the QIC Committee offering an apology for having made a mistake, and a proclamation that my hospital privileges had been restored. Even more distressing was the realization that if the state medical board yanked my license, seven years of advanced medical education—not including four years of college—were about to be rendered worthless. Given the circumstances, keeping an upbeat attitude was nearly impossible.

The more I dwelled on my troubles, the deeper my funk became. What I needed was a distraction, something to take my mind off myself. Then my gaze fell on my desktop calendar, and I realized it was Friday. The medical center would be hosting another CME program. *What would happen*, I wondered. *If I were to attend?*

I suspected that a majority of my peers believed the charges against me. As had been pointed out several times, the testimonies proclaiming my guilt were compelling. With no evidence to offer in my own defense, how could I fault my colleagues for accepting what they had heard?

As I sat there, pondering my dilemma, it occurred to me that there was one thing I could do that might limit the damage to my reputation. I could behave as if I was innocent, which I was. That meant holding my head high and refusing to cower in the face of public scrutiny. I slapped the surface of my desk. I would attend the CME conference, and damn the consequences. If they had a problem with me being there, they could tell me to leave.

Rather than enter a room with my colleagues already assembled, I arrived early. As unobtrusively as possible, I started to make my way to the back of the auditorium. I was halfway there when a voice called out, "You shouldn't be in here. You need to leave."

Marcus Eldridge rose from a seat toward the middle of the auditorium. He seemed agitated as he threaded his way along his row in my direction. Gesturing for emphasis, he declared, "You've been banned from the hospital. You're not welcome here."

"Actually," said a calm voice coming from behind me. "His admission privileges were suspended. That's not the same as an outright ban."

I turned to see who had spoken and found myself standing face-to-face with Sam Duncan. The chief of staff's cobalt-blue eyes regarded me keenly through his wire-rimmed glasses. He smiled and then returned his attention to Marcus. "I say he should be allowed to stay unless you can cite some good reason why his being here would present a problem. Surely you don't expect him to do something rash, do you?"

"I wouldn't put it past him," Marcus replied tersely. "Desperate men do desperate things."

"Seriously?" Sam laughed. "Isn't that a bit paranoid? Look, I'll take responsibility for his actions. If he does anything disruptive, you can blame me."

Several of the physicians standing nearby murmured in agreement. Apparently, Marcus sensed that he was outnumbered.

Reluctantly, he capitulated, "Very well, but these CME conferences are as far as he goes. I will not have him participating in other hospital functions. Is that clear?" He glowered at me.

"As a matter of fact—" I began.

Interrupting, Sam laid a hand on my shoulder and whispered, "Don't press your luck."

Grumbling to himself, Marcus retreated to his seat.

Rather than remove his hand from my shoulder, Sam said, "I never got the chance to speak with you after the QIC hearing. I wanted to tell you how sorry I am that things worked out as they did. I know you must think I'm responsible for your suspension, but I was just doing my job. If you find evidence that proves your innocence, let me know, and I'll make sure you get a fair hearing."

"I don't blame you, Sam. Like you said, it was your job, but one day I will be vindicated."

"I believe you." Sam removed his hand from my shoulder. Then in full view of those who were watching, he offered to shake hands.

I greatly appreciated Sam's public display of respect. With a twinge of humility, I heartily returned the handshake and then took my seat.

It wasn't until the speaker began his presentation that I learned what the subject matter for the day's lecture would be. A local physical therapist—a doctor of physical medicine by the way—had chosen to expound on the value of exercise.

For me, the topic was of only minimal interest. I felt I already knew that regular exercise was essential for good health. My problem has always been summoning the determination to commit to an ongoing program. Many times, with good intentions, I have begun an exercise regimen, but then after a few sessions, I typically find some excuse not to continue. I just can't seem to convince myself that the reward is worth the effort. Perhaps this lecture would help me turn that mindset around. I sat up and tried to focus on what the lecturer was saying.

And then a thought came to me that jarred me into a new level of awareness. I had remembered when, shortly after joining Pulmonology Associates, Jerry had invited me to work out with him at the Columbia Fitness Center. Specifically, I had recalled that as a regular member, Jerry had rented a locker at the facility.

A little over two months had elapsed since Jerry's passing. It was likely that his widow had canceled his gym membership and cleaned out his locker. On the other hand, maybe the locker was still registered in his name. If so, might it contain the book Jerry had referred to in the Emergency Department?

The possibility that the locker was where the book was to be found excited me—so much so that I very nearly surged to my feet and sprinted from the room. I was required to exert considerable restraint to remain seated until the lecture concluded. Then without hesitating, I drove straight to Jerry's house. En route, I called the office and canceled my scheduled patients, freeing up my entire afternoon. Again, I hated doing so, having come to appreciate what it's like waiting to see the doctor and then having your appointment canceled, but I had to know what, if anything, was in that locker.

Jerry's widow answered the door after I rang the bell a second time. She was wearing a rumpled cotton blouse and an old pair of blue jeans. She yawned and knuckled an eye. I wondered if I had interrupted a noontime nap. "Linda, I am sorry to barge in like this, but I need to ask you something. It's important."

"All right. Come in. What time is it?"

"A quarter to two."

She shook her head. "It's so easy to lose track of time these days." Then she straightened up. "Can I get you something? Is it too early for a glass of wine?"

"I can't stay, but there's something I need to know. Did you cancel Jerry's gym membership at the Columbia Fitness Center?" I held my breath while I waited for her answer.

"*Nooo*," she said slowly, as if searching her memory. "I meant to, but I completely forgot about it."

"So as far as you know then, there's still a locker registered in his name. Is that right?"

"As far as I know. I haven't been in touch with the gym. Why?"

"I need to find out what's in that locker. Now this is really important. Do you still have his locker key? It would probably be with his personal effects."

"I'm not sure. I'd have to look."

"Would you mind?"

"Okay, if you think it's necessary."

"Believe me, it is."

Linda moved off in the direction of the master bedroom at the back of the house. I remained in the entryway, shifting from one foot to the other, unable to let go of the anticipation I felt. She was gone probably no more than four or five minutes, but it seemed an eternity.

Eventually, Linda returned and held up a bronze key. "I think this is what you want. It was the only key on his key ring I didn't recognize." She held the key out to me.

It was all I could do to keep from snatching the key from her hand. "Thank you…so much. I'll let you know what I find."

"What exactly are you after, if I might ask?"

"The same thing as the last time I was here—Jerry's book, the one he mentioned the night he…when he got sick."

"Well, I wish you luck. You will keep me informed?"

"I promise."

After leaving Linda's house, I drove home to pick up a tote bag into which I stuffed a pair of gym shorts, a T-shirt, a towel, tennis shoes, a pair of white socks, and several other articles of clothing. In thinking ahead, it had come to mind that I couldn't simply walk in and ask to rummage through a locker to which I had no legal right of access. I would need to be more circumspect than that.

On my way to the Columbia Fitness Center, I had to repeatedly caution myself to keep my foot off the accelerator. It wasn't that I was worried that the facility was about to close—I remembered that in the evenings the exercise spa stayed open for people who like to work out after a hard day at the office. It was a burgeoning sense of anticipation that caused me to recklessly thread my way through traffic.

When I entered the building, it was the middle of the afternoon, and the place was as crowded as it had been during my previous visit. A throng of physically fit patrons, mostly young millennials, crowded the juice bar, and a majority of the machines in the exercise room were in use. Both the racquetball court and the handball court were occupied. I thought, *Not only is there value in exercise, there is a profit to be made as well.* I stepped up to the registration counter.

"Welcome to Columbia Fitness," said a young lady wearing a tight T-shirt bearing the company's logo. "How can we be of help?"

"I'd like to purchase a day pass."

"Have you been here before?"

"Yes, I have. It was four months ago approximately. I was the guest of a member."

"I see, and the member's name?" She prepared to type my response into the computer terminal at her elbow.

It was then I realized I probably should have lied and claimed this was my first visit, but it was too late to do so now. "Tucker, Jerry Tucker."

"Aw, yes, Doctor Tucker. We haven't seen him in a while." The young woman's comment provided me with a glimmer of encouragement. It suggested that Jerry's membership was still open, and that implied that the spa's staff had not yet cleaned out his locker.

"He's indisposed," I stated flatly. "This afternoon, I'm here on my own."

"And your name is…?"

"Sterling, Doctor Blake Sterling."

The young woman entered a string of keystrokes to call up my biographical data. After reviewing the information line by line, confirming it was still correct, she said, "That will be sixty dollars, please."

"Sixty dollars? No, this is just for one session."

The young lady seemed offended. "That is for one session."

"Oh. I didn't realize it was that much." *Ouch,* I thought.

I handed her my credit card. In return, she handed me a padlock with a key inserted and a receipt I was to keep on my person and produce if requested. She glanced at my tote bag. "I assume you know where the locker rooms are?"

"I do."

"Well then, welcome to the Columbia Fitness Center."

I slid my credit card back into my wallet, and after gracing the young woman with a forced smile, I headed for the men's lockers. The moment of truth had finally come.

I recovered the key Linda had given me from my pants pocket and again read its number—locker 126, which thankfully turned out to be in the far corner of the room, away from the main entrance.

Before stepping up to the locker, I lingered to confirm that no one was watching. I also offered up an arrow prayer. "Dear Lord, please let the truth come out."

Casually I stepped forward and deposited my tote bag on the wooden bench that ran between banks of lockers. When I inserted my key into the padlock, it turned easily with a satisfying click. After removing the padlock, I took a deep breath and slowly opened the locker. The first thing I noticed was a dingy towel and a pair of gym shoes that smelled worse than they looked. Gingerly moving the towel aside, I found a spiral-bound notebook lying flat on the floor of the locker. Otherwise, the shelves were empty.

Without hesitation, I picked up the notebook and quickly slid it into my tote bag. I did not stop to look inside. Either the notebook was the book Jerry had mentioned or it wasn't. I would have to wait to find out.

I closed the metal door and reset the padlock. The key I put back in my pocket.

I thought about leaving then and there, but that would look suspicious. Instead, I moved to an empty locker and changed into my gym clothes. After placing the tote bag in the locker, I set the padlock and headed for the exercise room. Thirty minutes later, feigning a leg cramp, I returned to the locker room to change back into my street clothes. As I limped past the registration counter, I shrugged at the young lady who had assisted me. She scowled but didn't say anything.

When I was back in my Nissan Sentra, I placed the tote bag on the seat beside me and drove off. It wasn't until I was safe at home that I took out the notebook and began to read.

Five minutes later, as I was reading Jerry's journal, I felt as if I had uncovered a powder keg primed to explode. An hour after that, I was struggling to wrap my brain around the magnitude of the conspiracy that was being laid out before me.

Meticulously and in great detail, Jerry had documented a paramilitary operation code-named Ophis Pterotos. He had documented names, dates, locations, objectives, mission parameters, and methodologies. He had described in nauseating detail the bocavirus infections the first five patients had endured, with him being the last patient mentioned in his journal. I and Hazel Marsh were excluded because by the time we suffered our infections, Jerry was already dead.

Jerry's coconspirators, Marcus Eldridge and Tyler Wickham, were explicitly named and their contributions to the operation carefully recorded. Jerry had even transcribed excerpts of conversations relevant to their involvement. Also named but not as well documented were two members of the New World Militia, Captain Jack Summers and The Angel, whoever he might be.

One thing I found particularly distressing was the dispassion with which Jerry chronicled the medical histories of his infected victims—up to and including his account of Leland Wright's death.

After my own battle with the virus, when I had nearly died, I had come away with a heightened awareness of the psychological trauma such an illness can cause. As a result, I was developing levels of empathy I had not experienced before. I was beginning to care.

Jerry's accounts, on the other hand, were devoid of compassion. He simply recounted facts as one might jot down a grocery list. How the man had become so insensitive to the plight of his fellow human beings, I could only imagine. I tried to envision a creature more deplorable than a physician who could care less if his patients lived or died.

Toward the end of the journal, I discovered an entry that I found quite intriguing, a signed and dated confession in which Jerry enumerated his crimes and took full responsibility for his actions. At least the man had the moral courage to stand accountable for what he had done.

At the bottom of the page was a statement that took me by surprise. A short paragraph declared Jerry's intent to infect himself and very probably take his own life. The reason he felt compelled to do this was not explained. I chose to believe that he was haunted by remorse for what he had done and needed to atone for his sins.

As I read the confession, I considered the impact the document would have on his widow. No doubt it would come as a horrific shock, but then she had lived with the man for decades. Surely, she must have gleaned some insight into his true character.

The final entry in the journal was the most intriguing of all. On the last page, a local address followed by a three-digit number had been recorded. Taped to the page below the number was another key. Beside the key, Jerry had hand drawn a skull and crossbones, the universal symbol for death. Clearly Jerry had intended that extreme caution should be used when recovering whatever was contained in whatever that key would unlock. I felt I had a fairly good idea what I would discover when his hiding place was opened.

An online search revealed that the address recorded in Jerry's notebook belonged to our local interstate bus depot. The key, I suspected, would open one of the depot's storage lockers. I checked the time on my phone. It was past my usual dinner time, but I had to know the secrets that key would reveal.

*What about the skull and cross bones?* I thought. For all I knew, Jerry might have set a trap or was warning about something worse. I would have to be very cautious indeed.

Before driving to the bus depot, I rounded up several tools I thought might prove useful: a flashlight, a dental mirror with a long handle, a pair of surgical gloves, safety goggles, and a tuna sandwich. This last item was because I was absolutely starving, having skipped lunch to attend the CME conference.

I dumped the clothes out of the tote bag and put in the tools and the journal. I then grabbed my winter coat. After one last look around to make sure I wasn't forgetting something, I climbed into my Sentra and drove to the bus station.

Besides the clerk behind the ticket counter, the porter handling luggage, and the janitor cleaning the waiting room, only a few people occupied the Metropolitan Bus Depot. I stepped inside and looked around. An elderly couple sat facing the double doors leading to the boarding zone. A young woman with a toddler in tow and a diaper bag over her shoulder paced nervously near the entrance. A homeless vagrant, by the look of him, lay curled in the corner of the waiting room, snoring loudly.

I immediately spotted the wall of lockers opposite the ticket counter, and I headed in that direction. It took only a moment to find locker number 78 and insert the key. At first, the key refused to turn, and I worried that maybe I had made a mistake, that I was in the wrong place. After reinserting the key a couple of times and jiggling it a bit, the lock finally clicked open. However, instead of fully opening the door to the locker, I reached into my tote bag and retrieved the flashlight and the dental mirror.

Cracking the door open barely an inch, I inserted the dental mirror. I then aimed the light through the crack, illuminating the interior of the locker. Peering inside, I searched for wires, explosives, or other booby traps. All I saw, however, was a brown paper grocery bag.

I put the flashlight and the dental mirror back into the tote bag and took out the surgical gloves and the safety goggles, both of which I put on.

Very carefully, I opened the locker door and examined the brown paper bag. It was folded closed at the top, but otherwise, it seemed perfectly ordinary. Proceeding slowly, I undid the top of the bag and peeked inside. I counted five slender bullet-shaped metal cylinders with screw caps. There were also several amber pill bottles in the bag. Each contained a few tablets which I didn't take the time to count.

Although I felt 98 percent certain that I knew what was in the containers, curiosity got the best of me. I removed one from the brown paper bag and unscrewed its lid. With extreme caution, I tilted the container to expose a stoppered test tube padded in cotton gauze. It was half full of amber liquid. The label on the test tube was encrypted.

Straightaway, I knew I was holding a bocavirus culture in my hands. I returned the test tube to the cylinder and screwed the lid back on. I then retrieved my tote bag from the floor beside me and the brown paper bag from the locker. When I started to leave, I noticed the ticket clerk eyeing me suspiciously. I held up the brown paper bag and said cheerfully, "Homework for my son's high school chemistry class." I smiled at the clerk and hastily left the depot.

With five cultures of a lethal virus resting on the passenger seat beside me, I drove home.

I sat at my small dining room table, poring over the journal and periodically looking toward the viral samples, confirming that they were still there. I had not yet fully come to grips with the fact that they were now in my possession.

The natter of what to do with the journal and the virus samples burned within me. There was no question that the information contained in the journal should be made public—eventually. However, several considerations needed to be taken into account before that could happen.

First was the matter of credibility. If I were to simply publicize the journal, people might claim I had created it as a self-serving hoax. As far as I knew, no one other than Jerry and myself had read the notebook; and therefore, no one could validate its authenticity.

My second concern was accountability. The people named in the journal would have to be brought to justice, but that wasn't my job. I had forgiven Marcus—Tyler as well—but they would still have to answer for their crimes. The victims' families and society at large would demand justice.

The final consideration was that by themselves, the journal and the viral samples would do little to disprove the allegations against me. As far as the medical community was concerned, based upon the unopposed testimony presented at my hearing, I had prescribed the wrong medication, contributing to a patient's death. I had then tried to cover up my error by resorting to blackmail and intimidation.

As I sat there mulling over my options, it came to me that there might be a way I could leverage the journal to reveal the truth. Whether or not I could make it happen, I would have to wait and see.

In light of these concerns, I realized that obviously I would have to involve the authorities. In great detail, the journal documented a plot to commit domestic bioterrorism. In truth, I didn't have a choice. In the morning I would deliver the journal, the viral samples, and the pill bottles to the regional office of the Federal Bureau of Investigation. I would then have to convince the agents there that the plan forming inside my brain was worth pursuing.

Midmorning Saturday, I sat across the table from Special Agent Dallas Carlton, the man in charge of the FBI's local field office. We were the only two people in the room. For security purposes, everyone else had been excluded.

Agent Carlton and I had been talking for several hours. When we had first begun, it had been blatantly apparent that he was miffed at having been called in on his weekend off to deal with a crackpot spouting nonsense about a bioterrorism conspiracy. As we had continued talking, however, his attitude had changed especially after I had demonstrated that I could personally corroborate the case histories of the patients identified in the journal. Coupled with the viral cultures and the tablets I had turned over to the bureau, he had reluctantly been forced to conclude that I could be telling the truth; and when the scope of the operation described in the journal had become apparent, he had responded with tightly controlled outrage.

As we sat facing one another in the interview room, I regarded the man who would soon determine what happened next. Agent Carlton fit my mental image of what a federal cop should look like. His brown eyes gave the impression he was constantly looking past what was apparent on the surface and into areas more deeply hidden. His dark-brown hair had begun graying at the temples. Prominent cheekbones, a well-defined nose, and thin lips enhanced his stern facial expression, though I certainly hadn't given him a reason to smile—quite the opposite, in fact.

For the last hour, I'd been doing my level best to convince Agent Carlton that a sting operation should be the bureau's appropriate response to the material I had brought to their attention. Patiently I had described the plan I had stayed awake most of the night formulating. One by one, I had countered his objections while emphasizing the goals I expected my plan to accomplish.

"Of course, there's a chance that the sting won't succeed," I said, continuing our ongoing debate. "But what other options do you have? Without corroboration, the journal alone isn't going to convince a jury."

"I suppose that's true," agent Carlton admitted. I could tell I was wearing down his resistance. Still he continued, "If we do this, it's going to require a lot of preparation."

"You're the FBI. Don't tell me you don't have the resources to make it happen."

Agent Carlton sat back and eyed me critically. At length, he said, "Do you really believe we can predict how he's going to respond?"

"If we plant the idea in his head, I think we can."

"All right then. Let's make it happen. I hope you appreciate that I'm going out on a limb trusting you."

"I know, but if we pull this off, you can bring down the entire operation. That's got to be worth the risk. How long do you think you will need to get things ready?"

"We should be good to go in seventy-two hours."

"What can I do to help?"

"Just be available in case we need to talk to you. You do realize… until we gather additional evidence, we can't rule out the possibility that you are a fraud and this is some sort of elaborate sham."

I nodded solemnly. "I understand. Tap my phone. Put me under surveillance. Do what you need to do to determine that I'm telling the truth, but when this is said and done, I want my life back. I want things restored to the way they were."

"We will do what we can, but there are no guarantees. Now get out of here, and let us get to work."

We shook hands, and I headed home to wait.

# WHAT GOES AROUND

"Thank you for stopping by." Linda Tucker looked across to where Marcus Eldridge sat on her living room couch and said. "I could have brought it to the hospital and saved you the trip."

I thought I detected a quaver in Linda's voice, and I prayed that Marcus wouldn't notice—or if he did, he would assume her grief was responsible for her uneasiness. Agent Carlton and I were sequestered out of sight in Linda's garage, monitoring a video feed from the hidden camera that was recording their conversation.

"It's perfectly all right," Marcus said mildly. "I don't mind at all." Knowing Marcus, I assumed that the real reason he had agreed to come to her home was because he wished to avoid being seen in public with Jerry's widow. "On the phone, you mentioned that you had something for me?"

"Yes. Yes, that's right." Linda fished in the pocket of her apron and pulled out a brass key. "The other day, I was going through some of Jerry's things, and I came across an envelope that had my name on it. Inside was this key." She held it up. "Also, there was a note that said I should be sure to give this key to you." She rose from her armchair and stepped forward to pass the key to Marcus. "I believe it opens his locker at the Columbia Fitness Center. Why he wanted you to have it, I can't begin to imagine."

Marcus seemed unsure. "He specifically said he wanted me to have this key?"

"Those were his instructions."

"You wouldn't happen to have the note he wrote, would you?"

"Yes, I still have it."

"Would you mind if I see it?"

"Not at all." Linda reached into the pocket of her apron again and produced an envelope. She handed it over to Marcus.

*He really is a suspicious bastard,* I thought. I had to hand it to Agent Carlton. He had foreseen that Marcus might seek confirmation that Linda was telling the truth.

Marcus read the note and then asked, "Mind if I keep this?"

"If you feel you need to." Linda returned to her chair and sat down.

Marcus tucked the note back into its envelope, which he then folded and slid into his hip pocket. "Do you know what's in the locker?"

"I don't. Honestly, I had forgotten about his gym membership until I found the envelope."

"It's strange that your husband would leave me a key to his gym locker."

"I agree, though it must be important. Several times he mentioned that the work you were doing was crucial."

Marcus visibly stiffened. "Did he happen to mention what that work entailed?"

*Careful, Linda,* I thought. *Don't blow it now.*

"Not really. I always assumed it involved your efforts to bring all the practices under the hospital's banner. He was very passionate about that."

*Bravo, Linda. Well done.* I looked at Agent Carlton. For the first time since I had met him, he was smiling—if you call a relieved grimace a smile.

"I see." Marcus hesitated as if making a decision. "Okay, I'll check out the locker, and I'll let you know what I find. Look, um…I really would like to stay and visit, but I really must be getting back to the hospital."

"I understand, but before you go, would you mind if I ask you something?"

"Go ahead."

"Have you heard anything about what Doctor Sterling is up to?"

"What do you mean?"

"I was talking to one of the nurses my husband used to work with. She was saying that Doctor Sterling is planning on going to the FBI and demand that they start an investigation. I think the man is deranged. I wouldn't be surprised if he was somehow involved in Jerry's death. Somebody should alert the FBI that they need to investigate him. What do you think? Have you heard anything about this?"

Marcus's countenance brightened as if the spark of an idea had ignited in his brain. "No, I haven't, but you might be right. Perhaps it is time for the authorities to take a long hard look at Doctor Sterling— find out what secrets he's hiding."

"It would serve him right." Linda saw her guest to the door and then came into the garage. She was trembling. "How did I do?"

"You did fine," Agent Carlton replied.

"She did better than fine." Turning to Linda, I declared, "You were splendid. You got your lines just right."

"We'll see," Agent Carlton commented with obvious skepticism.

A look of sorrow spread across Linda's face. "Will this help us understand what happened to my husband?" I was reminded that she still had not been told about the contents of her husband's journal.

"We hope so," Agent Carlton said. He switched off the video monitor. "My men will stop by and collect our surveillance equipment. Remember, if he attempts to contact you again, please keep us informed."

We thanked Linda for her assistance. On our way back to my car—I had volunteered to drive— Agent Carlton said, "Do you think he bought it?"

"Hard to be sure. We planted the seed. Now we'll have to wait to see how he responds. I know he'll check out the locker. It would be foolhardy for him not to. What happens after he finds the copy of the journal we put there, well…"

"Right," Agent Carlton sighed. "Only time will tell."

That evening, I was at home, doing a poor job of watching the news. My thoughts were centered on Jerry's journal and how the bureau's investigation was progressing. A loud knock sounded at my front door. I went to see who was demanding entry.

Special Agent Carlton stood on my front stoop. Beside him stood Marcus Eldridge, a malevolent grimace on his face. Behind them stood three other agents whom I did not recognize. Their FBI badges gleamed in the fading sunlight.

"What is this?" I blurted out. I scowled at Marcus. "What do you want? What's going on?"

The lead agent stepped forward and identified himself. Matter-of-factly, he said. "I'm Special Agent Dallas Carlton. Mr. Eldridge, you know. These three men are here to assist me."

"Assist you with what?"

"With this." Agent Carlton fished in his inside coat pocket and produced a document that he handed to me. "This is a warrant to search these premises. Now if you would please stand aside…"

I didn't budge. Instead, I began reading the search warrant. It appeared to be valid. "What is it you hope to find?" I asked while I continued perusing the warrant.

"Materials related to criminal sedition. Specifically, we expect to find evidence that you have engaged in acts of bioterrorism that caused the deaths of three people."

"What?" I exclaimed. "Are you insane? I'm no bioterrorist. What are you talking about? What is this?"

"Sir," Agent Carlton said sternly. "I'm not going to ask again. Please stand aside, or we will forcibly remove you from the premises. It's your choice."

Begrudgingly, I stepped out of the way and allowed the five men to enter. One man headed into the kitchen, another to the master bedroom at the back of the house. The third man went upstairs. Soon I heard the sounds of strangers rummaging through my belongings. Such an invasion of my privacy made me nauseated. I wandered into the living room and sat down.

Marcus seemed agitated. With a pleading look in his eyes, he glanced at agent Carlton and then at me. "I'm sorry, but I've really got to go. Would you mind if I use your restroom?"

I wanted to tell him to hold it. Instead, with my attention focused on what was being done to my home, I replied numbly, "Second door to your left down the hall."

Marcus hurried off.

"I might as well begin in here," Agent Carlton said. Otherwise ignoring me, he began by opening drawers on the end table beside the couch. He then shifted to the bookshelf in the corner. With each book, he fanned through it to see if anything might be hidden inside. He then dropped the book on the floor and moved on to the next, leaving a mess for me to clean up later. I envisioned the same acts of legalized vandalism occurring throughout my home.

Soon Marcus returned from the restroom and stood off to the side, watching me and gloating. I paid him no heed.

Twenty minutes later, the agent who had begun in the master bedroom called out, "In here." He had moved into the downstairs bathroom. He stood waiting when Marcus, Agent Carlton, and I advanced down the hall. Holding open my linen closet, he pointed to the top shelf. "Up there," he said.

"Let's see it," Agent Carlton said brusquely. "Bring it down."

Very gingerly, the agent stepped forward and reached up. With great care, he lifted the top towel off a short stack and gingerly placed it on the bathroom counter. Lying atop the towel were five slender bullet-shaped metal containers with screw caps.

"That's them," Marcus proclaimed, pointing at the cylinders. "Those are the virus cultures I was telling you about."

I glowered at Marcus and snarled silently, *Gotcha, you son of a bitch*. Aloud, as if without thinking, I exclaimed, "What are those doing here?"

Agent Carlton regarded me with an accusatory frown. "So you have seen these before."

Intentionally, I stammered, "I…I…I have nothing to say—not until I speak with my attorney."

I could tell Marcus was itching to deliver some scathingly snide remark, but he refrained from offering a comment.

One of the agents produced a camera and began taking pictures of the cylinders and their environment. He also photographed Marcus and myself. When he finished, Agent Carlton said, "Let's take these into the living room where there's more space."

We all complied, and I sank down into the recliner in the corner but did not lean back. Instead, I sat tilted forward at the hips, elbows braced on knees, waiting to see what would happen next.

Rather than sit down on the couch, Agent Carlton remained standing next to the coffee table where the towel and the metal cylinders had been deposited. Marcus also remained standing, two feet from Agent Carlton. The other three agents had casually stationed themselves around the two men, equidistant from one another.

Agent Carlton turned to face Marcus. "Well, it looks like you were right…if these are what I think they are. How did you know they would be here?"

Marcus drew his shoulders back as if whatever he had previously told the FBI had just been vindicated. "As I explained this morning, I overheard Blake making a phone call. He didn't know I was listening. He was talking to someone about having to get rid of the virus."

"And where were you when this phone call took place?"

"We were in the main lobby of the hospital. I was standing behind a pillar."

"So…he was on his cell phone?"

"That's correct." Marcus nodded to confirm his assertion. He seemed irritated by the questions.

"What was he doing at the hospital? Didn't you tell me he had lost his privileges?"

"Maybe he was visiting his girlfriend. How should I know why he was there? All I can tell you is what I heard."

"Is that so?" Agent Carlton said mildly. "Well, it might interest you to learn that we've had Doctor Sterling under surveillance since Saturday and we've had a tap on his phone. There have been no phone calls."

Suddenly flustered, Marcus countered, "Maybe he was using someone else's phone—perhaps his partner's."

Agent Carlton turned his head to look at me. "Did you borrow someone's phone?"

"I did not," I responded.

"He says he didn't." He then looked at each of the three agents and asked, "Did you see him borrow a phone?"

Each man answered in turn, "No, sir."

Agent Carlton faced Marcus again. "They didn't see anybody. Besides, with Doctor Sterling's permission, we searched his home this morning. These weren't here then. Care to try again? No? Then let me tell you how you knew. The only way you could have known we would find these items is if you had planted them yourself."

"That's ridiculous," Marcus sputtered. "Why would I do such a thing?"

"Because you want me out of the way," I retorted angrily. "I was getting too close."

Marcus was about to respond, but Agent Carlton cut him off. "To plant these items, you first had to acquire them, and to accomplish that, you had to have read Doctor Tucker's journal. We know you had access to the journal because Linda Tucker gave you her husband's locker key. By the way, knowing where to find these cylinders constitutes means— as in means, motive, and opportunity. The journal told you where to look, and that gave you the means to plant them as incriminating evidence against Doctor Sterling.

Agent Carlton gestured toward the cylinders lying on the towel. "Let me ask you something. Have you ever seen these before?"

"No, never," Marcus said, shaking his head.

"Then how did you know these cylinders contain viral cultures?"

"Because the journal said so."

"No, it didn't," Agent Carlton snapped. "The journal you found at the gym was a doctored copy—one we created. It never mentions the words virus, bocavirus, cultures, or samples. It only refers to 'Items.'"

"You'll never be able to prove that."

"Why? Because you destroyed the doctored copy you found? Don't worry. We have a certified duplicate of the one we planted. Also, destroying the journal speaks of motive. When you read the journal and learned about the incriminating evidence it contains, your guilt compelled you to attempt to frame someone else for your crimes."

It pleased me greatly to see that Marcus had begun to sweat.

"All right," Marcus exclaimed after giving the matter some thought. "I opened the cylinders and read the labels on the test tubes inside. That's how I knew what they were."

Agent Carlton cocked his head at Marcus. "When? You've been under constant observation since we got here."

"Not when I used the restroom. I was alone."

"So…you admit you were alone in the place where the cylinders were found."

"That's right. That's when I read the labels."

"No, that's when you planted the cylinders you had concealed on your person, and that's opportunity. Means, motive, and opportunity—we can now prove beyond any reasonable doubt that you sought to use the cylinders to frame Doctor Sterling. Under federal law, a person convicted of tampering with evidence can face a prison term of not more than twenty years."

Marcus vehemently shook his head. "That's absurd. I told you what happened. I learned that the cylinders contained virus cultures when I read the labels on the test tubes."

"No you didn't," Agent Carlton declared forcefully. "The labels on the test tubes inside these cylinders are encrypted, and the test tubes themselves are empty. You would have known that had you actually looked inside, but you didn't. You were afraid of getting infected, and I must say I don't blame you for that. It's a nasty virus you were helping to develop.

"The truth is you simply assumed these cylinders were the originals, and for you to have known that the originals contained test tubes filled with virus cultures means you'd encountered them before, and that, sir, puts you at the heart of a bioterrorism conspiracy."

Marcus paled. His knees began to shake. He looked as if he was about to pass out. I felt an intense rush of satisfaction. I had forgiven the man, but I could still feel pleased at seeing justice done.

Special Agent Carlton nodded to one of his team members, who then stepped forward with a pair of handcuffs.

"Marcus Layton Eldridge," Special Agent Carlton announced. "I'm arresting you on charges of domestic terrorism, murder, assault with a biological weapon, tampering with evidence, and whatever else I can think of down the road. You have the right to remain silent…"

I stopped listening. We had successfully completed the most problematic part of the plan we had devised. When Agent Carlton had informed me that Marcus had contacted the bureau, we knew we had him. From there, it was only a matter of giving Marcus enough rope and allowing him to hang himself. The part of the plan that would determine my future in medicine was yet to come.

Two days later, I sat in the front row of the Flintridge Medical Center's auditorium. Instead of the CME program previously scheduled, a special press conference had been announced by the FBI. The room was crowded with spectators—to the point that there was standing room only. Madison sat beside me, and I held her hand while we waited for the event to begin. There were so many people murmuring throughout the auditorium it was impossible to pick out any one conversation.

The double doors at the side of the auditorium opened, and Special Agent Dallas Carlton entered. The room fell silent as he strode to the lectern. He laid down the manila folder he carried and gazed out at the audience.

After introducing himself and the other members of his task force, he began by saying, "It is with great pleasure and immense satisfaction that the FBI would like to announce the arrest of the following individuals: Marcus Eldridge, Tyler Wickham, Captain Jack Summers, and Edward Garcia—also known as The Angel. These individuals have been charged with a variety of offenses including domestic terrorism and murder."

Agent Carlton then signaled a member of his team at the back of the room. The large projection screen at the front of the auditorium began to unfurl.

"What you are about to see," Agent Carlton said, speaking directly into the lectern's microphone. "Are segments of bodycam footage taken over the last forty-eight hours. These clips are also going to be broadcast tonight on the evening news." He again signaled the projectionist. The lights dimmed, and a sequence of video clips were projected onto the screen.

"This first scene," Agent Carlton narrated. "Shows the New World Militia's compound where Captain Summers is being taken into custody. Captain Summers is the militia's commanding officer. As you may notice, the militia members we encountered were heavily armed. Fortunately, we were able to affect this arrest without bloodshed. This second clip was taken at the home of Mr. Edward Garcia, aka The Angel. Mr. Garcia is reputedly the New World Militia's principal benefactor. He is currently under investigation not only for the charges I mentioned previously but for other acts of sedition as well."

Next came a video clip of Tyler Wickham's arrest. A rumbling murmur arose throughout the auditorium as the assembled medical professionals recognized one of their own. Seeing Tyler, I was transported in my mind back to the previous afternoon. The FBI had invited me to monitor via closed circuit TV the interview in which Marcus and Tyler were being questioned together.

I was one of four observers sequestered in a small featureless room across the hall from the FBI's main interview room. A large flatscreen television was mounted on the wall of the observation room. Several tables faced the TV. I sat at one of the tables. Agent Thomas Morris—one of the three men who had accompanied Agent Carlton when he had searched my house—sat beside me. Two other agents whom I did not recognize were seated at other tables. They appeared to be taking notes.

"Normally," said Agent Morris. "We shy away from interviewing subjects together. It creates an opportunity for them to coordinate their stories. However, in this case, we decided to make an exception. Hopefully, we can play one man against the other and see which one will rat out his compadre first."

A wall-mounted surveillance camera in the interview room looked down from near ceiling level to give a clear view of what looked to be a room even starker than the one we now occupied. There were no windows. There were no pictures on the walls. The only illumination came from an array of recessed ceiling lights. The only furniture was a nondescript table and three straight-backed aluminum chairs. Marcus and Tyler sat facing one another on opposite sides of the table. Agent Carlton sat at the end of the table as if moderating between them.

"For the record," Agent Carlton began, glancing up at the camera. "You both have waived your right to have your legal representative present. You both have been advised of the charges against you. You both have been provided a summary of the evidence we have accumulated thus far. Our purpose here today is to see if there is anything else you'd care to tell us. The value of whatever you share will be taken into consideration when it comes to recommending sentencing."

Agent Morris leaned in my direction and whispered, "This is where things get interesting. The first rat to sell out his buddy gets the cheese."

Tyler glowered across the table at Marcus. "You keep your mouth shut. Don't tell them anything."

"I warned you before," Marcus hissed in return. "Don't tell me what to do. It's your fault I'm in this fix."

"My fault!" Tyler exploded. "Are you crazy?"

"You should have kept better tabs on your buddy, Doctor Tucker."

Tyler raised his hands palms up. "How was I supposed to know he was keeping a journal?"

"Maybe if you'd been paying attention—"

"Mr. Wickham," agent Carlton interjected before Tyler could respond. "You've had a chance to review the evidence we've collected. Not only do we have Doctor Tucker's documentation of your involvement, we have the virus culture we recovered from your thermos—the thermos we found in your storage cabinet in the Respiratory Therapy Department. There's not a jury in the world that would fail to convict you on all charges. Are you sure there's nothing new you want to tell us, or would you rather face the death penalty?"

Tyler blanched. "You can't pin this on me." He stabbed an index finger in Marcus's direction. "It was his idea—just like it was his idea to frame Doctor Sterling."

Agent Carlton scowled. "You mean by planting what he thought were the original bocavirus cultures in Doctor Sterling home?"

Tyler nodded. "Yeah, that…and the way he got him kicked off the medical staff. That was all his doing."

With my eyes glued to the TV screen, I sat up straight, listening intently.

"Just how did he make that happen?" Agent Carlton asked mildly.

Tyler regarded his former boss with a look of disdain. "He bribed the pharmacist—paid him $10,000, and he threatened the nurse."

Agent Carlton cast a curious glance at Marcus, who looked away. The agent then addressed Tyler again. "Threatened her how?"

"He told her he would make it seem like she was stealing narcotics and then get the nursing board to yank her license."

"Could he really do that?"

"Oh, yeah."

"And what about the testimony you gave—that you had seen Doctor Sterling and Nurse Smith together?"

Tyler shrugged. "That wasn't true either—he made it up. Marcus told me what to say."

"Is that so?" Agent Carlton turned his attention to Marcus. With a penetrating gaze, he said, "How would you respond to these allegations? And remember, if you lie to us, we'll take the offer of clemency off the table."

Marcus heaved a heavy sigh. "I suppose it doesn't matter what I say now. What's one more charge against me? I'm going to spend the rest of my life in jail. Yeah, I tried to frame him. He was way too interested in the bocavirus patients. He was beginning to figure out that they were being deliberately infected. We had to get him out of the way."

"So you fabricated the entire narrative?"

"Yes, I did."

"You're saying that none of it was true? Doctor Sterling did not prescribe the wrong medication, and there was no cover-up. Is that what you're telling me?"

"Yes. It was all a lie."

Agent Carlton glanced up at the surveillance camera and winked.

When the video clips ended, Agent Carlton delivered a brief synopsis of what was now being called The Flintridge Conspiracy. He outlined how the leadership of the New World Militia, in anticipation of a rebellion that was soon to begin, had attempted to develop a biological weapon. Briefly he commented on the seriousness of the infections suffered by seven patients, including the loss of two lives. He finished up by saying, "Fortunately, there was one individual who had the fortitude, the determination, and the professionalism to bring this conspiracy to light—even at the risk of his own life. It is with sincere gratitude that the bureau would like to acknowledge Doctor Blake Sterling for his contribution to ending this biological attack against our citizenry. Doctor Sterling, we thank you."

A round of sustained applause erupted throughout the auditorium.

When it died down, Doctor Sam Duncan stepped forward. Gripping both sides of the lectern, he looked out at the audience. "For those of you who don't know me, my name is Sam Duncan. I'm chief of staff and chairman of the Quality Improvement Committee. I'll be brief. As I'm sure most of you probably know, the committee recently adjudicated allegations brought against Doctor Sterling. The charges were that he mistakenly prescribed the wrong medication leading to the death of a patient and then attempted to conceal his wrongdoing by threatening a nurse and ordering her to falsify a medical record.

"At the time, the evidence available to us supported these charges. Therefore, the committee decided to suspend Doctor Sterling's hospital privileges pending further review. In addition, a complaint was submitted to the state medical board requesting that Doctor Sterling' medical license be revoked."

Sam shoved his wire-rimmed glasses up the bridge of his nose with an index finger. "We have subsequently learned that the charges against Doctor Sterling are completely false and without merit. He is an innocent man. In light of these findings, the committee has unanimously voted to restore Doctor Sterling's hospital privileges effective immediately, and we have petitioned the medical board to withdraw the complaint against him."

Sam then looked down to where I sat and said with genuine sincerity, "Blake, welcome home."

Another round of applause filled the auditorium.

Sam gestured for me to join him at the lectern. "Come up here and say a few words," he prompted.

Madison squeezed my hand before letting go. I stepped forward.

Taking a deep breath, I spoke into the microphone. "Sam, thank you for the kind words spoken on my behalf. Agent Carlton, thank you for the FBI's unflinching efforts to bring this conspiracy to a satisfactory conclusion. To my partners, Doctor Adam Thayer and Doctor Fred Spalding, thank you for your unwavering friendship and support. I also want to thank my fiancée, Madison Lane, for her love and her faith in me—yeah, that's right. She said yes."

I waited for another round of applause to die down before continuing. "I especially want to thank my Heavenly Father and His son, my Lord and Savior, Jesus Christ. Without Them, I would not have survived. I owe Them everything I have. If you don't know the Lord, if you have never developed a personal relationship with Him, I would implore you to do so immediately. Not only is He the author of our salvation, He is a light unto our feet and the cornerstone of our faith. As I can personally testify, He will see you through. You can trust Him.

"Sorry. It wasn't my intention to deliver a sermon, but what I'm telling you is true. I'm living proof that if you put your faith in Jesus, He won't let you down. Anyway, may God bless you all, and may He continue to protect us from enemies—foreign and domestic."

I returned to my seat and sat down.

THE END

# EPILOGUE

Twenty-one months later, Madison and I sat on the balcony of our rented apartment in Santa Monica, California. We gazed out at the expanse of the Pacific Ocean as the sun slowly sank toward the horizon. It was one of the last glorious sunsets we would enjoy for quite some time. In the morning, we would be moving again, back to Flintridge to begin the next phase of our life together.

After having been exonerated of all charges against me, I had resumed my practice of pulmonary medicine. For a time, it had seemed as if I was where I belonged, but then I discovered that I had changed.

Shortly after Madison and I were married, I began to sense that I was in the wrong profession. As much as I loved private practice, I was increasingly troubled by the death and dying with which every physician must contend. The empathy that had awakened within me after my illness made it impossible for me to dispassionately treat the sick. I could no longer look upon their suffering without becoming emotionally entangled in their plight. In time, it became clear that to preserve my sanity, I would have to switch to a different profession. The one that immediately came to mind was hospital administrator.

In watching Marcus, I had discovered what hospital administrator should never be—overbearing, intolerant, vindictive. A good administrator never places corporate greed above seeking the greatest good for the greatest number. What's more, a conscientious administrator can help hundreds of people every day by striving to see that they receive the best possible healthcare.

The more I thought about making the change, the more convinced I had become that it was the right choice. To that end, and after much prayer, Madison and I had relocated to Los Angeles, where I had enrolled in UCLA's graduate program with a goal of earning a master's degree in public health. Madison had taken a position as an ICU nurse at the UCLA Medical Center. That was until her pregnancy had prevented her from working.

Ten months after William Sterling was born, along came Julia, who was now cradled in her mother's arms. William was seated on my lap.

A month before my graduation, the letter from Flintridge Healthcare had arrived. Apparently, the administrator they had hired to replace Marcus Eldridge simply hadn't worked out, and I had been invited to take over the position. It must have been a God thing because the board had even promised to hold the slot open for me until we could relocate to Washington State.

When Adam had learned that we would be returning to town, he had called to offer his congratulations and to say he was looking forward to seeing us again. He had also asked, "As our new administrator, what will be your highest priority?"

My answer had been straightforward. I hadn't even needed to think about it. "Always seek the greatest good so that God will be glorified." It was a simple concept, but it correctly encapsulated the attitude I wished to bring to the job.

"Well," Madison said as the sun disappeared below the horizon. "Should we finish packing?"

"Absolutely," I responded. "That way we can get the show on the road bright and early."

We both stood up and headed back indoors.

My heart was full as I considered the family God had given me. I sort of knew what the future would bring, but there would always be surprises. The important thing was that I had learned to trust God, and going forward, I was resolved to follow wherever He chose to lead.

www.ingramcontent.com/pod-product-compliance
Lightning Source LLC
Chambersburg PA
CBHW061346310726

48974CB00001B/226